W9-BKG-139

CRYSTAL MASK

The
— Echorium Sequence —

CRYSTAL MASK

Katherine Roberts

Scholastic Inc. / New York

For Jerry,
husband and Horselord

© The Chicken House 2002

Text copyright © 2002 by Katherine Roberts
Illustrations copyright © 2002 by Chris Down

First published in the United Kingdom in 2002 by The Chicken House,
2 Palmer Street, Frome, Somerset, BA11 1DS.

All rights reserved. Published by Scholastic Inc., *Publishers since 1920,*
by arrangement with The Chicken House. SCHOLASTIC and
associated logos are trademarks and/or registered trademarks
of Scholastic Inc.

No part of this publication may be reproduced, or stored in a retrieval
system, or transmitted in any form or by any means, electronic,
mechanical, photocopying, recording, or otherwise, without written
permission of the publisher.
For information regarding permission, write to Scholastic Inc.,
Attn: Permissions Department, 555 Broadway, New York, NY 10012.

Roberts, Katherine, 1962-
Crystal mask / Katherine Roberts. — 1st Scholastic ed.
p. cm. — (The Echorium sequence ; v. 2)
Sequel to: Songquest.
Summary: Renn, a novice Singer, and Shaiala, a girl raised by centaurs,
battle against a great evil and try to restore harmony to the world.
[1. Fantasy.] I. Title. II. Series.

PZ7.R54325 Cr 2002
[Fic]--dc21   2001042888

ISBN 0-439-33864-6

10 9 8 7 6 5 4 3 2 1   02 03 04 05 06

Printed in the United States of America 37
First American edition, February 2002

CONTENTS

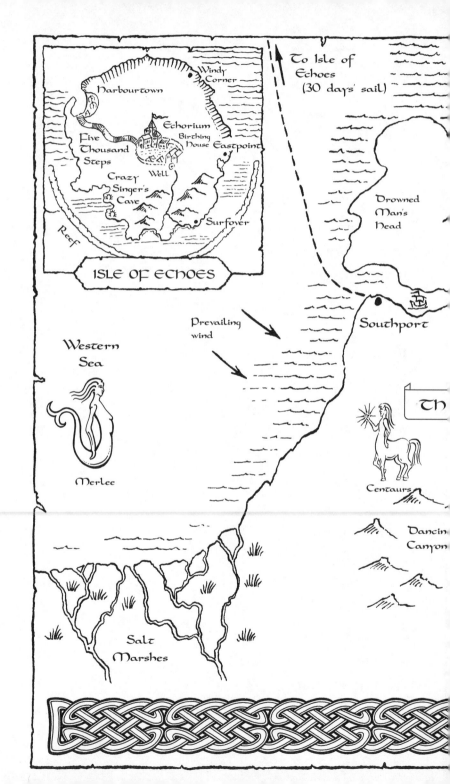

The Echorium Sequence

Long ago, before human history began, the world was inhabited by beautiful creatures — half human, half animal — who knew the secret of using the ancient power of Song to control their environment. These Half Creatures lived in harmony with their human neighbors.

But the humans, impatient for progress, began to turn their backs on the old ways. They made tools and built great towns and cities, ships to sail the seas, and wheels to travel the land. They made war on one another, destroying the very things they had built. The Half Creatures fled to the remote regions of the world — deep into the forests, to the bottom of lakes, and far beneath the waves — taking their secrets with them.

Not all humans forgot the old Songs. Those who saw how destructive their way of life had become set out across the sea to find a haven. On an island of enchanted bluestone, they built a school and taught their children the five ancient Songs of Power: *Challa* for healing, *Kashe* for laughter, *Shi* for sadness, *Aushan* for discipline, and *Yehn* for death.

News of the enchanted isle where people were healed by the power of Song quickly spread to the farthest corners of the world. The island became known as the *Isle of Echoes*, the school became the *Echorium*, and the people who lived there became the *Singers*.

The Singers made it their mission to restore harmony to the world. They dyed their hair blue to enhance the power of their Songs and added diplomatic skills to their lessons. Any youngster whose voice could not manage the Songs was trained in self-defense so he or she could help protect the Echorium. Singers negotiated treaties with the world's leaders and ensured that these treaties were kept. When necessary, they sailed to the mainland to stop wars and put an end to cruelty. Their children were able to speak with Half Creatures and became friends with them. But as the fame and influence of the Singers grew, so did the number of their human enemies.

Twenty years after the events described in *Song Quest*, enemies of the Echorium are once again growing strong.

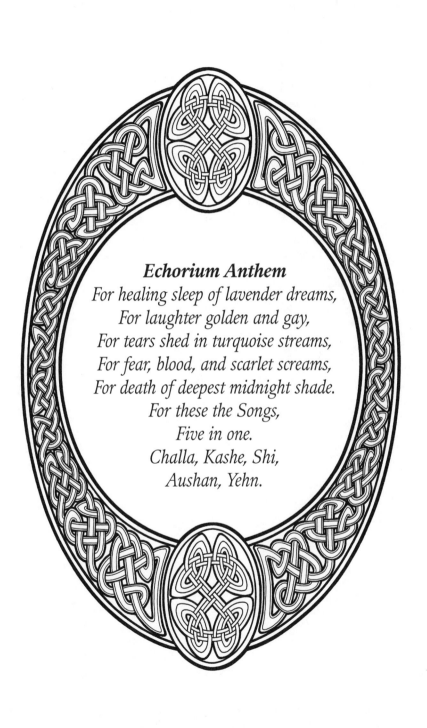

Echorium Anthem
For healing sleep of lavender dreams,
For laughter golden and gay,
For tears shed in turquoise streams,
For fear, blood, and scarlet screams,
For death of deepest midnight shade.
For these the Songs,
Five in one.
Challa, Kashe, Shi,
Aushan, Yehn.

1

NIGHTMARE

Shaiala crouched on a moonlit ledge beneath a sky dizzy with stars. The unruly mountain wind stirred her hair, which was long and black and heavy with lumps of purple mud. Below lurked the shadowy folds of the canyons that had swallowed her friends. She was shouting a warning. She shouted until her throat was as sore as her bleeding feet. But the wind stole her words and whirled them away.

What frightened her was the endless file of Two Hoofs running silently along the trail below. The men wore dusty black robes and had crimson-and-black-striped scarves wrapped tightly around their faces so that only their eyes showed. At their hips, curved blades glittered in the moonlight. The small blue centaurs, their human torsos clad in mare's-tail tunics, their ears drooping around pale human faces, and their horse bodies patchy with the last of their fluffy foal coats, hadn't seen the danger. So far from the herd, separated from one another by the steep-walled canyons and exhausted after a night of cracking rocks, they were pathetically vulnerable.

A group of Two Hoofs drove a lilac filly, so pale she was almost white, down the canyon toward its narrow end. The filly stumbled along, her coat streaked with sweat, not even trying to kick her way to freedom. In one delicate hand, she clutched a small green stone still glowing from the heart of the rock.

"Use it!" Shaiala shouted. "Use it, Kamara Silvermane! Fight!"

But the Two Hoofs pinned the filly against the cliff. One of them prized the herdstone out of her hand and tossed it away. Kamara Silvermane reared up. But before she could strike, a Two Hoof blade slashed at her legs. The filly screamed and dropped back to earth, blue centaur blood dripping from one fetlock. The blade at her throat kept her quiet as the Two Hoofs fixed rope hobbles to her forelegs. Then they drove her through a crack in the canyon wall, out of sight.

Shaiala's heart twisted for her friend, but the nightmare wasn't over yet. The Two Hoofs had spotted Kamara Silvermane first because her coat shone fatally in the moonlight, but they soon flushed out the other foals. First the lighter blues, then the purples, and finally the blacks. All were driven into corners, where their herdstones were taken away and hobbles applied. Few put up much of a fight, though a tall, dark colt called Rafiz Longshadow scored a kick that shattered a Two Hoof skull before they got the hobbles on him.

By the time she'd scrambled down to the canyon floor, all her friends had been driven through the crevice. She ran through after them. The sight beyond brought her to a halt. Nearly a hundred exhausted and frightened centaur foals shivered in the natural trap formed by the inner canyon, hobbled and taunted by Two Hoofs. Yet more Two Hoofs were tying the centaurs' small wrists behind them and linking their necks with loops of rope. Most of the foals looked too shocked even to realize what was happening to them. Kamara Silvermane and Rafiz Longshadow had been separated and were trying to move closer together. The Two Hoofs prodded them apart.

"No!" Shaiala screamed, seeing fresh blood on the filly's coat. "Not hurt they! They my friends!"

The men swung around, crimson-and-black scarves billowing loose around their necks. The alarm on their faces turned to amusement when they saw she was alone.

Even in her dream, Shaiala's entire body ached. It seemed as if she'd *been shouting and running all night. All she wanted to do was crawl into a corner and sleep. But she launched herself into the air and let fly with one foot at the nearest Two Hoof. It was a kick she'd learned from the centaurs, called a* Snake *because it would kill an attacking grass serpent before the creature had a chance to bite. Her heel caught the Two Hoof on the back of the thigh. She heard a satisfying crack. Before he'd started screaming, Shaiala had landed and whirled to face the next.*

Three more came at her, the laughter dying on their lips as they realized she'd broken their friend's leg. A sideways Dragonfly *kick took care of another. Sobbing with a mixture of fury and fear, she spun on her heel and cracked an exposed knee with a well-aimed* Hare, *then whirled again and snapped someone's arm with a second* Snake. *Unintelligible Two Hoof yells echoed in the canyon. The cliffs soared, high and black on all sides. A blade went spinning under her and away, like a slice of the moon.*

Everyone seemed to be shouting at once, including the centaurs.

"No, Shaiala Two Hoof!" Kamara Silvermane screamed. "Run!"

"Go fetch someone who can kick properly!" shouted Rafiz Longshadow. "Get stallion. Get mares."

"Sneaky Two Hoof spy!" a stocky colt called Marell Storm Temper spat through his cloud of purple mane. "You lead Two Hoofs here. You tell Two Hoofs about herdstones. You betray herd!"

Before Shaiala could protest, more men ran at her. One threw a rope. It tangled in her ankles, fouling her hasty Snake. *The ground rushed up and she choked on dust. Their rough hands were on her, tugging her hair, pulling her away from her friends, and slamming her against the canyon wall.*

A Two Hoof face, his ugly copper-colored skin glistening with sweat, pushed close to hers and snapped out a question. Shaiala shook her head helplessly. After the centaurs' language, his words were harsh and made no sense. Another Two Hoof pointed to her feet and repeated the question. She shook her head again. Her mouth was far too dry to ask him to say it in Herd. The first man gave a disgusted snort and raised his blade above her head. Terror poured into Shaiala's legs, stealing the last of her strength. She couldn't move.

But the blade did not fall. After a moment, she became aware of a face-less Two Hoof silhouette watching from the shadows. The silhouette floated closer, plumes of glowing color fluttering around its head, making her dizzy. Its black face blotted out the canyon, the captive foals, the stars, the raised blade, everything. Through two glittering holes in the night, eyes stared at her, colder than death.

Black lightning flashed.

Shaiala screamed.

The pain that signaled the end of the nightmare exploded in her head.

As always, Shaiala woke with sweat pouring off her, panting as though she really had just run down from a high ledge and fought a herd of Two Hoofs.

She lay still in the darkness while her heartbeat slowed. Then she pushed her hair out of her eyes and tried to stand. Her head hit something hard, and she lost her balance as the floor tipped sideways. She sat down again in a hurry. Not the first time she'd done that.

Gripping her knees, she tried to remember where she was. A line of light slid across the floor where she was sitting, turned a sharp corner, and rose until it reached the height where she'd hit her head, then turned back until it was above the start of the first line. All three lines swayed from side to side along with the rest of her prison. There were strange noises outside, mingled with the slap and echo of water against wood. Water far deeper and wider than the little streams the herd drank from during their travels across the Plains. Shaiala considered this for a moment, then gave a cold shudder.

She must be inside an enchanted Two Hoof building that could move over water. She had seen them sometimes, floating up and down the Two Hoof river with huge cloths billowing above them in the wind. The centaur foals had laughed and said Two Hoofs built them because their legs got tired if they galloped too far. Which reminded her . . . she shifted her feet experimentally, heard the clink of metal, and swallowed a cry of terror.

They'd hobbled her too.

"Kamara!" she called. "Kamara Silvermane!"

A moment's thought produced another name from her dream. "Rafiz Longshadow!"

Only the creak of the Two Hoof building and the slap of water answered. But centaur hearing was sharper than hers. The horse-ears that pushed through their cloudy manes could swivel to catch the slightest sound. They might be able to hear her even if she couldn't hear them.

She drew a deep breath. "Marell! Marell Storm Temper!" Even the purple colt who never lost an opportunity to tease her about her differences would be welcome company now. At least, he couldn't try to blame her anymore for the attack.

Still no answer.

"Anyone!" Shaiala screamed, thumping the wall. "Answer I! Not leave I here with Two Hoofs!"

Footsteps approached and a heavy blow shook the wood that imprisoned her. She held her breath. A black shape, taller than any centaur, blocked the vertical line of light. A rough Two Hoof voice shouted something she didn't understand, then laughed coarsely and went away. The wood creaked, the hiss and slap of water grew louder, and the floor tipped in a different direction. She was thrown sideways, the hobbles digging into her ankles.

A sick, cold feeling lodged itself in her belly. Her friends weren't here, and the longer she waited the farther away they'd be.

She studied the lines of light. If the Two Hoof could survive on the other side of them, then so could she. She rose carefully into a crouch. Keeping her head low this time, she leaped at the wall, striking with both heels simultaneously. *Flying Snake.*

She'd forgotten the chain fastened her ankles to the floor. It gave a rusty clatter and snatched her off balance before her toes touched the wood. She landed awkwardly in a twisted heap of hair, metal, and damp straw.

She panicked then, kicking wildly, trying every maneuver she knew — *Snakes, Flying Snakes, Hares, Double Hares, Dragonflies* — desperately attempting to land a blow on the walls of her prison. The only part of it she could kick with any kind of force was the floor, which refused to break. Its strange motion kept knocking her off balance and her feet were getting sore.

"Crack, stupid Two Hoof floor!" she screamed, slamming her bruised heels into the straw again and again. "Crack!"

But it was hopeless. As Marell Storm Temper was so fond of reminding her, you needed four legs to do a successful *Canyon* — the kick that could crack the ground. Shaiala's eyes filled. Her head throbbed terribly. But worst of all was the pain of separation from the herd and her friends. Even in her darkest nightmares, she'd never imagined it would happen like this.

Tears rolled down her cheeks and dripped into her hair. "Kamara Silvermane?" she whispered. "Rafiz Longshadow? Where you go? How I get here?"

She frowned, trying to remember what had happened after she'd been caught.

Glittering holes in the night. Eyes staring through them, colder and blacker than death.

Her mind shied away. She clutched her head. It hurt when she tried to remember, as if the Two Hoofs had chained her thoughts as well as her ankles.

She relieved herself in a corner as far as the chain would reach, then returned to the middle of her prison and lay down like a centaur, legs folded beneath her, every sense alert. The air was damp and tasted of salt. An eerie, wild song teased the edge of her hearing, only to fade when she tried to understand. An unsettling song, like the wind blowing from a far place.

She shivered, wrapped her arms around the rips in her tunic, and fixed her eyes on those swaying lines of light. Centaurs did not have a word for *door*, but she guessed the Two Hoofs must have put her in here through that part of the wall. Eventually, they'd have to open it again to let her out. When they did, she'd be ready.

This was the hope that kept her courage from failing as the ship sped across the Western Sea to the Isle of Echoes, home of the Singers, where people sent Crazies like Shaiala to be cured by the power of Song.

2
WILD GIRL

Isle history was not the Eighth Year's favorite lesson. Out of a class of twenty-three novices, Renn was the only one listening to Singer Ollaron. At least, he was *trying* to listen. Not easy when everyone else seemed more interested in what the orderlies would serve up for lunch.

The whispers and giggles found their way around the cool bluestone walls to where Renn sat on the front bench, straight-backed, his skinny knees pressed together and his pale hands clasped in his lap. A fresh bruise on his arm showed clearly against his tunic. He surreptitiously covered it with a fold of white silk. Novices of the Echorium weren't supposed to do things that damaged them physically. Especially not novices like Renn whose small frame, serious gray eyes, and pure voice made him definite Singer material, but on the downside meant he was bullied by everyone, even the girls.

Not that there was much danger the old Singer who took them for history would notice Renn's injury. Ollaron was almost as ancient as the events he was trying to teach the reluctant Eighth Year. He had only three strands of hair left to dye blue and his eyes obviously weren't sharp enough these days to see the others messing around at the back. Renn suspected their teacher was also going deaf. If Singer Ollaron had been able to hear properly, the entire class would have been sent for a disciplinary Song long before now.

Today, their teacher was telling them about the Battle of the Merlee, which had taken place twenty years ago around the shores of the Isle of Echoes and ended with the death of the First Singer. The Half Creatures had helped the Singers somehow, but the room was too noisy to catch the details. Frustrated, Renn turned his head. "Shut up!" he hissed, aiming his pallet-whisper at Alaira and Geran, the class troublemakers. "Some of us are trying to listen."

"Don't know why," Alaira hissed back, barely bothering to lower her voice. "Who cares about a bunch of old priests who tried to destroy the Isle way before we were born? Didn't succeed, did they? Our Songs are too strong." She flicked back a strand of long blue hair.

"Worse luck," Geran put in. "If they had, we wouldn't be stuck in here listening to this junk now. Isn't it lunchtime yet? I'm starving!" Several people giggled. Geran was the largest boy in the class with a bottomless stomach to match.

"Shh!" Renn hissed, casting a worried look at Singer Ollaron. But their teacher was chanting through his material as fast as possible, clearly as anxious to end the lesson as they were.

Renn sighed and stared at the narrow window. A curtain of flapping gray silk kept out the westerly breeze. It made the room dim, especially when the sun went behind a cloud. He shivered without knowing why. It was as if something had just breathed on the back of his neck. While his defenses were down, faint words formed in his head.

Son of stone-singer help.

He clenched his fists and shook the words out.

When he returned his attention to Singer Ollaron, the class

had gone quiet. For a wild moment, Renn thought they'd heard the words too. Then he realized that the lesson had reached the part where Singers punished the people who'd attacked the Isle.

The death-song, *Yehn*, was about the only subject that still had the power to interest the Eighth Years. The boys leaned forward with gruesome interest. Alaira's blue eyes shone. The old Singer blinked in surprise at all the eager faces.

He continued a little uncertainly. "The priests' accomplice and supplier, the lowland Lord Javelly, was discovered the next morning at his banqueting table facedown in a bowl of his own greasy quetzal soup. His servants assumed he'd drunk too much wine, passed out, and drowned himself by accident. But we know better — don't we?"

He peered around the room again to check that they were all still listening, then took a deep breath and asked, "How do you think Lord Javelly died?"

"It was the *Yehn*, of course!" Alaira called out in her clear voice. "Singers sang him to death!"

"Yes, very good — um — Aleera." He ignored the giggles that rewarded him for getting her name wrong and plunged on. "But Lord Javelly was in his castle on the mainland, remember, whereas the Singers were here in the Echorium, singing on the Pentangle. So how did the Song work?"

Silence. Alaira reddened as the old Singer squinted hopefully at her. She caught Renn looking and scowled at him.

Their teacher glanced around. "Anyone?"

People shuffled their feet, beginning to lose interest. Renn put his hand up. Ollaron looked relieved.

"Yes, Renn?"

"It was the stone, Singer. The big bluestone they put on the Pentangle stool. It amplified the *Yehn* and transmitted it to the mainland where the bluestone in Lord Javelly's Trust-Gift, which he was wearing at the time, picked it up and killed him."

"Know-it-all," Alaira muttered.

Singer Ollaron smiled at him. Renn flushed, feeling guilty. Their teacher obviously thought he was genuinely interested in all this dead stuff. He didn't know the real reason Renn listened so carefully.

"Excellent, Renn!" he said. "I'm glad someone's been paying attention. First, the Song traveled through the bluestone of the Echorium, then down into the rock of the Isle itself, and from there into the sea. . . ." He pulled aside the curtain to demonstrate and his voice trailed off as he frowned at something below.

"But what about the chief priest, Singer?" Renn blurted out, earning scowls and hisses of *"Shut up, you little idiot!"* from the rest of the class.

Renn persisted. "He didn't have any bluestone on him like Lord Javelly, did he? So how did the *Yehn* kill him?"

"It didn't kill him, stupid!" Geran shouted out. "Everyone knows that."

Their teacher's frown deepened as he retreated to his podium. "You haven't been listening, Geran. I told you the delegation sent out after the battle failed to find the chief priest's body. That doesn't mean the *Yehn* didn't work. There are lots of reasons for not finding a body, especially at sea." He kept glancing at the window as he spoke.

Geran winked at his friends. "Yes! And one of them is because the body is still walking around on its own two legs!"

The class laughed.

"Don't be such a salad-brain, Geran," Alaira said. "Dead bodies don't walk. It's perfectly obvious the priest was turned into a zombie. The *Yehn* scrambled his brains." She climbed onto the bench and pranced from one end to the other with a hand on her throat, rolling her eyes and making choking sounds.

Singer Ollaron closed his eyes.

"Yes, but how did it *work*?" Renn asked again.

His question was lost in a fresh eruption of giggles as the others followed Alaira's lead, some of them humming what they could remember of *Yehn*, others melodramatically "dying" on the stone floor beneath the rows of benches. In the process, someone rolled on the hem of the curtain. The silk tore, letting in a blaze of stormy sunlight.

"Look!" Alaira said, abandoning her zombie act to point at the harbor. "A new ship!"

Immediately, everyone crowded around the window, jumping on the benches and standing on tiptoe to see. Renn, left alone at the front of the room with their teacher, clutched his knees in frustration. He suspected Singer Ollaron didn't know how the *Yehn* had killed the chief priest anyway, which was why he'd let the Eighth Years disrupt the lesson. Sometimes Renn wished they had First Singer Graia for history. She'd never let the class get away with behavior like this. Then again, she wouldn't let things slip like old Ollaron did — morsels of information about Half Creatures that Renn seized upon and secreted away for future use, in the same way Geran's gang hid honeycakes under their tunics for midnight feasts back in the pallets.

He sighed and squirmed his way through the crush at the window, getting an elbow in his eye for his trouble. Might as well have a look, since it was obvious he wasn't going to learn anything useful today.

Their classroom was on the west side of the Echorium with a good view of the harbor when the weather allowed. For once, the clouds had broken at exactly the right time. There was an unfamiliar ship, flying a tattered purple banner. The ship was too distant, and the sun shining on the water too dazzling, to see the design. But the sailors were slowly making their way up the Five Thousand Steps, dragging in their midst a filthy, tangle-haired creature that fought them wildly every step of the way.

"What is it?" Alaira was leaning dangerously out of the window to see better.

"An animal?" one of the girls hazarded. "A mainland monkey, maybe? I've heard they keep 'em as pets over there."

"No," Geran said. "It's much too big for a monkey. Besides, it don't look very tame to me." He grinned. "Hey, do you think it's edible?"

Everyone groaned.

"Don't be silly," Alaira said. "Why would they go to all the trouble of bringing us live animals from the mainland when we have plenty of fish in the sea? Anyway, it's walking on two legs. And it's chained. Maybe it's some kind of Half Creature?"

"I know!" said Geran. "It's gone crazy and bitten someone, so they're bringing it for Song treatment!"

Alaira gave him a scornful look. "Singers have better things to do than sing to Half Creatures."

"I think it's human," Renn said, uneasy with all this talk of Half Creatures. "Looks like a girl."

For the second time that morning, the bluestone walls seemed to close in on him. The sun dimmed. The chamber chilled. Someone — or something — was whispering in his head, clearer than ever before.

Son of stone-singer help child of stone-dancers.

He looked around suspiciously. Alaira and Geran were arguing about whether Echorium Songs would have any effect on Half Creatures. Everyone else was hopping up and down, trying to see.

"THAT'S ENOUGH!" Singer Ollaron roared.

In all the excitement, they'd forgotten their teacher was a trained Singer. Forgotten that however old and decrepit Ollaron might be now, he'd sung on the Pentangle and his voice had once been powerful enough to reach halfway around the world.

The fear-song, *Aushan,* thrummed around the walls and through the soles of their sandals into their very bones.

The class fell silent. One by one, they crept back to the benches and sat meekly in their places, backs straight and eyes wide, casting sideways glances at the window.

"I know you think the things I'm talking about have nothing to do with you," Ollaron continued. "But some of us are old enough to remember the Battle of the Merlee. You saw that ship down there. Imagine what the world would be like if people had nowhere to bring their sick and their Crazies to be healed. We came *this* close to losing the Echorium and all it stands for." He held up a finger and thumb, slightly parted — an effect ruined by the way his hand trembled.

The class relaxed slightly.

Ollaron sighed. "All right, off you go — and while you're having lunch, try to remember how lucky you are to be here." His final words were lost in their undignified rush for the door.

Shouts and whoops echoed in the bluestone corridors as the Eighth Years fought to be first into the dining hall. Renn, still thinking about the girl on the Steps, waited until the room had emptied. He shook his head. He had other things to worry about.

When the last novice had gone, Renn quietly fell into step a few paces behind Singer Ollaron and trailed after him until the old Singer turned up the stairs to his private chambers. This usually enabled Renn to creep into lunch, bolt his fish soup, and get to his next class before anyone noticed him.

Not today.

Alaira and Geran were waiting for him in the deserted corridor. As Renn hesitated, wondering if he could maybe duck up the stairs after Ollaron and work his way around to the dining hall by another route, Geran seized his arm. The boy's large fingers dug painfully and deliberately into Renn's bruise.

Alaira smiled. "We think you work too hard," she said. "We think you need some fresh air — and don't you dare yell, or we'll tell the First Singer you hear things in your head."

Renn's heart sank. "It's starting to rain," he pointed out.

"We're going to take a closer look at that Crazy," Geran said. "And since you're such a Half Creature expert, you're coming with us. So it looks as if you're going to get wet, doesn't it?"

He had no choice. It was either go along with them or have his awful secret revealed to the whole Echorium. Which was how he came to be on the wrong side of the wall when the main gates creaked open and the last person they wanted to catch them out here hurried down the Steps, escorted by two orderlies, to meet the sailors.

*

The Second Singer of the Echorium didn't normally concern himself with common Crazies, not even during the rare times he was on the Isle rather than taking care of Echorium business abroad, but Shaiala had no way of knowing this. All she heard was that amazing song coming out of the clouds. The notes dripped into the edges of her thoughts and soothed her head, in the same way that the rain was washing the grime of her prison from her skin. For the first time since the Two Hoofs had dragged her off their floating building with her feet still hobbled, she stopped fighting and took a good look at her surroundings.

Wherever they were taking her was a long climb. The Two Hoofs were out of condition and breathing heavily. Fish odors mixed with some foul Two Hoof brew wafted into her face, turning her stomach. They were ascending an endless flight of gleaming blue steps. Below, she could still see the tiny harbor with its Two Hoof houses clinging to the cliffs. Up here, the hillside was steep and treacherous with loose stones. The steps disappeared into the clouds, where an enormous building of bluestone shimmered in and out of the mist, all towers and turrets and sky-piercing spires. Shaiala had never seen anything like it and stopped to stare.

One of the Two Hoofs prodded her with his stick. Her foot shot out instinctively, only to be snatched back by the hated chain before it could do any real damage. Nevertheless, the men stepped away from her, wary. Even hobbled, she'd landed several kicks on the shins and ankles of her escorts as they'd climbed.

The clouds drifted together again and the building disappeared. Only that song remained, flowing down the steps like a cool stream.

Relax, it whispered. *Shh, calm, rest.*

All at once, Shaiala realized how tired she was. She lowered her foot. Her hair swung across her eyes in greasy black tangles. The Two Hoofs closed in again and seized her arms. This time she didn't have the strength to kick them. She expected them to drag her onward, but felt them stiffen. She looked up.

A slender Two Hoof clad in swirling gray had appeared out of the cloud. His face had been burned by sun and wind, and raindrops glittered on his faded blue curls. He stood three steps above them, humming under his breath. He wasn't as tall or physically strong as the sailors but his brilliant green eyes caught and held Shaiala's as surely as her captors held her arms. She had a vague impression of two more gray-clad men standing behind him. The dark-skinned one seemed to have bones braided into his hair but she couldn't look away from the singer long enough to check.

An uneasy image sprang into her head. Of other, darker eyes staring at her through glittering holes in the night. She tore her gaze free with a shudder.

The singer frowned and said something to her escort that almost made sense. His voice wasn't rough like the other Two Hoofs'. It had music deep down, like a centaur's. She listened carefully, forgetting her unease. The singer said something else and gestured angrily at her ankles. His hum grew louder and *changed*. Little ripples of fear prickled Shaiala's spine.

Her escorts muttered under their breath. One of them ventured a reply, which provoked another angry hum from the singer. Still grumbling, the one who'd protested produced a key and crouched by Shaiala's feet. He unlocked the hobbles and quickly scrambled away. The others took hasty steps backward.

Shaiala caught her breath. Were they really letting her go?

The green-eyed singer gestured to his companions and descended another step, still humming. *Relax, calm, dream.*

She shook the song out of her head in alarm. The singer was now so close she could smell salt on his robes and traces of bitter seaweed in his sweat. His eyes never left hers as he sang.

Shh, calm, forget.

She'd done enough forgetting. With a final shudder, she aimed a lightning kick at his legs. *Snake.* Her heel cracked against bone.

The song stopped mid-note.

Her escort scattered, yelling warnings. The gray-uniformed men hurried forward to help the singer who had doubled over to clutch his knee. But it hadn't been a clean kick. Stiff after the long, cramped voyage, her muscles weak from lack of food, and still half expecting the chain to restrict her legs, Shaiala had merely bruised bone with the kick that should have been capable of killing a snake. Almost at once, its victim swallowed his pain and straightened, fury blazing in his green eyes.

Shaiala didn't give him a chance to start singing again. Before the Two Hoofs could recover, she leaped off the side of the steps, splashed through a stream, and swerved around the blue boulders into the thickest mist. With her hair blown across her eyes, she didn't see the danger ahead until it was too late. Little screams came from a concealed gully as three Two Hoof foals flung themselves out of her path. One wasn't quick enough and she tripped over him. They went down together in a tangle of legs and arms.

"Gerroff me!" he cried. "Go away. You'll get us all caught!"

"It your fault! You trip I —"

Shaiala spoke before she realized. She'd understood him. He was a Two Hoof, yet his words made sense.

For an instant they knelt in the bottom of the gully, winded, staring at each other. She had time to notice his eyes were wide and gray and frightened. Then the singer called out in a furious voice, and the other Two Hoof foals dragged the gray-eyed boy away from her. They waved their arms at Shaiala, hissing unintelligible words and pointing furiously back the way she'd come.

She scrambled after the boy. "Wait! I know you understand I!"

But the boy-foal slammed his hands over his ears. "Stop it," he whispered. "Leave me alone. You're crazy." He fought his way free of the other two, grabbed a pebble, and threw it as hard as he could over the edge of the gully so it rattled across the hillside.

There was a shout and feet pounded toward their hiding place. The Two Hoof foals groaned, grabbed the boy again, and scrambled out into the mist.

Shaiala gave up on the boy and fled downhill. She'd had enough of running in clouds. She needed to see where she was going. Loose shale slid under her feet; thorns snagged her tunic and grabbed at her hair. More shouts followed as the Two Hoofs spotted her and gave chase. But they hadn't been taught to run by centaurs.

Lungs sore with the unfamiliar air, Shaiala raced recklessly toward the sea. She had no idea where she was going, nor did she care. As she ran, the rain stopped and the sun came out. Suddenly, it was warm. Nothing in this place made sense except the boy-foal with the gray eyes.

And he had betrayed her.

*

Temporarily united by the need to get clear before the Second Singer spotted them, the three truants made their way across the hillside under cover of the mist, then followed a streambed down to the sea, finally slithering to a breathless halt in the shadow of the cliffs at the far end of the West Beach. Despite the trouble they were in, Alaira and Geran were laughing between gulps of air. Renn held his side, feeling sick and scared. The wild girl's words still echoed in his head. *I know you understand I.* She'd come this way. The tide was out, and he could see her footprints glistening in the wet sand. It looked as if she'd headed straight for the sea but at the last moment lost her nerve and swerved around the headland. The footprints melted as they slowly filled with water.

"Never seen anyone run so fast!" Geran said in admiration. "A girl too."

"What difference does that make?" Alaira's blue eyes flashed a challenge, but Geran was too full of what had happened to notice.

"Did you see what she did? She kicked the *Second Singer*!"

"Stopped him from singing!"

"I didn't even know he was back on the Isle. He's going to be furious when he catches her."

This reminded Renn that the wild girl wasn't the only one the Second Singer would be furious with when he caught them. Besides being the youngest Singer ever to be promoted to such an important position, Kherron had a reputation for being ruthless, both with the lords on the mainland and with any novice who had the misfortune to get on his bad side. Pallet rumor said Singer Kherron could kill an armed warrior with a single hum. Renn didn't really believe this anymore, not now that he knew how Songs worked. But he didn't want to test the theory on himself. He glanced up the cliffs to where the highest towers of the Echorium were still hidden by cloud and wondered how he'd gotten himself into this mess.

"Don't you think we should get off this beach?" he suggested. "They're bound to follow her trail and then they'll find us." Renn stared at the girl's footprints, his head aching. He hoped Alaira and Geran would see sense now that they'd satisfied their curiosity about the Crazy.

Alaira scowled at him. "If we're going to be in trouble, we might as well get into some real trouble. Come on, I want to see where she went."

"I don't think that's a very good idea," Renn said, turning cold.

"What's the matter?" Alaira said. "Are you scared?"

"No, but —"

"*Hearing* things again?"

"No!"

"He is!" Alaira giggled. She stared into Renn's eyes and smiled coldly. "If you don't come with us, I'll tell the Second Singer you understood every word that Crazy was saying."

Renn's stomach gave a wild flutter. "I did not!"

Alaira laughed. "Oh come *on*, Renn! We saw your face. I think Singer Kherron would be very interested to know you hear Half Creatures in your head. Perhaps I should tell him anyway to make up for what you did back there."

Renn turned even colder. "I don't hear Half Creatures."

"Everyone knows that's what voices in the head mean. And you're supposed to tell the First Singer if you hear them." She turned to Geran. "What Song do you think he'll get for keeping his talents secret? *Shi*? *Aushan*, maybe?"

"You can't prove it," Renn whispered. But he knew he'd do exactly what they wanted to stop them from telling.

Geran started to say something about Half Creatures but Alaira held up a hand. "Shh!" she hissed. "Someone's coming. Hide!"

They flung themselves behind the rocks, leaving Renn the smallest and most exposed one. He crouched behind it anyway, heart hammering, as the sailors who'd brought the wild girl to the Isle pounded past not an arm's-length away. Speckled blue sand sprayed into his eyes and he smothered a cough. Close up, the men were rough, dirty, and hairy. Their breeches and tunics had been patched many times. They carried stout sticks. One of them spotted the footprints going around the headland and gave a triumphant shout. Then every single man froze as a low, dangerous note echoed down the cliff. Renn peered farther around his rock.

Blue curls steaming in the sun, the Second Singer stood on a ledge above the beach, flanked by the two orderlies who had accompanied him from the Echorium.

"Don't chase her!" he called, reinforcing this with more *Aushan* as he limped down the narrow path to the sand, followed by the orderlies. "Return to your ship. I'll be responsible for her from here."

"But, Singer —"

"I *said* I'll be responsible." Warnings vibrated in his voice. The sailors backed off, grumbling. The captain fingered the manacles he'd taken off the girl. Some of the others swished their sticks in a threatening manner. The orderlies stiffened. The one with bones in his hair rested a dark hand on his sword.

"The Echorium thanks you for bringing her," Singer Kherron continued, changing smoothly to *Challa* with a skill that made Renn sigh in admiration. "Since this is a special case, we won't require any payment for healing her. You can keep whatever fee her people gave you for the Echorium. That'll save us both the trouble of haggling over your percentage." The *Challa* gave way to *Kashe*.

Some of the men chuckled and tossed their sticks away. But the captain swung his chain and bared his black teeth.

"She's been a lot of trouble, Singer. Almost sank us before we even left Southport Estuary, then kicked half my crew black an' blue when they tried to feed her. I was all for chucking her overboard and lettin' her kick the sea monsters to her heart's content. But it's not quite as simple as that."

Singer Kherron frowned and glanced down the beach. "What do you want?"

One of the men plucked at his captain's sleeve and mumbled something. The captain shook him off. His tone grew wily.

"I knew you'd understand, Singer. They didn't exactly send your fee with us, as such. But they promised you could collect it from the mainland when you're next over there."

The Second Singer's eyes narrowed. "Didn't trust you, huh?"

The captain scowled. But at Singer Kherron's hum of disapproval, he rushed on. "They said if you sent one of your little blue stones back with us, they'd contact you." He scratched his head. "Don't say as I understand it myself, but they only paid us half the transportation fee, see? We get the other half when we bring the stone back to prove we delivered the girl safe and sound. This island's the only place you can get 'em, innit? Must be pretty valuable, I'm thinkin'. But you got no worries we'd make off with it, 'cause a coffer of gold's more use than pretty stones to simple folk like us." He chuckled and the bolder members of his crew laughed with him.

Kherron's eyes narrowed still further. "The Echorium usually expects goods in payment for Song treatment," he said. "Yet you expect *us* to give *you* valuable bluestone for the privilege of healing your wild girl?" *Aushan* thrummed through his words, making Renn stiffen even though the Song wasn't aimed at him.

The captain backed away.

Singer Kherron held up a hand. "Wait, I haven't finished. Who's supposed to be paying for this girl's therapy? What did they look like?"

The bloodshot eyes shifted. "Er . . . well, we was contacted by this bloke wearing a mask, see. Very shifty-lookin', if you ask me, all these weird colored feathers hangin' off it."

"But whoever he is, he must be filthy rich," added one of his men, "'cause his mask was made of some fancy black crystal with jewels around the eyes and — Yeech!" He staggered to his knees in a spray of sand as his captain's chain caught him across the ear.

"Hmm," Singer Kherron said, looking thoughtfully at the felled sailor. "Black crystal, you say? No informed guesses? Men of the world like you, eh?" Undercurrents of *Kashe* mixed skillfully with his words.

The captain shifted uneasily from foot to foot. "I did think, er, it might've been a Horselord, Singer. They're not seen much around the coastal towns, bein' nomads and all, but I've heard some of 'em have riches that'd make your eyes pop out. And their women have a reputation for bein' a bit wildlike. My guess is the girl must've been too wild even for the Horselords, so they sent her here to have her tamed." He rubbed at a bruise on his shin and winced. "She could do with some taming, if you ask me."

Something about the way the captain avoided the Second Singer's eyes suggested he wasn't telling the whole truth. Renn listened, fascinated, hoping for more. But it seemed the interview was over.

The Second Singer stared hard at the southern sailors, then smiled. "Good. It always helps to know a patient's background. I'll send an orderly down to the harbor with the bluestone you require. In the meantime, I'd advise you to ready your ship for departure — the weather's about to change. And I'm sure you're anxious to get back to Southport to claim the rest of your gold as soon as possible."

The sailors hurried back toward Harbourtown, slapping one another on the back and congratulating their captain in loud, rough voices. It was clear they hadn't expected to see either the bluestone or the second half of their fee, which made Renn wonder why they'd bothered bringing the girl all the way to the Isle in the first place.

The Second Singer must have been thinking the same thing. While the orderlies knelt to examine the girl's footprints, he gazed thoughtfully down the beach. Renn relaxed a little. The sailors had done them a favor. With all the running around, they'd obliterated the tracks he, Geran, and Alaira had left in the sand.

He was just wondering if he could get away with pleading indigestion as an excuse for missing Rhythm Practice when Singer Kherron turned and looked straight at the rock where he was hiding.

"All right," the Second Singer said with a strong undercurrent of *Aushan* that froze Renn's blood. "You can come out now. All of you."

*

There was no point even trying to explain. Every trained Singer could hear the difference between truth and lies, and Renn hardly dared open his mouth lest Second Singer Kherron should discover the real reason he'd let Geran and Alaira bully him into coming outside. Fortunately, this worked both ways. The other two kept their mouths shut as well, in case they got into trouble for bullying Renn.

They waited meekly while the orderlies collected the wild girl from a small cove around the headland where she'd been trapped by the rising tide. The climb up the Five Thousand Steps was like a dream where nothing mattered because it was so unreal — no doubt a side effect of the *Challa* the Second Singer was singing to keep the wild girl quiet. By mid-afternoon, all four runaways were in the treatment levels of the Echorium, locked in separate cells.

3
PENTANGLE

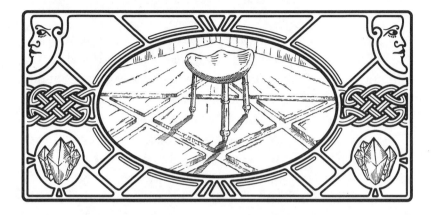

Renn was curled up on his pallet, staring nervously at the door, listening to footsteps approach then fade along the corridors. He wished the orderlies would hurry up and come for him. It was difficult to estimate time without sight of the sun, but he reckoned he'd been down here at least two days. The more he tried to tell himself the *Shi* that Singer Kherron had recommended wouldn't be so bad, the more nervous he became.

At night when they were supposed to be asleep, the boys used to pass stories around the dormitory in pallet-whispers, giving Renn nightmares: about the novice whose brains had spurted out of his ears during his *Shi* and splattered the five Singers on the points of the Pentangle; about the Final Year who'd turned into a Crazy afterward and thrown himself out of one of the high windows. If you wanted proof, there was a dark patch on the rocks below that was supposed to be where the unfortunate boy's head had smashed open like a sea-eagle's egg. It looked exactly like the scorch marks left by the orderlies' bonfires, but the rumors must have started somewhere.

Shi makes you cry.

Renn squeezed his hands into fists. The treatment levels were belowground and full of eerie shadows cast by lanterns with blue silk shades. If it hadn't been for the meals an orderly thrust through the door at regular intervals, he'd have thought they had forgotten him. His cell was at the end of a row, where it was quietest. Listening as hard as he could, Renn still couldn't make out what was happening. They'd taken the wild girl to the Pentangle several times, but so far no one had even brought him the Song Potion to drink. He had no way of knowing whether Geran and Alaira had been given their *Shi* yet.

When the footsteps finally stopped outside his door and a key turned in the lock, it was actually a relief. Whatever they did to him, it couldn't be worse than this awful waiting.

It took him a moment to realize the orderly hadn't brought the Song Potion, as anticipated, but a visitor. In the blue shadows outside his cell, his robes smelling of salt and with a deep crease between his startling green eyes, stood the Second Singer.

Renn scrambled to his feet, heart thudding. "S-Singer!" he said. "I'm sorry —"

"Quiet," said his visitor. He turned to the hovering orderly. "The boy hasn't had the Song Potion yet?"

"No, Singer. We — ah — were busy with the new girl and what with everyone so tired after her therapy we didn't think we should give it to him too early."

Singer Kherron waved the orderly silent. He gave Renn a very searching look. "So you find the Echorium boring, do you?"

Renn flushed. "I —"

Singer Kherron cut him off. "Don't bother me with your excuses. I know the inside of novices' heads better than you think and, if you want my opinion, a few more punishments wouldn't hurt any of you. Discipline is far too slack these days." He pressed his lips together. "But it seems you've been lucky this time. No *Shi* for you — First Singer's orders. Hurry along to the baths and change into a clean tunic. You're expected on the Pentangle a sunstep from now. Don't be late."

Renn's mouth fell open. The Second Singer was halfway down the corridor by the time he recovered enough to stammer, "The P-Pentangle? But if I'm not going to have a Song, then why?"

He turned to the orderly, hoping for clues. The orderly shrugged. "Don't ask me. Singers have been rushing around like Crazies ever since that girl arrived. Classes canceled, novices milling around like schools of lost fish. I haven't seen anything like it since after the Battle of the Merlee when all them wild Karchholders crowded in here with their death-braids and red swords. You'd better do what the Second Singer says and thank the echoes you've been let off so lightly."

Lightly? Renn's stomach churned as he hurried up the stairs and fought his way through huddles of whispering novices. He had to squeeze past a knot of Eighth Years, but they didn't even notice him. He couldn't see Alaira or Geran among them. In any other circumstances, this would have been a relief, but today their absence only made him more nervous. He bathed and changed as quickly as possible, glanced out the dormitory window to check the shadow cast by the sun pole, dragged a comb through his mussed hair, and took the stairs to the Pentangle two at a time, arriving breathless at the big double doors just as the sunstep was up.

They were closed. There was no sign of the orderlies who usually stood guard outside during a Song. Renn smoothed his tunic and moistened his lips. He was about to knock when one of the doors opened a crack, spilling lavender light into the corridor — the color used for *Challa*. Renn relaxed slightly, only to tense up again when he saw who had opened the door.

"Come in, Renn," said First Singer Graia, her eyes crinkling at the corners as she smiled. "We're waiting for you." She'd

coiled her hair around her head in a thick blue braid, making
her seem taller and more imposing than ever.

Nervously, Renn stepped into the five-sided chamber. The
domed roof soared overhead, making him dizzy when he looked
up. The viewing balcony seemed to be empty. Echoes of old
Songs haunted the shadows as he followed the First Singer
along one edge of the five-pointed star etched into the floor. He
eyed the stool in the center as they passed, but it seemed he
really wasn't going to be given a Song today. Graia led the way
to the far side of the Pentangle where a slender woman with the
longest, palest hair Renn had ever seen stood in the shadows
watching them approach.

At first, he thought she was a patient who had just been given
Challa, she was so quiet and still. Then he realized she wore
Singer gray, only the silk was so tattered and salt-stained, it
clung to her legs like feathery seaweed. Her hair had been
threaded with tiny colored shells that tinkled as she stepped forward to greet them. A thick red bracelet encircled one arm just
above her elbow. Her cheeks were freckled by the sun and her
eyes were wide and gray, the same color as Renn's own. The
lavender light of the Pentangle shifted in them like the ever-
changing sky over the Isle.

"This is Singer Rialle," said the First Singer. "She's got something important to ask you."

Very slowly, Renn let out his breath. A Singer who didn't dye
her hair blue? He'd never seen her in the Echorium before or
he'd have remembered.

As he glanced at Graia in confusion, Rialle said softly, "Why
didn't you tell anyone you could hear Half Creatures, Renn?
How long has it been happening?"

He stared wildly at her, then back at the First Singer. Graia
had her head tipped to one side. Truth-listening.

"Since the First Year," he answered stiffly.

The silver-haired Singer blinked. "You've hidden it that long?"

"Not exactly hidden it," Renn mumbled.

Now that he knew what this was about, his heart slowed. He remembered his breathing exercises and completed one there and then, noting the First Singer's approval. Geran and Alaira must have told, of course. Probably trying to reduce their punishment. In a strange way, it was a relief to have it out in the open. At least, they'd never be able to make him do anything so stupid again.

"Geran and Alaira have known for ages," he explained, unable to meet those disturbing gray eyes. "They threatened to tell on me. That's why I was outside with them when the wild girl came."

The First Singer frowned. "You were more afraid of us finding out you could hear Half Creatures than of having *Shi*? Why, Renn?"

"Because —" He closed his mouth on what he'd been about to say. *Everyone knows the people who hear them go crazy.*

"Because what?" Graia asked.

Renn shook his head. "I'm sorry, Singer. I didn't know what the voices were at first. Then, when I did, it was too late to tell because I was already in trouble for not telling."

The two Singers glanced at each other.

Renn looked curiously at Rialle. "If you're a Singer, why isn't your hair blue? Why don't you teach any of us?"

"Renn!" Singer Graia hummed disapproval, but Rialle held up a hand.

"It's all right, the boy should know." She turned to Renn. "I don't dye my hair because I don't sing officially on the Pentangle, so there's no need. And I don't teach because I no longer live in the Echorium."

Renn frowned at her. "Where do you live, then?"

"I live on the beach where I can be near my friends."

"What do you do when it rains?"

Rialle laughed and the shells in her hair tinkled merrily. "I take cover in the caves, of course. I'm not as crazy as all that. I'm surprised you don't have stories in the pallets about the Singer who still swims with the merlee."

Renn stared. "But I thought only novices could hear Half Creatures!"

"You heard right," Singer Graia said, giving Rialle a warning look. "Which is why you're here. Rialle has a special bond with the merlee, and we hoped she'd be able to understand the girl you saw outside. We've managed to discover a few things. But unfortunately Shaiala speaks a Half Creature tongue that's strange to us. It's not purely an inside-tongue like the merlee's, nor an outside-tongue like human speech, but seems to be a mixture of both. According to Geran and Alaira, you understood what she was saying —"

So they had told about that, too? Renn wasn't really surprised.

"— and we'd like you to try translating for us." The First Singer looked hard at him. "There might be some unpleasant things. Shaiala seems to have had a hard time of it lately. I don't really want to involve you with your Final Year coming up, but this is the only way I can think of to get her story straight. Are you willing to try, Renn?"

Rialle was watching him in a very disturbing manner.

"All right," he mumbled, curiosity overcoming his reluctance to go anywhere near the wild girl again.

Singer Graia smiled. "Good! This'll make things much easier. You shouldn't have to translate every word. We were able to open some of the communication doors in Shaiala's head because it seems she had already learned a certain amount of human speech before she was adopted by the Half Creatures. I think she understands most of what we're saying to her. But it was a long time ago, and we can't hope to teach her an entire lifetime's vocabulary overnight. It's still a struggle for her to speak to us and she's having trouble remembering everything. I wish we could take more time with her, but something's come up and we need to hear her full story as soon as possible. I expect she'll be only too pleased to have someone her own age who can talk to her in the tongue she knows best. It'll help her feel more at home."

The First Singer exchanged another glance with Rialle. Neither of them noticed Renn wince. The whispers were back in his head.

Son of stone-singer help child of stone-dancers.

He stared determinedly at the floor. The whispers usually went away if he concentrated on something that definitely couldn't talk. This time, however, the trick didn't work.

He looked up to find Rialle watching him in that way that made his skin creep. He wished she'd go back to her cave but dared not say so in front of the First Singer. Instead, he said, "These Half Creatures who adopted the wild gir — I mean, Shaiala. What sort are they?"

"Well . . ." The First Singer coughed. A little *Kashe* entered her voice as she said, "We're not exactly sure. Shaiala seems convinced she was brought up by centaurs. They're supposed to be half human, half horse. Different shades of blue, or so she says."

Renn giggled. "But centaurs are just stories to frighten First Years! And everyone knows horses aren't blue."

Again, that exchanged glance.

"It was probably our hair dye that suggested the color," Singer Graia said. "But it's what Shaiala believes — among other things."

Her words contained dark undercurrents that made Renn shiver. She stared at the doors a moment, then smiled brightly.

"Don't worry, we'll get to the truth soon. I doubt it's as bad as Singer Kherron thinks. All right, Renn. I'm going to ask the orderlies to bring her up now. Be ready for her."

*

Renn was beginning to have second thoughts about the whole thing. But the First Singer had already opened one of the doors and called to someone outside. After a short wait, during which the two Singers held a whispered conversation Renn could *not* overhear despite sidling closer and straining his ears, the doors opened a second time. Singer Kherron strode in followed by a tall, dark-haired girl dressed in the Echorium uniform of white silk tunic and skirt. An orderly steered the girl gently by one elbow.

At first Renn didn't recognize her. Her hair had been washed and neatly braided. With all the dirt scrubbed off, her skin was a different color. Deep gold, like honey. He had time to think she looked rather nice and that maybe it wouldn't be so bad translating for her, after all. Then she broke free of the orderly, took a flying leap across the Pentangle, and kicked him on the ankle — hard!

"I you hate!" she screamed in Half Creature speech.

As Renn clutched his foot and hopped clear, the orderly rushed to restrain the girl. Before he could touch her, however, Rialle started to sing. *Challa.* Soft and sweet. The orderly backed off, leaving Shaiala standing stiffly in the center of the floor, black eyes flashing. Singer Kherron simply watched, arms folded, a little smile on his lips. He didn't seem very surprised.

Renn fought a battle with tears and won. Tentatively, he tried his weight on his injured leg. It wasn't broken in eight places as he'd feared, but he could already feel the bruise swelling around his left ankle.

The First Singer shook her head. "Stop that, Shaiala," she said in a stern voice. "Renn's here to help you. He seems to be the only person in the Echorium who can understand your Half Creature voice, so I'm afraid you're stuck with him." Her words were expertly laced with *Kashe,* though the laughter-song didn't seem to have much effect on Shaiala.

She glared at Renn. "I speak good now!" she announced, shaping the human words slowly and carefully. "I not his help need. He not friend! Send he away."

Silence. The orderly gave the Second Singer a questioning glance. Rialle was still humming *Challa* under her breath.

Singer Graia frowned. "Now then, Shaiala. We're only trying to find out what happened to you."

The girl stamped her foot, sending alien echoes crashing around the Pentangle. One of the lanterns flickered out. "I tell truth!" she said. "Why not you believe I?"

Singer Kherron tightened his lips. He seized Shaiala's arm and dragged her to the stool in the center of the five-pointed star. "You sit right there, young lady!" he said. "And no more kicking or stamping, or I'll get those chains back off the sailors and put them on you myself."

His final words thrummed with *Aushan*. Renn's stomach fluttered as Shaiala's black eyes flashed under her freshly trimmed bangs. But the Second Singer's threat had the desired effect. She stayed seated, hands clasped in her lap.

"As for you, Renn," the Second Singer continued. "Stop hopping around like a one-legged gull and come over here where everyone can hear you. We've wasted enough time."

Reluctantly, Renn limped across. He kept a wary eye on the girl.

"Relax, Shaiala," First Singer Graia said, taking up a position on one of the points. "You're safe in here. There are orderlies standing guard outside the doors who'll die before they let anyone interrupt us. The Pentangle is warded, so you can speak freely with no fear of your enemies overhearing."

Renn looked curiously at the points of the star, but they were in shadow and he couldn't see what the Singers had done. He shivered and moved a little closer to the stool. The lanterns flickered. Ancient echoes breathed down his neck. He became aware of Singer Rialle watching him again with those disturbing gray eyes. She gave him an encouraging smile.

Renn quickly looked away. There was only one seat and that was the treatment stool Shaiala already occupied. Careful to stay out of range of the girl's feet, he sat cross-legged on the bluestone nearby and rubbed his ankle.

Singer Graia dismissed the orderly, who pulled the doors shut behind him. Rialle stopped humming, retreated into the shadows, and calmly began to rethread the shells in her hair. The First and Second Singers exchanged fierce whispers. They seemed to be arguing about something.

Shaiala seized this opportunity to lean forward and whisper in Half Creature speech, "You not betray I this time, Two Hoof! Or I kick you again."

Renn scowled and replied in a pallet-whisper. "I was only trying to stop you from getting into any more trouble. You shouldn't have kicked the Second Singer like that. And you nearly crippled me just now."

"Little *Dragonfly* not enough to tickle foal! If I give you *Snake*, you not walk again. I learn kicks from centaurs!"

Her threat lost all its force with this boast. Renn giggled. "Centaurs aren't real, stupid. You must've dreamed them."

She blinked. It took him a moment to realize the glitters in her eyes were tears. He looked away, embarrassed.

The First and Second Singers broke off their argument. "Stop that, you two," said the Second Singer, frowning suspiciously at Renn. "Speak Human so we can all understand. You'll have plenty of time later to get to know each other."

Renn missed the significance of that, but Singer Graia gave Kherron a hard look. When she spoke, her words contained an undercurrent of disapproval that reminded them all she was older and wiser than everyone else present, Singer Kherron included.

"This is merely a trial session to see if Renn can help us," she said firmly. "I absolutely forbid you to push Shaiala too hard, Kherron, do you hear? Our Songs are powerful, but they can't work miracles. Even if Renn manages to translate for us, Shaiala won't remember everything at once. I'm afraid this is one case where you'll have to curb your impatience."

The Second Singer refolded his arms. He said nothing.

Graia sighed, then continued in a softer tone. "Now then, Shaiala. Let's go back to the attack in the canyons, shall we? Take your time. We're still a bit puzzled about the little green stones."

*

When the Two Hoofs had caught her down on the beach, the last thing Shaiala had imagined was that three days later she'd be sitting meekly on a stool in their blue building, answering questions. But this Pentangle of theirs had strange powers.

The first time they'd brought her here, the awful feeling of being shut in had sent her racing to the doors, determined to kick them down and flee. But the blue-maned Two Hoofs sang, and soon she felt so drowsy and relaxed it was all she could do to sit on the stool without falling off. After her second session, she suddenly found their words made sense. And soon after that, she began to realize not all Two Hoofs were like the ones who'd invaded the Canyons and the sailors who had chained her inside their floating building. These Singers treated her gently, even when she fought them, while at the same time making sure she didn't get close enough to kick them. Fighting was not going to gain her freedom. She had to find another way.

"After I tell, you let I go?" she asked, forcing her tongue to shape the alien sounds. They made her mouth ache, but it was important that these blue-maned Singers understood. She didn't trust the human boy. What was his name? Renn?

The male and female Singers who had been present at all her Pentangle sessions so far glanced at one another. She watched them carefully, trying to see what they were thinking. At first, she'd assumed the man who had caught her on the beach was in charge. But it was the woman who held the position of herd stallion in this back-to-front place.

"We'll help you, Shaiala, don't worry," she said with a smile that crinkled the corners of her mouth.

"And help friends?"

"Your friends too," the First Singer promised.

Shaiala relaxed slightly. She turned her attention back to the boy. She didn't understand how he spoke Herd so well. But so many things in this place didn't make sense. All she could do was store the unanswered questions at the back of her mind and concentrate on what was important.

She shook her memories into order.

"We call they *herdstones*," she said, and waited.

Renn licked his lips and translated hesitantly, stumbling over the word.

"Every adult centaur carry one, or not run with herd. Herdstones found only in Dancing Canyons. When foals old enough, they crack rock to get stones out. Adults not help, wait outside on Plain. When Two Hoofs come, us long way from herd. Foals very tired. Shaiala shout warning, but Two Hoofs —" She faltered.

Rafiz Longshadow, hobbled and bound, trying to comfort Kamara Silvermane whose lilac coat dripped blue blood.

"Go on, Shaiala," the First Singer said gently, once Renn had stumbled his way through this explanation. "What happened then?"

She swallowed hard. Renn was looking curiously at her.

"Marell Storm Temper think I betray herd." She stared fiercely at the First Singer and groped for the human words. "Me not stupid! Me know not born centaur. But Shaiala Two Hoof *never* betray friends!"

Renn colored and avoided her eye.

In the pause, the Second Singer asked, "Why do adult centaurs need the green stones?"

Shaiala shook her head helplessly. "I not remember."

With an exasperated sigh, the Second Singer began to pace up and down, his long robes causing a draft that made the lanterns flicker. "You must *try* to remember, Shaiala! We can't help you unless you tell us everything. Those tribesmen came to the Canyons on that particular night for a reason. We need to know what it was."

To her relief, the First Singer interrupted. "I don't think the stones are important, Kherron. It seems the men left them behind anyway when they took the — er — foals. My guess is they were more interested in trapping the youngsters away from the herd, and this stone-dancing ritual was an ideal opportunity, that's all. What happened next, Shaiala? You said you tried to help your friends?"

Immediately, she was back in the nightmare.

Black cliffs rising sheer on all sides. The Two Hoofs rushing toward her with drawn scimitars —

Someone began to hum. The Song went through her like warm southern rain. She sagged on the stool, suddenly very tired.

"That's enough, Rialle," said the First Singer. "Don't put her to sleep. We have questions that need answering first."

The Song stopped. Shaiala's eyes snapped open. For an instant, the stool spun beneath her thighs and the shadows rushed at her, making her dizzy and sick. Then she noticed the scornful expression on Renn's face and gritted her teeth. She sat up straighter and gave the First Singer a tentative smile.

Graia smiled back. "That's better," she said. "That was a very brave thing to do, Shaiala, putting yourself in danger to help your friends. I know the next part isn't pleasant, but I'm afraid we need to ask you to remember a bit more for us. You obviously weren't taken to the same place as the foals, or you wouldn't be here now. What happened after they caught you?"

The sweat started again, making her palms clammy. "Nothing."

Renn didn't need to translate this. The First and Second Singers exchanged a glance. "Nothing?"

"It all go black."

"Yes, so you said before. The Two Hoof leader must have knocked you out. Did you see his face? I know you told us they were all wearing tribal sharets around their heads, but anything you can tell us about him would help. Do you remember what color his eyes were?"

Glittering holes in the night —

"I not remember!" she said desperately, clutching the stool.

The Second Singer's green eyes narrowed. He pushed Renn out of the way, limped to the stool, and frowned down at Shaiala. "You must remember something! What about when you woke up? It's a long way from the Dancing Canyons to Southport, and there's no road. The fastest way they could have got you there was by horse. Surely you weren't unconscious all the way? Did you see the leader again? How old was he? Did he have any injuries? Anything wrong with his hands or face? Scars, for example? Think carefully, Shaiala. This could be important."

Her hands were trembling. But as Renn translated the word *scars,* something slipped into place in her head. "He wear rock over his face," she whispered.

Singer Kherron's eyes flashed. "Now we're getting somewhere! The sailors said the man who paid them wore a mask. What did it look like, Shaiala? Describe it!"

Shaiala's mind shied away. "I n-not see."

The Second Singer gripped her shoulders. His voice lashed her like the whips she'd seen Two Hoofs use on horses. "Try!

What color was it? What sort of rock? Did it glitter or was it dull?"

Tears sprang to her eyes. "I not remember!"

"Kherron." The First Singer stepped forward and laid a hand on his arm. "That's enough. It's obvious whoever captured the — er — centaur foals put some strong blocks in Shaiala's head. We'll give her another course of Songs to counter them, then she'll be able to answer some more of our questions."

The two Singers, young and old, locked eyes. Kherron's fists clenched. For a moment, Shaiala thought he was going to kick the female stallion. Then he shrugged her off and walked away, shaking his head and muttering to himself.

She sagged on the stool in relief. Her head ached and she felt as if she'd galloped the entire length of the Two Hoof river. Renn was staring at her again. He looked as if he wanted to ask something. She spun the stool until her back was turned.

None of them had noticed the Second Singer climb the stairs to the viewing balcony. Now he came back down, carrying something wrapped in gray silk. He marched across the Pentangle toward the stool, tearing off the layers so they trailed behind him.

The First Singer took a hasty step back. "Careful with that, Kherron!" she snapped. A small sound came from the shadows where the silver-haired Two Hoof had taken refuge. Renn was trying to see what was under the silk without getting too close.

Shaiala stiffened. There was only a single layer left now, and the thing in the Second Singer's hand glittered faintly through the thin material. Before he'd removed the final layer, she was off the stool and racing for the doors.

Hands caught at her. She tore free. Her head was a dark whirl. The Two Hoof faces spun. Shadows reeled around her. She flung herself at the barrier with a clumsy *Flying Snake* that hurt her heels, then she landed off balance and fell flat on her back on the floor. The doors remained closed but with a sound like a thunderclap a crack zigzagged from top to bottom.

A stunned silence fell. Everyone stared from the doors to Shaiala's feet and back again as if unable to believe their eyes. Shaiala only knew that she'd failed. All the wind knocked out of her, she lay helpless as the Second Singer strode across and stood over her. He turned the shard of crystal so that it glittered darkly in the eerie blue light.

"It looked like this, didn't it?" he demanded. "The leader's mask was made of crystal exactly like this!"

Shaiala whimpered and pressed her face to the cold stone floor, but the Second Singer brought the shard closer and forced her to look at it. "Yes," she whispered. Then, angry with him for having scared her, she sat up and screamed in his face, *"Yes! Yes!"*

4
KHIZ-CRYSTAL

Renn had never witnessed such chaos in the Pentangle. When Shaiala cracked the doors, he had scrambled to his feet in alarm but then didn't know which way to run.

The Second Singer left the wild girl sitting on the floor and strode around the five-sided chamber, sweeping up lengths of gray silk and wrapping them back around the splinter that had scared her so much. As he passed Renn, he was muttering furiously to himself.

"It's Frazhin, all right. No one else can use the khiz-crystal like that to mess with people's heads, and he'd know about our bluestone. A mask would tie in with injuries from the quetzal attack. Stupid Half Creatures! We should never have relied on them to finish the job in the first place. They probably got carried away mutilating him and didn't think to check if he was dead. The girl remembers just fine. All she needs is the right key."

The orderlies rushed through the doors with drawn swords. They exclaimed at the crack and looked to the First Singer for an explanation. For an instant, Graia seemed uncertain. Her gaze flickered over Shaiala, the damaged doors, the orderlies, and finally settled on Singer Kherron, who had planted himself in front of her.

"If Frazhin's involved, we can't afford to wait for the Songs to take full effect," the Second Singer said. "I'll set sail for Southport immediately and take Shaiala with me. She'll remember when she sees the place. Better take Renn too, since I can hardly understand a word the girl says."

Renn's stomach fluttered. He glanced at Shaiala, but she didn't seem to have heard. She was too busy eyeing the open doors. The orderlies stood between her and the corridor but their attention was on the two Singers.

"That's enough, Kherron!" Graia snapped. "You're letting your obsession with the priest interfere with your work. No one is setting sail for anywhere unless I say so. And you're certainly not taking the poor girl back into danger after all she's been through. She needs more therapy. Anyone can wear a mask. Besides, we haven't decided about the centaurs yet."

"If Shaiala's remembering the truth, slavery is a direct violation of the Half Creature Treaty and cannot be tolerated, no matter who's involved," Kherron said firmly. "And if her memories *have* been tampered with, then it's because Frazhin's up to something. She can finish her therapy when I bring her back."

"I — said — that's — enough."

The First Singer didn't need to shout. The Pentangle magnified her words and gave them power. Renn shivered. With all the excitement, no one had noticed the wild girl get to her feet. She edged toward the doors. Renn opened his mouth. But before she could make her bid for freedom, the First Singer gave Kherron a final stern look and came toward them.

"Don't worry, Shaiala," she said gently. "You won't have to go back."

"But me *want* go! Friends —"

"Singer Kherron will help your friends now."

"He not! He — him —" She turned to Renn, a desperate look in her eyes. "Translate! Please!"

He bit his lip and nodded.

She switched to Half Creature speech. "Him not find they! Centaurs not trust Two Hoofs, think Second Singer come to hurt they. I go, find herd, explain to stallion. Then mares help find foals."

Before Renn had finished translating, Graia sighed. "Shaiala, it's much too early. Maybe after you're better, you can visit the centaurs —"

The black eyes flashed. "I go now! Find herdstone, be in herd. Be with friends!"

The First Singer shook her head sadly. "Shaiala, I'm sorry, but I'm going to have to ask the orderlies to take you back to your pallet. They'll give you something to drink and when you wake up you'll feel much better."

"No! You *promise*!"

With the alarming speed she'd demonstrated on the Steps, she spun on her heel and aimed a vicious kick at the First Singer of the Echorium.

Renn gasped and covered his mouth. But the First Singer let out a low hum, the blue shadows shifted, and somehow the kick missed. By this time, Shaiala was halfway to the doors. The orderlies blocked her way. She launched herself at them with a desperate cry.

Renn wouldn't have been surprised to see her knock all five armed men out cold. But at that moment Rialle, whom everyone had forgotten, stepped out of the shadows. Humming softly, the silver-haired Singer fearlessly put her arms around Shaiala, drawing her so close the girl couldn't have kicked her even if she'd tried. The orderlies stepped back, looking relieved. Renn saw the tension trickle out of Shaiala as Rialle stroked her hair.

"Shai's not used to being shut up indoors for so long," Rialle said softly, still singing. "Why don't I take her down to the beach to see my cave? Renn can come too if he wants. The fresh air will do them both good, and they'll be safe enough with me. When you've decided what you're going to do, you can send an orderly down to collect them. In the meantime, we have some things to talk about."

She gave Shaiala a squeeze. But it was Renn she gazed at with her large sad eyes, the color of rain over the sea.

*

What a choice! Lunch at the Eighth Year table with Geran and Alaira trying to find out what had happened in the Pentangle. Or creeping around in caves with a girl who thought she was a centaur and a Singer who claimed to swim with the merlee.

Renn would have preferred to be locked back in his cell. Except he'd been let off his *Shi*, and First Singer Graia seemed to think it natural that Shaiala and Renn should want to stay together a bit longer. "But don't think this means you can sneak outside whenever you like, Renn," she added sternly. "There are good reasons we don't allow novices out of the Echorium unsupervised. You're not stupid. You know your Isle history. Think about it."

Renn thought about nothing else as he trailed farther and farther behind Rialle and the wild girl. All the way down the Five Thousand Steps, Singer Kherron's words echoed in his head. *Better take Renn too.* So casual, as if the Second Singer held their lives in his hand to use as he wished.

He scowled at Shaiala's thick black braid, which was already frizzing out of its thong. She was barefoot again, having left her sandals in the Echorium, and she gazed around her as if she'd never seen the sea before. Singer Rialle held her firmly by the hand as they walked along the beach. They'd hardly spoken a word since they'd left the Pentangle. Maybe they were communicating inside their heads like Half Creatures.

"I'm not going," he muttered, with a flicker of guilt at abandoning Shaiala. "Singer Kherron can translate for himself."

Rialle's head turned, shells tinkling. "Keep up, Renn," she said. "Don't you want to see where I live?"

He nearly said *no*. But curiosity got the better of him. If he had something interesting to tell Geran and Alaira when he got back, they might forget about the pebble he'd thrown out of the gully.

He caught up just as the silver-haired Singer slipped from sunlight into the shadow of the cliff. She seemed to vanish into the rock itself. When Renn looked more closely, he saw a narrow crack leading into darkness. He hesitated. In front of him, Shaiala dug in her toes and braced her arms across the entrance, shaking her head.

"Come on, you two," Rialle called, her voice laced with *Challa*. "There's nothing to be afraid of."

Shaiala's shoulders relaxed. She took a hesitant step into the dark. Then she, too, vanished. Renn's heart thudded. But he couldn't let the centaur girl think he was afraid. Ears straining, every nerve taut, he stepped after her.

He felt his way along a rough passage so narrow he could press his hands against both sides without stretching his arms. The passage made a sharp turn to the left followed by another immediately to the right. Ahead, turquoise light dappled the rock. Renn hurried forward, squinting at the sudden brightness — and bumped into Shaiala, who had stopped at the edge of an underground pool. He hurriedly backed off. But she didn't try to kick him. She seemed far too entranced by the sight before her.

They were in a large cavern partly filled with water that reflected eerie turquoise ripples on the roof and walls. The light filtered through an underwater sea tunnel, illuminating the depths. Soft plops and splashes echoed in the shadows. A slight draft tinkled strings of colored shells that Singer Rialle had hung from the roof. Sheets of dried seaweed formed mats on the floor. She even had a pallet down here in a little alcove curtained off from the rest of the cave by more strings of shells. Chests were stored on ledges out of reach of the tide and footprints in the sand showed where she had walked to the pool and back.

"It's a bit damp in winter when the storms come," Rialle said, smiling at their astonishment. "But I like being near my friends."

Renn thought he ought to say something, only his tongue had tied itself in knots. "The Echorium's damp too," he managed in the end. "Especially my pallet. Geran made me swap, so I'm right against the wall under the window where all the rain comes in and the voices —" He bit his tongue. Why did he have to remind her about that?

Rialle sighed. "You're not the only novice who's ever been bothered by Half Creatures, Renn," she said softly. "It happened to me, too, when I was about your age. And I was just as scared at first."

"I'm not scared!"

The gray eyes regarded him steadily. "Good. Then you won't mind if I call my friends now? They're anxious to meet you."

Renn peered uneasily through the turquoise ripples. "They come in *here*? But I thought merlee stayed far out at sea; least that's what I heard in the pallets."

Rialle laughed. "Oh, you don't want to believe everything you hear in the pallets! . . . Shai, stand back from the edge a little. They're a bit shy of strangers, but I'm sure they'll like you." She knelt at the edge of the pool and closed her eyes.

Renn stared at the silver hair trailing in the sand.

"How can you be so sure?" he whispered, wishing he were old enough to just get up and leave.

"Not talk!" Shaiala hissed. "Look!"

Deep green shadows rippled under the water, making straight for Rialle. Big fish, Renn told himself, though he knew before they surfaced that they wouldn't be anything of the sort.

The whispers in his head confirmed it. *Son of stone-singer!* came the delighted contact. *Swim with us!*

Renn staggered backward through the strings of shells, stumbled over one of Rialle's chests, and put his back to the wall. Out in the cave, the creatures broke the surface of the pool in fountains of silver and green. Even from his hiding place, Renn could see they were human to the waist with green skin, silver hair, and wide turquoise eyes. Rainbow tails splashed playfully as three of the creatures came closer. Shaiala laughed and stretched over the water, trying to stroke them.

Son of stone-singer not swim? came their puzzled whispers.

Renn shut his eyes in terror and pressed his hands to his ears.

There was a tinkle of shells as Rialle came into the alcove. "Renn?" she said. "The merlee won't hurt you. Come and say hello."

He shook his head. "Make them go away."

She frowned. "Come on. They've wanted to meet you ever since they discovered I had a son."

Renn's stomach did a peculiar dance. "What did you say?" he whispered.

"I said the merlee have been longing to meet you. I've also been looking forward to this moment. Just because I don't live in the Echorium doesn't mean I haven't taken an interest in your progress, Renn. I'm very proud of you, and I'm so pleased you can hear the merlee too."

"But . . ." Renn stared at her. "But, I'm not your son. I can't be! I was born in the Birthing House like everyone else. My mother was a Singer. A real Singer!"

A shadow crossed Rialle's face. "I am a real Singer. I —"

A loud splash from the cave interrupted them. Rialle snatched the shells aside. Shaiala was in the pool, fully dressed, clinging on to a merlee's tail and laughing in obvious delight.

Renn was still struggling with what Rialle had just told him. The crazy Singer who lived in this cave . . . his mother? She *couldn't* be! Oh echoes, if Geran and Alaira found out he'd never dare show his face in the Echorium again.

The silver-haired Singer had gone to check that Shaiala wasn't drowning. Apparently satisfied, she returned and pushed Renn down on the pallet. He tried to get up but she seized his wrist in a surprisingly strong grip and pulled him back.

"We need to talk," she said.

Renn set his jaw. "Novices aren't supposed to know who their mother is. If the First Singer finds out you've told me, she'll banish you from the Echorium!" Only when Rialle smiled did he realize how silly this sounded. "I mean . . . she won't be pleased. It'll interfere with my studies, and . . . and —"

"And you'll be embarrassed if your friends find out," she finished for him.

Renn flushed.

She put her head on one side and gave him that disturbing gray stare. "Why do you hate your gift so much, Renn?"

"I . . ." He colored again. "I just do."

"Because you don't want to end up like me, is that it?"

Renn couldn't look at her. He stared at his toes in their novice's sandals. The foot Shaiala had kicked was turning blue. "I want to be a *real* Singer," he whispered.

To his surprise, she wasn't angry. She hummed a few bars of *Challa,* then said softly, "I'm not down here because the merlee made me crazy like you think, Renn. In fact, they saved my life. If I hadn't been able to hear them, I wouldn't be on the Isle at all. There might not even *be* an Isle. Every Singer in the Echorium has reason to be grateful to those creatures you see in the pool. Being able to hear them is an honor, not a curse."

"Then why . . .?" He gestured helplessly at the walls.

She smiled. "Why do I choose to live in this cave rather than sing in the Echorium? Shai understands that better than you, I think. Like her, I'm happier when I'm not shut in by walls and doors. Things were done to me, Renn. It was a long time ago, but I remember them like yesterday."

"What things?" he asked, curious in spite of himself.

Rialle patted his hand. "It's best you don't know the details if you're going with the Second Singer on the *Wavesong*. Just don't condemn Half Creatures until you understand them better. All right?"

Renn found himself nodding. Then he realized what she'd just said. "But I won't be going with the Second Singer, will I? Singer Graia said he couldn't take Shaiala, and if he doesn't take Shaiala then he won't need me — will he?"

"Would you like to go with him?"

"No!" He thought of escaping Geran and Alaira. "I mean, maybe . . . I'm not sure."

Rialle sighed. "Kherron has a knack of getting his own way. All I'm saying is, be prepared. And if he does take you with him, listen to the Half Creatures and stay close to Shai. Because once you get to the mainland you're going to need all the friends you can get."

There was a sudden scream and frantic splashing from the pool. A single word pierced Renn's head.

Evil.

He leaped up from the pallet, forgetting how small the alcove was, and bashed his head on the low roof. "They're drowning Shaiala!" he said.

Rialle was already out of the alcove, shells swinging in her wake. He heard her sweet voice singing *Challa* and hurried out after her, rubbing his sore scalp and trying to understand why the merlee should suddenly attack the wild girl.

But Shaiala hadn't drowned. She stood dripping at the far side of the cave, her clothes clinging to her body and her hair stuck to her shoulders like wet seaweed. She was staring wide-eyed at something near her feet. Waves splashed over the edges of the pool but the merlee had gone.

Calmly, Rialle walked around the pool and picked up a shard

of crystal similar to the one the Second Singer had unwrapped in the Pentangle. She carried it to one of her chests and dropped it inside. She slammed the lid and wiped her hands on her tattered robe.

"Nothing to worry about," she said. "They're always bringing them to me. The poor things don't like them polluting their sea. The First Singer sends an orderly down here from time to time to collect the chest. No need to be afraid, Shai. There's very little power left in those pieces. The Khiz shattered into millions of them after the Battle of the Merlee, and they've been rotting in the ocean for twenty years."

"Khiz," Renn whispered, skin prickling as he connected Singer Ollaron's history lessons with what the Second Singer had been muttering about on the Pentangle. "That was the priests' secret weapon, wasn't it? And the man who sent Shaiala here had a mask made of the same stuff!"

"Which is why Kherron's so anxious to go after him," Rialle said, nodding.

"Frazhin," Renn said, slowly putting the pieces together. "He's —"

"The chief priest who led the attack on the Isle," Rialle finished for him. "He called himself the Khizpriest back in those days."

"Then he *isn't* dead! Geran always said he wasn't!"

Rialle raised an eyebrow. "So that's pallet-rumor now, is it? It's supposed to be a closely guarded secret, but Kherron always suspected he had survived. Worse, if it is Frazhin behind that mask as Kherron thinks, it seems he's found another source of khiz-crystal."

Shaiala had been listening carefully, hugging herself and frowning. Now she said in her clumsy way, "Why he want centaur foals? What do he to friends?"

A shiver ran along Renn's spine.

Rialle gave Shaiala a sympathetic look. "I don't know, Shai. But that's why Kherron wants the First Singer to send an expedition to Southport."

*

Singer Kherron got his way. Toward evening, the dark-skinned orderly who'd been with the Second Singer on the beach crunched into the cave and told Renn and Shaiala they were to go straight to the harbor and report aboard the *Wavesong*. Apparently, the Second Singer wanted to set sail for Southport on the midnight tide.

Renn's skin prickled. So soon? "B-but what about all my clothes and things?" he stammered. "And my lessons? If I miss the rest of this year, I'll have to go down a class!"

"Would that really bother you?" the orderly said, giving him an amused look. "Don't worry, a chest will be packed for you."

He flicked a bone-fastened braid over his shoulder and turned to Rialle. "I'm sorry, but Graia's decided it's the best way. I'll be taking Frenn, of course, and the best-trained orderlies in the Echorium — Durall, Anyan, Verris. We'll look after the boy for you, I promise."

Rialle waved the orderly silent and gazed at Renn in a most peculiar manner. Unexpectedly, she hugged him. "Remember what I told you, son," she whispered.

Renn's cheeks burned with embarrassment. He pulled free and glanced anxiously at Shaiala. But Rialle was giving the girl a good-bye hug too, whispering similar advice into her ear.

Renn experienced a sudden stab of jealousy. Rialle was *his* mother, not Shaiala's. He wondered briefly if centaurs hugged their children like humans did, then thrust the thought away in annoyance. Centaurs didn't exist, whatever weird dreams Shaiala might have. Hadn't the First Singer said as much?

Finally, Rialle released the girl and stepped back. Shaiala faced the orderly with a fierce gleam in her eye.

"Second Singer take I home now?" she asked, glancing at Renn.

Still confused and frightened by the way everything he knew was being turned upside down, Renn said nothing. The orderly, however, seemed to have little difficulty understanding her.

"Yes, Shaiala Two Hoof. You're going home." He patted her on the head.

Shaiala stiffened and lifted a foot. Renn winced, remembering how quick she could be with her heels. But she lowered the foot and gave the orderly a dazzling smile. "You come with we?"

"Oh yes," the orderly said, with another amused glance at Renn. "You don't get rid of me that easily! My name's Lazim, and I'm in charge of the pentad that'll be responsible for protecting you on the mainland." He grinned at them both. "The Second Singer and I go back a long way."

5
VOYAGE

The voyage was every bit as bad as Renn had feared. Though the *Wavesong*'s crew claimed the sea was calm, he was so sick for the first few days he could barely lift his head off his bunk. The very thought of food was enough to start his stomach retching up a thin clear bile. No one seemed to have much sympathy for his suffering. The Second Singer stayed in his cabin with the door locked, the orderlies busied themselves doing mysterious things to the sails that made the ship roll even more, and Shaiala galloped from one end of the deck to the other, her feet thundering overhead when Renn was trying to sleep.

The only person he saw during this time was the orderly called Frenn, who came in to empty his sick bowl. With a cheerful lopsided grin and a twinkle in his blue eyes, he wiped Renn's mouth, draped a wet cloth over his forehead, and assured him he'd feel much better in a day or two. Renn just closed his eyes and moaned. The orderly had a crooked left hand and limped slightly. Renn hoped he wasn't part of the pentad that was supposed to be protecting him.

He didn't think things could get much worse. But on the

third day, when he was feeling just about as wretched as he could get, Shaiala came thumping down the ladder and thrust her head around his door.

"You come out now?" There was a wild look in her eye.

"Go away," Renn mumbled, too weak to get up and close the door.

She fiddled with her hair and ventured a step farther into his cabin. "Please, Renn . . . Come see merlee-fish?"

That was the last thing he needed. "I've already seen them," he said, turning his face into the pillow. Then he roused himself. "Anyway, they're not fish, they're half human. And they're a lot more intelligent than your silly centaurs. *Merlee* wouldn't have got themselves trapped in a canyon and captured by slavers."

Shaiala's eyes glittered. For a moment he thought she was going to cry. Then she stamped her foot, making the boards creak alarmingly. "Horrid Two Hoof! I you hate!" She dashed out, slamming the door behind her. The whole cabin shook. The ladder Renn used to climb in and out of his bunk clattered to the floor.

"Thanks a lot," he muttered. But at least she'd gone.

Son of stone-singer help child of stone-dancers, came the familiar faint whisper from the sea.

Renn stuck his fingers into his ears. "And you can shut up!" he hissed before the guilt could set in. "This is all Shaiala's stupid fault. If she hadn't come to the Isle, I wouldn't be here. Anyway, it's true, isn't it? You wouldn't get trapped in a canyon because you haven't got legs to take you there in the first place —" His giggle turned into another moan as the ship rolled gently to one side and his stomach heaved to the other. "I wish I was back in the Echorium," he groaned. "At least the floor didn't go up and down there."

Even when his sickness passed, Renn stayed in his cabin and kept the door shut. Once, he asked Frenn, who was now bringing him food instead of sick bowls, for a lock like the Second Singer's. But the orderly just grinned in his lopsided way and said, "What in echoes for?" Renn couldn't think of a good enough reason, so he made do with jamming his clothing chest against the door and heaving it out of the way every time he wanted to use the toilet. It was about all the chest was good for. The stupid orderlies had packed it with scratchy gray goat-hair tunics several sizes too big for him. They seemed to have forgotten he was a trainee Singer. Renn stubbornly washed his white uniform in the buckets of seawater they brought down for his baths and ignored both the goat-hair tunics and Frenn's frequent attempts to lure him out of the cabin with promises to show him around the ship. While the uniform was drying, he wrapped himself in a blanket from his bunk and prayed Shaiala wouldn't choose that moment to burst in on him again. But he must have upset her more than he'd thought, because she didn't come back. "Good!" he muttered, trying not to think of that desperate look in her eye.

In truth, now that he was feeling better he would have liked to see how the ship worked. But he couldn't go on deck because Shaiala was always up there and the last thing he wanted was to get kicked in front of all the orderlies. He filled the time doing his breathing exercises and practicing the Songs, dividing up his days as they had been organized in the Echorium. And when he grew too lonely, lying in his bunk at night with the stars glittering above the black sea and the unfamiliar creaks of the ship keeping him awake, he reminded himself he was Singer material, not some common interpreter at the beck and call of a Crazy. The merlee didn't bother him much, either, now that he'd found a way to block their whispers and unsettling sea songs. All he had to do was think hard of the khiz-crystal they'd brought to Rialle's cave and they retreated from his head in panic.

In this way, the days slipped past. The weather stayed fair, the sea kind, their sails swollen with wind. He got the feeling they were making good time but resisted the temptation to ask Frenn how long before they landed. A Singer should know such things.

He was beginning to think he might survive this voyage after all when, after maybe two weeks at sea, he was woken by what sounded like a whole herd of Shaiala's imaginary centaurs trying to break into his cabin.

*

He'd been having an uneasy dream in which Geran and Alaira were chasing him down the blue corridors of the Echorium, which had somehow transformed into the caves under the Isle. They were waving sharp splinters of black khiz-crystal, and he knew if they caught him they would hurt him. Bad. The tunnels twisted until he was hopelessly lost. Then he rounded a turn and saw Shaiala blocking the way ahead, laughing. "What you afraid of, Two Hoof?" she jeered, and kicked the rock so hard the whole Isle came tumbling down in an avalanche of bluestone —

He jerked awake, relieved to see the familiar shape of his porthole bathed in pink light from the sea. Someone was knocking loudly and insistently on the cabin door.

Renn struggled out of his blanket, which had wound itself tightly around him while he slept, and staggered to the chest. He dragged it clear, wondering why Frenn was so early with his breakfast, and found himself looking up at the dark-skinned orderly, Lazim.

"Get dressed," Lazim said. "The Second Singer wants to see you in his cabin before breakfast."

Renn shook his dream from his head and peered out of the porthole. A long dark line of land was sliding past, spray dancing over rocks that looked far too close for comfort. "Are we nearly there?" he said, excited and terrified all at once.

Lazim frowned. "No, we have some way to go yet. That's

Drowned Man's Head. A tricky navigation problem for some, but luckily for us, the *Wavesong* has a certain amount of underwater aid. The merlee seem more anxious to please than usual this trip — they must like you." He missed Renn's guilty expression. "We'll follow the coast down to Southport. May have to head upriver from there, though that's up to Singer Kherron of course. Hurry, now. Shaiala's already with him."

Renn, who'd been struggling into his stained and crumpled uniform, hesitated. "What's *she* doing with the Second Singer?"

The orderly gave him a sharp look. "As to that, young Renn, if you don't know I'm not going to tell you. Considering all she's been through, Shaiala's taking this a lot better than you are. I think you're being very silly, hiding yourself away down here like this. It's not natural for a boy your age. And if you want my advice, you'll change that uniform for something more presentable before the Second Singer sees you."

Renn dragged his tunic straight and pulled at his breeches to get the creases out. "I don't want your advice," he said, lifting his chin. "You're only an orderly. What do you know?"

Lazim's face clouded.

Renn's heart thumped. The sword at the orderly's hip looked well used. Too late, he wondered if the bones in Lazim's hair could be those of disobedient novices.

But the orderly merely sighed. "Please yourself," he said. "Only remember what I told you when the Second Singer tells you the same."

Renn had a lot more on his mind than his clothes when Lazim ushered him through the door into Singer Kherron's cabin. As the orderly had warned him, Shaiala was there too. She stood stiffly amid an avalanche of rainbow silk cushions, haloed by the light streaming through the portholes, tears on her cheeks. The Second Singer's cabin was much larger and better furnished than Renn's. Lanterns swayed on hooks hung from the low roof, and by the look of it Shaiala had already smashed one. Splinters of blue glass and a puddle of oil glistened near her bare feet.

Singer Kherron was pacing at the far end of the cabin. He swung around and fixed Renn with a smoldering green glare. "About time! Echoes, boy, what are you up to? I thought I told you to stay close to Shaiala at all times so you could translate for her. Now I hear you've been hiding in your cabin like a frightened crab while she's been rampaging through the ship getting more and more upset. The orderlies have done their best, but in the end they had to bring her to me. I'm far too busy to spend the whole voyage singing to the girl, and Lazim can't always be looking out for her. It's not his job. That's why I brought you along."

He was forced to punctuate this angry speech with bars of *Challa* to keep the wild girl calm, so his words didn't have the power they might have had. But the Second Singer in a bad mood was terrifying, Songs or no Songs.

Renn swallowed. "Er, I didn't realize you meant stay with her *all* the time, Singer," he said. Which was the truth, otherwise he wouldn't have dared say it. "I thought you'd just need me occasionally."

He stole a curious look at Shaiala, who seemed to be trying very hard not to cry. When she saw him looking, she set her jaw and glared. Surely she couldn't still be upset over what he'd said about the centaurs? After all, it wasn't as if they were real.

The Second Singer stared hard at him. Renn shifted from foot to foot and tried to look innocent. But Kherron attacked from a different direction. "Why are you still wearing that uniform?" he snapped. "It's filthy! You're a disgrace to the Echorium. Didn't Lazim tell you to change?"

"Er, yes. But —"

"I don't want to hear your feeble excuses. From now on you're to wear the clothes the orderlies packed for you. I'm going to send Frenn down to your cabin to dye your hair black. You can be Shaiala's brother — yes, that should solve things nicely."

Shaiala stiffened. "Two Hoof *not* brother!" she said, stamping her foot. "Centaurs brothers."

"And as for you, girl —"

The Second Singer controlled his fury with visible difficulty, took a deep breath, and hummed a few bars of *Challa*. As the Song filled the cabin — s*hh, calm* — Shaiala's shoulders relaxed. She dropped her gaze.

"As for you, Shaiala," Singer Kherron continued more gently, "you'll put your sandals back on and wear them at all times. Your feet are far too dangerous to be flying around unsheathed. You're as wild as a half-trained orderly who's just got his hands on a real sword."

His words might have contained *Kashe*, but his gaze flickered to the smashed lantern and Renn could tell he was a lot angrier than he let on. He wouldn't want to be in Shaiala's shoes — not that she was wearing any, of course. He noticed blood on her feet and for the first time wondered if they hurt when she kicked things. She caught him looking and scowled.

"Now that that's settled," Singer Kherron went on, "you two can use the rest of the voyage to practice being brother and sister. We have a few days yet before we reach Southport. Once we land, there'll be no singing from you, Renn, and no kicking from you, Shaiala. If anyone asks, you're orphans who have grown up with only each other, so it's understandable you've developed your own private language that no one else can understand." He smiled at their horrified looks. "Don't worry, brothers and sisters fight all the time too. It's the perfect cover for you." He moved over to a chest and opened the lid. "Now then, Shaiala, I've got a present for you. Come here."

Shaiala stayed where she was, dividing her glare between Renn and the Second Singer.

"Translate for her, Renn!" Singer Kherron said, straightening from the chest. "Don't just stand there gaping like a fish."

Renn shook himself. "She understands fine," he muttered in Half Creature speech. But he mumbled, "He's giving you a present. No idea why. You don't deserve it."

His resentment faded, however, when he saw what the Second Singer had removed from the chest. A small, polished blue-stone with one flat side and a little hole bored through it. The Second Singer threaded the stone on to a goatskin thong, pushed Shaiala's hair aside, and firmly knotted the cord at the back of her neck. The bluestone nestled in the hollow of Shaiala's throat, collecting all the light from the sea.

Shaiala's eyes lit up. For the first time since Renn had known her, she looked truly happy. Her fingers came up to stroke the stone and she gave the Second Singer a dazzling smile. "Thank you," she whispered in nearly perfect Human.

Renn shot her a suspicious look.

The Second Singer was explaining the gift. "I know it's not a centaur herdstone. But it has power. You might like to wear it until you find your own." He patted her cheek and hummed a few notes of *Kashe*.

Shaiala's smile widened. "I wear it always!"

Renn frowned. "But that's —"

Kherron flashed him a warning glance. He closed his mouth. Serve the stupid girl right if she didn't know that you should never accept a gift from a Singer unless you meant to behave.

*

Shaiala hadn't meant to smash the Second Singer's lantern. But the very motion of the ship brought memories of her awful journey to the Singer island, chained in the dark, terrified and alone. When the panic rose, anything that got in her way was in danger of being smashed. She'd expected the Two Hoofs to be angry and lock her up again. Yet the Second Singer had given her the best gift in the world. Shaiala hadn't even tried to understand.

The gift was simply another example of Two Hoof eccentricity, which she would soon be leaving behind forever.

She stood at the rail with the salt breeze tugging at her hair, stroking the little blue stone and thinking of the centaur herd. The *Wavesong* had been following the coast for many days now, but this morning they'd rounded a headland and turned between two low hills where the wind snatched at the sails, sending the Two Hoofs running to their posts. Shaiala's blood ran faster as she caught the familiar smells of sun-baked earth and dung. The dark-skinned Two Hoof who seemed to understand her almost as well as Renn came over and leaned on the rail beside her, the bones at the ends of his braids clacking in the wind.

He squinted at the purple cliffs. "Nearly there," he said.

Shaiala's heart leaped, but she tried not to let her excitement show.

Lazim fingered a curl of her salt-stiff hair and gazed thoughtfully at her. "Are you excited to be going home?"

She laughed. She hadn't fooled him after all. "Yes!"

He smiled in his gentle way. "It'll be good to see the Purple Plains again. People say the Horselords breed the fastest horses in the world." Then his eye fell on the stone at her throat and his expression sobered. He glanced around and lowered his voice. "You will be sensible when we land, won't you, Shaiala? Kher's — Well, let's just say his temper gets the better of him sometimes. It makes him a good Second Singer, but the rest of us can suffer for it. I wouldn't like to see you hurt any more than you have been already."

Shaiala's stomach gave an uneasy lurch. "How him hurt I?"

But Lazim couldn't have understood. "Just remember we're on your side, Shaiala Two Hoof." He grinned and gave her cheek a pat. "Now run along. We'll be docking soon, and I've got things to do. Look, there's Renn! Isn't it about time you two made up?"

Shaiala frowned at the skinny figure dressed in badly fitting gray goat hair who had emerged, blinking in the sunlight. Despite what Singer Kherron had said about them practicing being brother and sister, she hadn't seen the boy since that morning in the Second Singer's cabin. His hair was black now, making his skin seem even paler than before. As far as she knew, this was his first time on deck since they'd left the Singer island.

More to please Lazim than anything else, she went over to the boy. She didn't have the first idea what to say to him and hoped he'd say something first. When he didn't speak, she asked, "Why you not come outside before?"

"Leave me alone." He pushed past her and gripped the rail with white knuckles. His gaze lifted nervously to the cliffs.

"You afraid of sun?" she asked, curious.

This earned her a scowl. "*Singers* don't race around all day getting sunburned and sweaty," he said in a haughty tone. "We've got more important things to do." He looked her up and down and wrinkled his nose. "You smell like a Half Creature. Haven't you ever heard of a bath?"

Shaiala's cheeks burned. She lifted a foot. "I wear Two Hoof sandals now, but I still kick good," she warned.

"And I can still sing! If you don't leave me alone, I'll sing you *Yehn*. I've been practicing."

They glared at each other. Sunlight glittered off the waves. The coast drew slowly closer, the cliffs giving way to sand dunes and spiky grass waving in the sea breeze. Spray blew over the rail and soaked their hair.

Suddenly, she began to giggle.

"What's so funny?" Renn said, still sulking.

"You! I never hear you sing one note! I not believe you can."

He raised his chin and said self-righteously, "Eighth Years aren't allowed to use Songs on people. It's dangerous until we're fully trained."

"Then why Second Singer bring you?"

He looked at her as if he didn't believe she'd said that. "You know very well I'm here to translate your stupid Half Creature speech! I wish I'd never left the Isle. I wish I'd never set eyes on you. I wish you'd go away and dream about your silly centaurs and leave us all in peace!"

Shaiala clenched her toes, disliking him more with every moment. "Centaurs teach I to run good," she whispered.

He gave her a sharp look. "What's that supposed to mean?"

She stared at the waves, dancing in the sunlight. In her head, she was already galloping barefoot through the purple grass of the Plains.

Renn frowned. She even thought she saw a hint of concern in the gray eyes. "If you're thinking of running away, think again. That stone —"

"Renn," said a quiet voice, making them both jump.

Shaiala whirled around and found herself face-to-face with the Second Singer. He wore the same gray ankle-length robe that he had been wearing when she first saw him back on the island. It billowed around him in the wind. His curls had been freshly dyed bright blue and he'd trimmed his beard.

His eyes rested on Shaiala a long moment. She looked down at her feet in their Two Hoof sandals. Had he heard them arguing?

"That's better," Singer Kherron said, including Renn in his gaze. "Now listen, you two — translate this, Renn, I want to be absolutely sure Shaiala understands. You're both to stay close to me when we go ashore. We'll take a little tour of Southport. As soon as you remember anything, Shaiala, I want you to tell Renn at once. Doesn't matter if it seems silly. I'll decide what's important and what isn't. These Southerners can be a rough bunch, so no sneaking off and getting yourselves into trouble that I'll have to waste time and energy getting you out of. Stay in sight of the orderlies at all times, and if they ask you to do something, do it quickly without arguments. It's their job to protect you and they can't do that unless you cooperate. Understand?"

His voice thrummed with power. Renn licked his lips and mumbled a translation. Shaiala had understood the first time and opened her mouth to say so, then closed it again. It might be better to let these Singers think she needed them. That way they wouldn't watch her so closely when they landed.

She squinted at the approaching town. The estuary was wide here, but it was possible to make out Two Hoof dwellings of purple stone covering the hillside, so close together it didn't seem possible to walk between them. Dark warehouses lined the riverbank and more buildings clustered behind them, filling every available space. At one end of the wharf a large harbor heaved with ships, while the hot southern sun baked the rocks to the color of Kamara Silvermane's coat.

Impatiently, Shaiala shifted her feet in their sticky sandals. *Soon now*, she silently promised her friends. *Soon.*

6
PRINCE

Slipping away from the Singer party proved more difficult than Shaiala had anticipated. Not only did the five orderlies who made up Lazim's pentad keep her and Renn carefully surrounded as they made their way through the town, but almost every person they passed turned to stare. Some sketched peculiar signs in the shimmering heat, which the Second Singer and the orderlies ignored but which Renn twisted his head and stared at nervously. Also, Southport proved to be a lot larger and busier than it had seemed from the sea. Everywhere Shaiala looked, Two Hoofs were poling laden barges along the narrow canals that separated the buildings, loading and unloading ships, gutting fish on the wharves, or emptying buckets of crabs into the enormous rusty tanks that lined the quay. The entire harbor area stank of rotting weed and fish, making her stomach turn.

Shaiala began to wish she hadn't eaten so much for lunch. The idea had been to fill herself up so she wouldn't need to worry about food until she was clear of the Two Hoof town. But the honeycakes sat heavily under her ribs, making her feel more like curling up in a corner than running. The goat-hair tunic made her itch and the sandals rubbed her sweaty feet. They seemed to have been tramping these hot, dusty streets forever.

At last, the Second Singer raised a hand and went to question some merchants who were taking a mid-afternoon snooze in the shade of a scarlet awning. At Lazim's nod, two of the orderlies accompanied him, hands resting lightly on their swords. That left Lazim and two other orderlies. And Renn.

Shaiala studied them through her hair. The orderlies were sweating freely, slapping at the little blackflies that were intent on making a feast of their blood. The one with the crooked hand kept glancing at Renn, who avoided his gaze, scarlet-faced. Since they'd left the ship, the boy had barely spoken a word to anyone. Which suited Shaiala fine.

She edged away. Feigning weariness, she stumbled to the side of the street and sat on a low wall. Lazim's watchful gaze followed her. She smiled at him and bent to unlace one of her sandals.

"Keep them on, Shaiala!" Lazim called.

"Sweaty. Blisters," she explained.

Renn flashed her a scornful look as he translated. Shaiala controlled an urge to give him a *Dragonfly*. She plucked the final lace free and sighed, making a show of massaging her foot. Lazim lost interest and returned his attention to the Second Singer, who was using his powerful voice on the merchants. Shaiala needed only an instant to unlace the second sandal and slip off the other side of the wall.

Renn's gray eyes widened. "Where are you going?" he called in Herd. "We're supposed to stay with the pentad."

But Shaiala was already racing down a steep, cobbled alley between two rows of houses, the sandals thrown blindly behind her.

Lazim cursed. "Echoes! Stop her!"

The orderly with the crooked hand and the other man who'd

stayed vaulted the wall and gave chase, but she had a good start. Then the Second Singer's voice came pouring down the streets of Southport, filling the sunlit spaces between the buildings and stirring the surface of the river.

"SHAIALA TWO HOOF! STOP RIGHT THERE!"

Something tightened around her throat, making it difficult to breathe. The hairs on the back of her neck rose. She leaped over one of the smaller canals without breaking stride, ignoring the little humpbacked bridge where people tried to get out of her way but ended up blocking one another in their panic. As the first two orderlies reached the bridge and shouted for the people to move, Shaiala plunged into the shadows between the warehouses that lined the river. She turned her back on the sea and ran faster. Now that her muscles had warmed up and her legs were at full stretch, she felt better. She'd been cramped too long on ships and that tiny island. The air in her lungs was polluted with Two Hoof smells, and she had no idea how far it was back to the Plains. But she was going the right way, with the southern wind in her hair. All she had to do was get out of these Two Hoof buildings. Then she could start to look for her friends.

Easier said than done. Soon after entering the warehouse district, she was hopelessly lost. Too late, she realized she should have stayed up on the hill, where she'd have been able to see the way out. Down here in the shadows, everything was confusing. The quays twisted and turned. The huge, gloomy, fish-reeking buildings blocked the sun. Chains stretched across her path like metal snakes. She avoided the clattering crates and Two Hoof voices, selecting alleys where she could run unhindered. But every time she thought she'd got a clear run inland, another canal cut across her path, too wide to leap, forcing her to turn aside and look for a bridge. She couldn't even find her way uphill again — not that she really wanted to. The Second Singer was up there, maybe still looking for her.

Tired and thirsty, she squeezed behind an empty crate and sat against the wall, knees drawn up to her chest. She'd wait until sunset. Then, when she was sure they'd given up the chase, she'd try to find a barge willing to take her upriver.

*

When they lost Shaiala among the warehouses, Renn fully expected the Second Singer to be in a foul mood. The race down the hill must have hurt the knee Shaiala had kicked, for he was limping worse than Frenn. But after a perfunctory search of the immediate area, Kherron called the orderlies to abandon their efforts. He told Frenn and the muscular Durall to take Renn back to the *Wavesong*. Then, as if nothing had happened, he strode off with Lazim and the two remaining members of the pentad to continue his interrogation of the Southport merchants.

Renn studied the two orderlies as they made their way back to the harbor. Frenn wasn't making his usual jokes. He kept his good hand firmly on his sword and both men's eyes swiveled from side to side as they walked. Renn closed in a little.

"Why did Singer Kherron stop looking for Shaiala?" he asked.

Frenn gave him his lopsided smile. "The Second Singer's got his own way of doing things, as you're startin' to find out."

"But he said Southport was dangerous —" He bit his tongue, and the orderlies misunderstood.

"Don't worry," said Durall, resting his huge hand on Renn's shoulder. "The two of us are quite capable of protecting you from anything Southport cares to throw our way."

Renn thought doubtfully of Frenn's limp but said nothing. The orderly had been first over the wall when Shaiala ran off.

Singer Kherron arrived back on board well after sunset, disappeared into his cabin, and locked the door. After a moment, a few notes of *Kashe* danced out of the open portholes. The Second Singer of the Echorium was whistling like a novice.

Though this surely meant they could all go home now, Renn couldn't sleep. He kept thinking guiltily of Shaiala and how he might have stopped her from running off if only he'd talked to her a bit more, made an effort to be friends as everyone had advised. He'd selfishly thought they were concerned for his welfare, not hers. Now he saw how wrong he'd been. He turned over for the thousandth time and thumped his pillow in frustration. Too late now.

As soon as they got back to the Isle, he'd ask Singer Graia for *Challa*. Get the wild girl out of his head once and for all.

*

The last thing Shaiala meant to do was fall asleep, but the tension of the last few weeks caught up with her and the heat dulled her senses. When she started awake, alerted by the rattle of a chain, it was fully dark. The Two Hoofs working on the wharves had locked up and gone home. The warehouses remained like sentinels, black and silent under the stars. Beyond their roofs, an orange glow in the sky showed where torches burned in the more populated parts of town. She crept from behind her crate, stretched the kinks out of her legs, and set off at a slower pace than last time.

It didn't take as long as she'd feared to find what she was looking for. A barge, moored and heavily laden for its journey inland, with its owner sitting on deck in the starlight puffing on a pipe. A red circle glowed in the night as he inhaled. When he exhaled, sweet smoke drifted across, bringing a flood of memories. The smoke smelled of the aromatic leaves the centaurs liked to chew. Shaiala smiled and watched for a while to make sure the man was alone. Then she smoothed her hair and tunic and ventured out of the shadows.

She cleared her throat.

The man jumped, spilling ash from his pipe. Sparks showered into the black water as he stared at her in astonishment. "By the river, girl, you gave me a fright!" He peered suspiciously up and down the quay. "Are you all alone? Dangerous place for a young girl, down these parts at night."

Shaiala raised her chin and took what she hoped was a confident step toward his boat. At least she could understand him. Now the test.

"Need go Plains," she said slowly and clearly in her best Human. She gestured to his barge, pointed upriver, then at herself.

The man squinted at her. His gaze traveled slowly from her bare feet to her throat, where it remained a long moment before moving to her face. He shook his head, got stiffly to his feet, and shuffled toward a flap that led into the belly of his barge. Yellow light flooded out as he raised the canvas. "Go home, girl," he muttered. "You're far too young to be out on your own at this time of night." The flap swung closed, shutting off the sweet smoke and the light.

Shaiala clenched her fists in frustration. He'd understood, she was sure. She eyed his cargo. The canvas wasn't tied very securely. There were gaps between the crates where she might be able to hide until they reached the Plains. But the gaps were small and dark. Even as she was searching for a good place to crawl in, the panic returned.

Eyes. Staring at her through glittering holes in the night.

Suddenly, the Two Hoof buildings seemed like a trap. She fled to the end of the wharf where moonlight poured through a break in the warehouses. Raising her face to the stars, she took deep breaths until the nightmare retreated. The buildings down at this end were derelict. Broken glass glittered beneath the windows. She stepped carefully around the shards, looked behind to check that the man hadn't come after her, then started down an alley that looked like a shortcut to another promising canal. She was about halfway down when a muffled Two Hoof whisper came from the shadows.

Heart thudding, she froze and stared at the spot. She should have taken the long way around. She broke into a run. Her frightened breathing echoed between the buildings and her footsteps sounded too loud. No — not hers, she was barefoot. Someone else's boots. She looked wildly over her shoulder and sprang for the end of the alley.

A mistake.

The rope came out of nowhere, hissing across her shins. She leaped to avoid it, kicking out instinctively. *Snake. Flying Snake.*

Too late, she saw the dark figure who had thrown the rope step out of the doorway where he'd been hiding. Then the weights attached to the ends whipped around her ankles, and she was falling. Sliding across cold cobbles, out the other end of the alley and across the narrow wharf toward the canal she'd glimpsed. All the breath was knocked out of her and her feet were bound tightly together.

She must have hit her head when she fell because it was spinning as it had during her Song therapy. She lay stunned for a moment, staring over the edge. The water was black and deep, reflecting stars. A rotten timber floated past, nudging a dead fish.

Stupid! What was the first thing the herd taught its foals? Always look before you gallop.

She rolled onto her back and kicked frantically at the weights as the Two Hoofs pounded up. Scruffy boots with holes in the toes straddled her. "Get the sack on 'er, then!" one of the men shouted, his words almost as difficult to understand as the Singers' had been before their Songs opened the right place in her head. "Quick, before someone hears."

"Necklace looks like it might fetch somethin'."

"Leave it for later!"

Shaiala struggled furiously, but her captors were big men. The fat one with holes in his boots sat on her legs, while the other dragged a musty sack over her head and tied it around her neck. As he did so, his rough hands tugged at the bluestone thong, but Singer Kherron's knots held firmly.

Shaiala choked, fury giving way to terror. Now she could neither kick nor breathe.

"I said *leave it*!" snapped the first voice.

There was a smack and a grunt. The pressure around her neck eased. While she gulped air, too thankful she was still alive to think about anything else, the Two Hoofs picked her up. They carried her, legs still entangled in the rope, into a place where their boots echoed. The weights were unwrapped from her feet. Then they dropped her.

Shaiala fell, arms flailing, the sack muffling her screams. Down, down, down . . . She landed on something soft and rolled against another soft thing that said, "Oof! Gerroff me, you great lump!"

She scrabbled away from the voice, dragging at the knots around her throat. Somehow she got the sack off and sprang to her feet. A rather wobbly *Snake* hissed out at her assailant.

"Oy, steady!" he said, expertly dodging her foot.

As he backed away, Shaiala glimpsed a wary copper-colored face covered in bruises and dirt. He wasn't the only one down here. In the faint light filtering down from above, a ring of frightened eyes glinted in the shadows behind him. Then the light vanished with a clang that echoed around invisible walls and the darkness rushed back.

A couple of the smaller children began to cry.

"I thought it was food," said one.

"They ain't never goin' to feed us!" wailed a girl.

"We'll starve to death down here, an' no one'll ever know."

Shaiala lowered her foot and took a deep breath. Not being able to see, even a tiny bit, made her dizzy. She needed both feet on the ground. She hadn't thought anything could take away the stink of the fish, but the smell down here was worse. Unwashed bodies, urine, vomit. The stench was thick and frightening in the dark.

She began to tremble uncontrollably. "Where I?" she whispered. "What place this?"

"What's she saying?" grumbled a boy. "I can't understand a word."

"Must be foreign from over the sea. There's monsters live there, and people wiv three heads."

Someone giggled, the sound high and strained in the dark. "She's only got one, stupid. They'd have needed three sacks otherwise, wouldn't they?"

At the mention of sacks, someone let out a choked sob.

"Don't cry, Imara," said a gentle voice. "They got to let us out soon. There ain't much more room. They can't keep on throwing people down here. . . . What's your name, new girl? Where you from?"

The panic came and went in waves. Every time someone spoke it receded, only to rush back again in the silence between their words.

"Shaiala Two Hoof," she whispered in her best Human. "From — Plains."

An interested rustle. They'd understood.

She stood very still as hands tentatively reached out of the darkness, feeling her borrowed Singer tunic, stroking her bare arms, gently tugging at the tangles in her hair. Then someone touched the stone at her throat.

"Not take!" she said, jerking back.

The boy who'd touched it chuckled. "Worth somethin', is it? They'll have it from you soon enough. Had all our stuff, what there was of it. Not that it was exactly ours in the first place, of course. Lifted mine from a drunk merchant just in from Silvertown — rich 'n' easy pickin's when they're like that. I was goin' to trade it for food."

At the mention of food there were several moans.

Then a quiet, clear voice behind Shaiala said, "*I* didn't steal anything. They took the dagger my father gave me for learning to ride. When he finds out how they've treated me, he'll feed their bones to his horses!"

The voice was drowned out by whistles and heckles.

"There he goes again, tryin' to impress us all!" said the boy she'd tried to kick. "That's Erihan, our resident prince! Claims he's one of the Plains people and his father's a Horselord. Got lost, or somethin'. Ha! I use that old story when I can't think of anythin' else. Sometimes gets me a coin or two out of a soft-hearted lady."

Shaiala frowned. "He speak tongue of Plains," she said, hugging herself. More memories.

"Huh?" said the boy. "Talk sense, can't you? Your accent's nearly as bad as his is!"

"Maybe Shaiala's a lost princess?" someone suggested.

A few people laughed, but not for long. The darkness was too close, the smell too bad, the fear never far away. In her corner, Imara began to cry again and the girl with the gentle voice hushed her.

Shaiala slipped through the captives toward the clear voice. "Erihan?" she said carefully, kneeling beside him. "Can you understand I?"

There was a stillness beside her, a whiff of spices just detectable above the stench. "Yes."

"I Shai — Shaiala Two Hoof. I run with centaur herd."

Another silence.

"Centaurs aren't real," Erihan said in the end, but there was a wistfulness to his tone.

Shaiala set her jaw. "They real!" she whispered fiercely. "Is you real Horselord prince?"

There was a rustle in the dark as Erihan drew himself up beside her. "The Kalerei do not lie," he stated in his clear voice.

"How you here get?"

He sighed. "I was stupid. Father's going to skin me alive for losing my dagger, and I've ripped my sharet. I lost all my jewels and things on the way downriver. The men who grabbed me probably thought I was a street scavenger like the others, but when I get out of here they're going to be sorry! The Kalerei won't rest until they find me. They'll be here soon, you'll see."

His words were as fierce as hers had been when she defended the centaurs. Yet deep under them lay the same hollow uncertainty. Shaiala felt a sudden kinship with the Two Hoof prince. She reached for his hand. It was very cold.

"Us get out now," she said, pulling him to his feet. "Not wait for Kalerei or centaurs!"

*

Although Erihan claimed there was no way out, he joined her in a careful exploration of their prison, testing the walls for weak spots. No one tried to stop them. Nor did they help.

Shaiala's fingers sank into thick slime she was glad she couldn't see. Cold puddles lapped at her ankles. She tripped over musty straw mattresses shared by several bodies clinging to one another in the dark. The only empty mattress had been positioned beneath the trapdoor where Teggi, the boy she'd almost kicked, sat on guard. It seemed the children preferred to huddle together on the wet mattresses rather than challenge Teggi's authority. Or maybe they just didn't want to get squashed by the new captives as they fell. At one end of their prison, a metal grille blocked off a tunnel along which slow-moving air brought the smell of dead things.

There must have been around fifty Two Hoof children in the cellar, but they were quiet now that the excitement of her arrival had worn off. Just the occasional muffled sob or whisper came out of the dark. Shaiala longed to rush around the cellar and kick them all. Scream at them to *do* something, anything! But it was obvious they'd long ago given up trying to escape.

She led Erihan back to the grille and pushed her fingers through the squares in frustration. The water here was knee deep and the floor sloped downward. She inhaled, trying to identify other smells above the stench of rotting fish. Impossible. When she listened, all she could hear was the plink, plink, plink of drips falling from the roof of the tunnel. She shook the grille until it rattled, then pushed Erihan out of the way, twisted on her heel, and sprang into the air.

Double Hare.

Her feet struck the metal with a clang that echoed around the cellar. Erihan staggered clear. The others leaped to their feet in alarm. There were several screams.

The blow had jarred her legs. Shaiala landed awkwardly, recovered her balance, and kicked again. *Snake. Flying Snake.*

Rough hands grabbed the back of her tunic. "What do you think you're doing?" snapped Teggi.

She fought him off. "Trying get out!"

"We already tried that." Teggi sounded weary. "Save your energy. It don't open."

"It must!" Erihan said. "Shai's right. This is the only way out!"

"No it's not," Teggi pointed out. "They could put a ladder down the way we came in. Or a rope."

"I can't climb a rope all the way up there!" one of the youngsters wailed. "They'll leave me behind and then the river monsters'll come up the tunnel and eat me!"

"Don't be silly," said Teggi. "River monsters would never get through the holes in that grille."

"Maybe they're goin' to open it and feed us to 'em," someone else suggested.

There was a frightened silence.

"That's stupid!" Teggi said firmly. "If they was goin' to use us as monster fodder, they'd be fattening us up, wouldn't they? Not starvin' us like they are."

Uneasy mutters filtered out of the dark. Then a small voice said confidently, "I know what they's going to do wiv us! They's going to take us all to the Singing Palace! It's nice there, wiv lots of food and drink and clean clothes wiv no holes in 'em and soft warm beds and —"

Several people groaned and said in chorus, "Shut up, Imara. That's just silly kids' tales."

"No it ain't! It's true! Ain't it, Laphie? Tell 'em it's true!"

Weary sighs. It seemed they'd had this argument before. The girl with the gentle voice hushed her sister, while the others crept back to their foul mattresses. Imara started to cry again.

Shaiala, Erihan, and Teggi were left standing in the dark by the locked grille. A draft stirred their hair. Shaiala's heart thudded uneasily.

"What Singing Palace?" she whispered, catching Teggi's arm.

"Oh, it's just some stupid story they tell on the streets," he told them in a low voice. "Keeps the little ones happy when people disappear. Don't make a fuss over it. Poor Imara's frightened enough already. Let her believe it if she wants."

"But *is* place like that!" Shaiala whispered back. "Across sea. Big Two Hoof palace of blue stone. I inside it been!"

The boy sighed. "Don't you start."

Shaiala resisted an urge to give him a *Dragonfly* on the ankle where it would hurt. As Teggi groped his way around the slimy wall back to his post, she thought uneasily of Renn and the other Two Hoof children she'd seen in the Echorium. Had they come from a place like this? Taken by force, sent to the Isle, and turned into Singers against their will? It might explain why Renn was such an idiot all the time. She shook her head. She couldn't imagine Second Singer Kherron ever doing anything he didn't want to do.

Erihan's whisper broke into her thoughts. "We have a story too," he said. "The men tell it around the campfire at nights when they think we're all tucked up safely in our bedrolls. Me and the other boys used to creep out of our tents and listen. Do you want to hear it?"

Shaiala's head was still whirling with river monsters and

Singing Palaces and how she was going to break that grille. She was hardly in the mood for stories. But when Erihan led her back to their mattress, settled himself, and lowered his voice, she found herself captivated by his words.

"Far to the south," the prince whispered, obviously repeating something he'd learned by heart, "deep in the Mountains of Midnight, there's a valley where the sun never shines. There's a way in, but no way out, because no one who ventures into the Sunless Valley ever returns. In this valley live demons as dark as the caves they haunt. The demons guard a fabulous treasure that would make a man rich beyond his wildest dreams, but the treasure is hidden in narrow cracks under the mountains and only a child can fit through them. That's how children disappear. Greedy men take them up there and send them into the caves. When the demons catch them trying to steal their treasure, they cut off their ears, gouge out their eyes, and steal all their memories, even the memory that makes a child able to grow up and die. The husks that are left when the demons have finished with them stumble around and around the valley in the dark, getting hungrier and thirstier until their flesh melts off their bones, their blood fizzles away, and only their skeletons remain. These child-skeletons rattle over the black rock, wailing terribly because they cannot rest unless they find their way out of the valley, which of course they never do. Sometimes, on clear nights, you can hear them on the other side of the Plains. That's when my people say the children of the Sunless Valley are screaming."

"You them hear?" Shaiala whispered, gripping the moldy mattress with trembling fingers.

Steal all their memories.

"I think so," Erihan said seriously. "Sometimes when I couldn't sleep, there'd be this strange noise outside the tent. Never sounded very human to me, though. More like an animal."

Shaiala shuddered. *Centaurs screaming?* she wanted to ask. Except that voicing such fears down here in the dark would make them all too real.

*

Renn's dreams churned with muddled images of the wild girl who had grown four legs and sharp hooves like a horse. He kept half-waking to find the blanket tangled around him, then drifting back to sleep before getting comfortable.

Once, he thought he heard voices outside his door discussing the girl and her bluestone. He rolled over and tried to get back to sleep but one of the voices was too familiar to ignore.

"You know what I think," it said. "I think the boy's too young for this. He had a rough time on the voyage, an' he's worn out with new experiences. I'm not goin' to wake him in the middle of the night, whatever Kherron says."

"You and Kher were only a year older than he is when you left the Isle."

"A year's a long time at that stage in a boy's life. No one's goin' anywhere till dawn, so it don't matter if he sleeps till then. I'll tell Kherron myself if you don't want to."

A sigh. "I'll convince him somehow. But the boy's his own worst enemy. If you'd heard what he said to Rialle in the cave when she told him she was his mother . . . if I'd spoken to *my* mother like that, I'd have been bent over her knee and thrashed!"

Frenn chuckled. "Singers don't need to thrash people, remember? But he'll come around now that the girl's out of the way, you'll see. He's just scared an' confused and tryin' to hide it. You have to admit Kherron doesn't help much."

"No." A rueful laugh. "Kher's never been renowned for his patience. But I hope you're right, for the boy's sake as well as ours. Because if we do find what we're looking for, he's going to need every scrap of his courage. . . . We all are. . . ."

The voices drifted away.

Renn turned over with a sigh and buried his face in his pillow. A dream, just a bad dream. He could think of no reason why Frenn and Lazim should want to wake him in the middle of the night, especially now that they'd lost Shaiala.

*

The children huddled in the cellar soon found out why their captors hadn't fed them. Not long after Erihan's story, they were woken by splashing feet and rough voices that echoed loudly in the enclosed space. Shaiala jerked upright, blinded by a red blaze, her head whirling with fragments of nightmares all mixed up with Erihan's demons.

For a horrible moment, she thought the cellar was on fire and they were going to be roasted alive. Around the walls the other captives were cringing too, hands raised against the light. Then her eyes adjusted, and she realized the "fire" was a single lantern hung in the bows of a barge that had crept up the flooded tunnel on the other side of the grille. Unlocking the grille was the fat man Shaiala recognized from the quay.

Her panic eased. She grabbed Erihan's arm. "Quick! We get past he! Run!"

Erihan held her back. "Wait, there's more of them in the boat."

Even as he spoke, the hatch that led into the belly of the barge was thrown open and a delicious aroma of soup and fresh bread invaded the cellar. The captives gave a low, collective moan. Beside her, Erihan's stomach rumbled loudly.

"Children!" called the fat man in a sickeningly sweet tone. "If you want to eat, get in the boat. Otherwise, we'll lock you back in and you can starve."

There was a pause, followed by a mad rush that sent Shaiala and Erihan staggering back against the wall. The barge rocked dangerously until the men aboard sorted the children into some kind of order.

"Walk, don't run!" they bellowed, using their fists to reinforce their instructions. "Single file! Anyone who pushes gets locked back in and left behind!"

The rush slowed slightly. Somehow, everyone managed to scramble aboard and get through the hatch without drowning themselves or anyone else.

"They're lucky we're all feeling so weak," Erihan muttered. "Otherwise Teggi's gang would kill them for that food."

Now that Shaiala could see them clearly, the street children were quite a frightening sight. They wore an assortment of rags and some had tied strips of cloth around their heads to keep their hair out of their eyes. Their faces were thin and determined, every pore was black with dirt, and even the girls had scarred knuckles. The way they attacked the soup and bread made it obvious they were used to fighting for food a lot less appetizing than this. She stole a look at Erihan. His clothes and face were as ragged and dirty as everyone else's, but he wore a tattered green sharet around his neck in Plains fashion and the way he watched the others told her he wasn't one of them.

She tugged his arm again, anxiously eyeing the grille.

"Not yet," he whispered.

Now that the initial rush was over, the fat man took a long pole off the barge and ventured deeper into the cellar, poking the hooked end into dark corners.

Erihan drew her farther into the shadows. They huddled together, hearts beating rapidly. "Shh," he whispered. "When he's gone past, we'll make a run for it. . . . Ready?"

The fat man must have heard. Before they could move, his pole slammed into their hiding place. The metal hook struck sparks off the wall as they jumped apart.

Shaiala kicked out at him. *Snake.* But the fat man slammed the pole into her legs. She overbalanced, slipped on the wet stone, and crashed down on her back. The hook pressed into her throat, pinning her to the cellar floor.

At once, Erihan leaped out of his hiding place. "No! Don't hurt her!"

The fat man chuckled. "Thought I heard someone skulking back here. Not hungry, children?"

"Not want eat!" Shaiala said, still trying to reach him with her feet.

He shrugged. "Please yourselves. We're not coming back down here for a long time, maybe not at all. Depends how much we get paid for you lot."

He moved the hook under the thong around Shaiala's neck. She stiffened. If he tried to take the stone . . . But after a chuckle, he pulled the pole back, allowing her to rejoin Erihan.

The prince squeezed her hand and whispered, "Did he hurt you?"

Shaiala shook her head, though when she checked to see if the bluestone was still safe her fingers came away smeared in blood.

The pole bumped the backs of their legs. "Come on, you two. Be sensible and get in the boat with the others, eh?"

Shaiala would have tried to kick him again, but Erihan tugged her toward the barge. "We'll get another chance later," he whispered. "We'll be able to run faster with food inside us."

His words made sense, but the space inside the hatch was very small and crowded. Shaiala experienced a moment of panic as the low roof and narrow sides closed around her. But Erihan let her have the end of the bench nearest the opening, and with an effort she managed to control her fear. The other captives were sitting in well-behaved rows down each side of the boat, quietly and happily gorging themselves. Someone placed full bowls of soup on their knees and thrust hunks of bread into their hands. Then the last man squeezed out through the hatch and slammed it, plunging the narrow space into darkness. As the bolts latched, Shaiala experienced another wave of panic.

"Steady." Erihan felt for her hand and gave it a squeeze. "At least we're out of the cellar and we have food. Getting out of a boat is simple. We're as good as free."

His words made Shaiala uneasy, though she couldn't say why. This was what she'd wanted, wasn't it? A lift upriver to the Plains.

There was a pause in the contented slurping as the metal-tipped pole chinked against stone and the barge began to slide backward through the tunnel.

"See?" piped a small voice from the far end. "They're takin' us to the Singing Palace!"

This time no one told Imara to shut up. They were all too busy licking every last drop of the delicious hot soup out of their bowls. Before she'd even finished her meal, a strange heaviness spread through Shaiala's limbs. She fought it a moment, then rested her head on Erihan's shoulder and closed her eyes with a sigh.

Soon every child inside the barge was sound asleep.

7

ΛUNT YΛSDRΛ

As the sky was paling over Southport harbor, the Second Singer summoned Renn to his cabin, thrust something small and blue into his hand, and ordered him to think as hard as he could of Shaiala.

Renn just stood there, staring dumbly at the little bluestone the Second Singer had given him to hold. It had one flat side, as if it were part of a larger stone that had been sliced in two.

"You're not trying," Singer Kherron snapped with a warning note of *Aushan*.

Renn's stomach clenched. "But I don't know how —"

"Don't give me that! You know the theory well enough. Singer Ollaron tells me your eyes always light up at the part where Lord Javelly gets his *Yehn*."

"Not mine," Renn whispered, beginning to suspect what the Second Singer wanted. "Geran's and Alaira's —"

"Don't split quavers. You're not in the Echorium now. The farther away Shaiala gets, the harder it'll be for us to trace her. Concentrate, boy. Echoes, but I wish I could do this myself!"

"Why can't you, Singer?"

Kherron rounded on him with a look that might have cracked the Echorium. But even as Renn cringed, the Second Singer took a deep breath and turned away. With supreme control he changed the shades of five lanterns, humming under his breath. *Challa, shh, calm.* Lavender light filled the cabin, softened further by the dawn filtering through the portholes.

He began to pace, his shadow swinging across the sloping ceilings. "Want a reason for everything, don't you, Renn?" he muttered, half to himself. "Can't say Ollaron didn't warn me. Always asking questions in class, too curious for your own good." Unexpectedly, he kicked a cushion across the cabin. "Sit!" he ordered.

Renn didn't need telling twice. He collapsed onto the cushion, the bluestone cupped carefully in both hands.

The Second Singer stared out of a porthole as he spoke. "Knowledge doesn't make things any easier, you know. Often when you're starting out, the more you know about something the harder it is, because you're so worried about the details you forget what you're aiming for. Normally, you wouldn't learn the use of bluestone until you'd finished your Final Year and sung on the Pentangle, but I suppose these are exceptional circumstances. I need you to work with me, not against me." He sighed and swung around. "Better put that stone down a moment. We don't want any accidents. Graia and Rialle would never forgive me."

Renn placed the bluestone on the floor and stared at it. "What accidents?" he asked, his heart thudding uneasily.

"Never mind. Now, you ought to know from your Isle history that we give bluestones to selected lords and princes and other significant people as Trust-Gifts. If they behave themselves, we never have to use the stone. But if not, Songs can be given over any distance using a special stone on the stool in the Pentangle."

"Like Lord Javelly's *Yehn*," Renn said, nodding. "We sing them to death if they step out of line."

"Hardly ever *Yehn* — that's rare. But often *Shi* or *Aushan*. Sometimes *Challa* if it's necessary to heal a lord whose physicians can't cope alone."

Renn frowned. "I never heard that."

"No. Eighth Years might like to think they know everything. Fortunately for the rest of us, they don't." He chuckled. "The stones work like this because they were all originally mined on the Isle of Echoes. They were once part of the very same stones used to build the Echorium."

Renn blinked. But before he could ask any of the questions bubbling inside his head, Kherron was talking again.

"The stones already know how to sing to one another, so it's fairly simple to persuade them to sing our Songs of Power. Similarly, we can use the small stones to pass messages back to the Echorium from anywhere in the world and the First Singer can pass messages the other way around."

"That's what you were doing during the voyage!" Renn said, suddenly understanding the Second Singer's anger the morning Shaiala had smashed his lantern. "That's why you didn't want to be disturbed, isn't it? Were you talking to Singer Graia? Can you use the stones to talk to anyone in the Echorium? Can I do it?" He glanced at the little bluestone. "Could I talk to my . . . friends?" That'd give Geran and Alaira a shock. He could call them at night while they were asleep and —

Singer Kherron let out a warning hum. "The Second Singer's business is not for Eighth Years to know," he said darkly. "But you have the right idea. Among other things, I was trying to track the sailors who brought Shaiala to the Isle. You remember they asked for a bluestone to prove they'd delivered her safely? Unfortunately, with the small stones it's not so easy. In theory we should be able to use them in exactly the same way as we use the Echorium. But in practice it's necessary to tune them very carefully if we want them to sing to one another, otherwise they revert to the Echorium because it's so large and powerful. I lost track of that death trap of a ship soon after we cleared the reef, but I doubt it sank. You see, most Singers can only use the small stones over short distances —"

"And now Shaiala's too far away for you as well!" Renn finished for him, picking up the undercurrents in his words. "That's why you want me to try."

The Second Singer's green eyes regarded him with a mixture of frustration and satisfaction. "Exactly," he said.

Renn wrinkled his brow. "But I'm not fully trained yet."

"I told you, training doesn't always help. There are things even the First Singer doesn't understand, but in this case I suspect it's more to do with novices having a greater range of hearing. You hear Half Creatures, whereas grown-ups lose the ability —"

"Except Rialle."

"Don't interrupt. Except Rialle, yes, but her gift is restricted to the merlee. We think novices probably pick up a greater range with the stones too, so you should be able to track Shaiala all right. Now, pick up that bluestone — *carefully!* — and let's try again, shall we?"

Renn's head was spinning with the theory. His pride swelled at being able to do something the Second Singer of the Echorium couldn't. But he didn't miss the true meaning lurking beneath the Second Singer's words.

"This is the real reason you brought me, isn't it?" he whispered, touching the flat side of the stone and remembering the conversation outside his door last night. "You prepared this ages ago. It's the other half of the one you gave Shaiala. You *expected* her to run away and you brought me along so you could follow her. It's got nothing to do with needing me to translate her words. You *tricked* her! And you tricked the First Singer!"

The green eyes watched him with amusement. "That bothers you, does it?"

"Yes! No! I mean . . ." Renn angrily shook his head.

"In spite of what you think, I didn't set out to trick Shaiala," Singer Kherron said, serious again. "I merely made sure we could follow her if she did give us the slip. Her therapy wasn't finished and I guessed she might act unpredictably. You'll learn there's never any harm in taking precautions in this job." A faint smile hinted that being right about Shaiala pleased him. "And as for tricking the First Singer, don't be silly. Graia knew very well I might need you for more than just interpreting Shaiala's words, which is why she let you come. If I've deceived anyone, it's you. I'm sorry, but you do see I couldn't have you bragging about bluestones to all your friends? The next thing we know, the entire dormitory would have had them, and you'd be calling one another up in class. The Eighth Year is quite unruly enough already, thank you!"

Kashe. Renn set his jaw and squeezed the stone. "We wouldn't be so stupid," he said.

"Maybe *you* wouldn't," Singer Kherron said, "but I'm not so sure about some of the others. I admit I hadn't expected Shaiala to leave us quite so soon. I'd hoped for some clues about these centaurs of hers first. I thought she'd at least wait until we reached the Plains before she ran off. But this way is just as good. Provided you can use that stone, of course."

His words contained a challenge.

"What do I do?" Renn heard himself say.

Singer Kherron smiled. "Try singing to it. That's what the Second Singer in my day used to do when things were difficult. Hopefully, you'll get an echo. When you do, *listen*."

Renn knew about listening. It was one of the first lessons they learned in the Echorium. Cupping the little stone in his hands, he completed a short breathing exercise and concentrated. Ignore the cabin, ignore the watching green eyes. Think of Shaiala, only of Shaiala. His head began to hurt. He hummed some *Challa*, probably influenced by the lavender light. Gradually, the stone warmed. Then it began to glow. Blue light spilled between his fingers and across the floor. He willed himself not to drop it.

"Shaiala?" he whispered, concentrating on her tangled black hair and dirty knees. "Where are you?"

The stone vibrated gently in his hands. Then all of a sudden he *knew* — though when he tried to work out how he was so sure, the stone stopped singing, cooled, and dulled. But not before he'd got the direction.

"It's moving," he reported with a little shiver. "Over water. Inland."

*

Late that afternoon, the cargo of an anonymous barge heading upriver from Southport began to stir and let out small moans of protest.

Warm hair twitched under Shaiala's cheek, waking her from pleasant dreams. She stirred, eyes still closed, and snuggled closer with a sigh. "Kamara Silvermane?" she mumbled in Herd.

The hair tugged free, replaced by a knobbly elbow. "Eeow," grumbled a voice she vaguely recognized. "My shoulder's gone to sleep." As the owner of the voice pushed her off and sat up to rub his arm, there was a clink and something dug into Shaiala's left ankle.

Darkness. A floating building. Two Hoofs who held her down so they could —

She jerked awake and kicked in panic. The thing around her ankle bit hard, rattling a ring set into the wall below the hatch and jerking Erihan off the bench. "*No!*" she screamed, thrashing blindly. "Not again! Let I out! Let I *go!*"

Erihan threw his arms around her and held her tightly. "Steady, Shai! Don't kick! It's all right, I'm here, we're linked — see?" He lifted his own foot.

His voice helped. Shaiala stared in horror at the manacle around Erihan's left ankle. Like the one around hers, it was firmly shut with a metal pin. A chain ran through a metal loop at the side. All along the barge, children were stirring and rubbing their eyes, blinking blearily at the spilled soup bowls, at their ankles, and especially at the long chain that joined them all together and secured them to the bench.

"They must have put something in the soup," Erihan said, amazingly calm. He rubbed his shoulder and looked around. "It's light outside. Wonder how long we've been asleep?"

Shaiala's gaze snapped up. Dusty sunshine forced its way through a narrow slit above the hatch and through tiny holes in the sides of the barge, picking out two rows of confused, sleepy faces. They were moving and the snap of a sail above suggested how. Trembling, Shaiala let Erihan help her back up onto the bench. She stretched toward the hatch. The manacle kept her from reaching it with her feet, but by pressing her eye to the slit she at least had a view of the outside world.

She saw a wide expanse of muddy river bordered by reeds. The water level was so low, the bank obscured what lay beyond. The occasional hut with a roof of woven grass slipped past against the sky. Then there was a dull thud. Boots thumped across the deck overhead and a dark leg blocked her view. She snatched her eye back, jerking instinctively against the chain. Erihan jerked, too, sending a ripple effect down the line.

"Don't," he said, still calm. "No point fighting metal."

"Yeah, sit still, can't you?" grumbled the boy on Erihan's other side. "I got enough bruises as it is."

"Shh!" hissed Teggi, who had his eye pressed to one of the holes on the opposite side of the barge. "Someone's just come aboard. I'm tryin' to hear what they're saying."

Everyone shut up. Two Hoof voices rumbled outside and more feet clumped overhead to join the man at the hatch. Snatches of their words came through the slit.

" . . . should be awake by now . . ."

" . . . sure you've stripped 'em of all their treasures?"

"Shut up, you fool! She'll hear . . ."

A lighter, quicker tread stopped outside. The men coughed and shuffled their feet.

"Well?" demanded a new voice, sharp and female. "Open it up then, Greth! I can't check the goods if they're locked away, can I?"

Shaiala froze.

"Er, they smell a bit, your Ladyship," said the fat man from the cellar. "You might not want to get too close."

"Open it up, you miserable lump of horse excrement! Quickly. I haven't time to waste on this crate. I'll let you know which ones I want delivered to my camp, then you can get rid of the rest. No sense dragging the lot upriver, and you'll save on food." She gave a dry laugh.

Only when that laugh faded did Shaiala become aware of Erihan's stare. "What's wrong?" he whispered. "You look as if you've seen a demon."

"That voice . . . I hear before," she breathed.

Erihan frowned. But there was no time for explanations as the hatch was suddenly flung open, letting in a blaze of fierce sunlight that made them all cringe and squint.

A tall woman ducked inside. She wore the traditional long robe of the Plains with an embroidered tunic over the top, its laces stretched tight across her plump stomach. Her head was wrapped in a crimson-and-black-striped sharet that hid most of her face. The fat man, Greth, followed her in, his bulk blocking most of the light. The other men stayed out on deck.

Shaiala sat very still, but it was no good. She was the first person the woman saw. The large black eyes stared at Shaiala, puzzled. Then they widened and, for an instant, uncertainty flashed through them — gone as soon as it had come. Shaiala turned hot, then cold. But the woman recovered her poise and strode past her up the narrow aisle between the two rows of captives.

Erihan stiffened. "Those are Harai colors," he whispered. "The outcast tribe. I might have known." He spat on the floor.

The woman ignored him and loosened her sharet, spilling midnight hair down to her waist. She turned to smile at them all. Her teeth were very white against her smooth copper-colored skin. She was so pretty and she looked at them with such pity in her black eyes, some of the smaller ones smiled back.

"Don't be afraid," she told them. "My name is Yashra. You can call me Aunt Yashra, if you like. Those of you who please me will come with me to a beautiful place where you'll never be hungry or hurt again. Would you like that?"

Silence, broken by suspicious mumbles from Teggi and the older ones. Then Imara piped up. "Are you taking us to the Singing Palace, Aunt Yashra?"

"Shh!" Laphie hissed, giving the smaller girl a dig in the ribs with her elbow. But Yashra's head turned and her large liquid eyes fixed on Imara. She smiled again. "That's right, little one. Have you heard of it? How lovely. But first I need you to do something for me. It's very easy, so don't worry. I'd just like you each to sing something so I can be absolutely certain you'll be happy in such a beautiful place. Can you do that for me?"

The captives glanced uncertainly at one another. Teggi stuck out his tongue behind Yashra's back. The fat man saw him and clipped Teggi's ear. "Enough of yer cheek, boy!" he said. "You better sing for the lady or I'll throw you overboard with that chain still on yer foot. See how well you make faces then."

"I know you don't trust me," continued Yashra, casting a reproachful look at Greth. "But I understand you're used to singing for your suppers and I'd like to hear you, too."

There were a few giggles.

"That's true enough," Erihan whispered into Shaiala's ear. "They deliberately sing like cats. People pay them to stop."

Yashra glanced Erihan's way, her eyes lingering on his tattered green sharet. She walked slowly up and down the aisle, patting some of the little ones on the head. "There's nothing to be afraid of," she murmured. "After you've sung for me, these nice men will give you something to eat and —"

"Ha! We know all about the food in *this* place!" interrupted Teggi. "Think we're stupid, or something?"

Greth swung his fist again, but this time Yashra whirled and caught his wrist in a firm grip. She looked hard at Teggi. "All right. Since you're so eager to be heard, you can go first."

Teggi scowled. "Take this stupid chain off me first."

"After you've sung," said Yashra with a note of finality. "Come on, anything you like."

The street boy glared at her. For a moment he looked as if he would defy her. Then he drew himself up straight and bawled out a song that made Shaiala blush before he'd reached the end of the first line. She didn't even understand the last line, though she had a feeling it was about something centaurs didn't do.

Beside her, Erihan was scarlet with trying not to laugh. "He must've learned that from the sailors in the taverns," he whispered. "Knows all the words, too! Watch Yashra now."

They all watched with interest. But if they expected a reaction they were disappointed. Yashra's expression did not change. When Teggi had finished, she nodded. "He'll do," she said. "He's a bit rough but he's certainly got volume."

After Teggi's lead, the others sang or hummed without protest when Yashra asked them to. Imara's song was the sweetest of all. Finally, Yashra reached Erihan. "Where did you pick this one up?" she asked, fingering his sharet. "I said street children only, ones that won't be missed — or did you steal it, boy?"

Erihan met her gaze. "I don't need to steal," he stated in his clear, ringing voice. "I'm Prince Erihan of the Kalerei! When Father finds out how you've treated me, he'll ride you down and feed your bones to his horses!"

Having the woman so close made Shaiala's head spin with half-remembered fears. She plucked Erihan's sleeve, filled with an urgency she didn't understand. "Not make she angry! She . . . power . . . bad."

Yashra's gaze flicked sideways. She narrowed her eyes, then laughed. "Kalerei, mmm?" She snatched Erihan's sharet free and tucked it under her tunic. "Now you look just like all the other boys. Don't worry, we'll soon train the haughtiness out of you."

An angry flush spread across Erihan's cheeks. Shaiala reached hurriedly for his hand. "No," she whispered.

Yashra turned to the fat man. "I'll take him. But I'll expect him to come complete with whatever you took off his person when you found him. Otherwise, his tribe might get to hear about you and your friends. There are plenty of others we can use to find children for us, men willing to work for half what you demand."

"He didn't have nothin' on him," protested the fat man. "That's why we thought he was one of the street boys —"

"Liar!" Erihan said. "You took my dagger!"

Yashra smiled. "I want everything you stole off these poor children," she said. "And don't try lying to me again, or you know what'll happen."

Greth shot Erihan a vicious glance then hurried after Yashra, who had twisted her hair back into her sharet and was heading for the hatch. "What about the last one, your Ladyship? The girl?"

Shaiala gripped Erihan's hand harder. Her muscles went rigid as Yashra thoughtfully fingered a rip in her borrowed tunic. *Kick her!* screamed her centaur instinct. But Erihan was squeezing her hand in warning.

"Not her," Yashra said coldly, stepping out of range. As she clambered through the hatch she added, "And if you took anything off that last girl, I'd advise you to tie it back around her neck and get rid of her as soon as possible. Some jewels are a lot more trouble than they're worth."

Shaiala choked. She snatched her hand free of Erihan's and

slammed it to her throat. Greth chuckled at her furious expression. "Want it back, girlie? Maybe I'll just get rid of you an' keep the stone. No one'll know any different once you're at the bottom of the river, will they?"

*

After Yashra had gone ashore, Greth and his men made a half-hearted attempt to clean up the mess the children had been forced to make beneath their benches. Erihan seemed embarrassed, but Shaiala was too worried about Greth's threat to throw her overboard to be concerned about such things. Then more soup and bread was brought around and the hatch bolted again. An uneasy silence descended over the captives as those who had been chosen by "Aunt Yashra" eyed those who had not.

People sniffed suspiciously at their soup, then at the bread. No one seemed eager to eat, though they were certainly hungry enough. In the end, Laphie spoke up in her gentle voice. "We either sleep or starve. I know what I'd rather do. At least, sleeping makes the journey pass quicker." She dipped her bread into her soup and took a large bite. Imara did the same.

The boy next to them watched enviously. He turned to the others and said, "What are you all waiting for? This here's free food, and it tastes a lot better than what I've been eating lately, I can tell you!"

Grunts of agreement. About half the children started eating, relieved someone had made the decision for them.

Shaiala stared at her own meal, feeling sick. Surely they weren't going to eat it, knowing what it would do to them? Erihan glanced at her, then very deliberately poured his soup onto the floor and dropped the bowl on top. The clatter made some of the guzzlers look up. "I'm not *that* hungry!" he said.

Shaiala began to breathe again. But the boy chained on Erihan's other side said, "Please yourself, *Prince* Erihan. Just don't come whining to me when you're hungry. You're not getting any of mine."

Snickers rippled along the barge. Erihan colored.

Shaiala threw her bowl against the hatch as hard as she could, splashing soup everywhere. At the same time she jerked her manacled foot against the chain. It worked. Everyone on their side of the boat lowered their bowls and glared at her, which disturbed those on the other side long enough to distract them from their stomachs, too.

"You Erihan *listen!*" she hissed. "Aunt Yashra bad. I memories!"

The snickers were fewer this time. People glanced at one another, as if trying to decide whether to laugh at her accent or ask what she remembered.

To her relief, Erihan spoke up again in his clear voice. "We have to escape, and we can't do that if we're asleep. Night's the best time. There's a lock at this end of the chain that threads through all our shackles. All we need to do is get the key off the fat man and we'll have a chance. Once the chain's off, I'm sure we can find a way to open the hatch. We can wait until the men are asleep then slip over the side into the water."

"I can't swim!" wailed a small boy.

"Yeah! We'll all drown with these shackles still on," a girl said, lifting her foot to demonstrate. "They're heavy!"

"The river's not that wide here," Erihan said. "You'll have to kick as hard as you can. Those who know how to swim can help the ones who don't. Now, we need a plan to get hold of the key."

People made faces and went back to their soup.

"I'm not sure I want to escape," said Laphie. "You heard Aunt Yashra. We'll be well fed and looked after where we're going. It's all right for you. Your father's a Horselord. You don't have to beg a living off the streets, worryin' about the little ones all the time. There's worse things than being taken to the Singing Palace." She stroked Imara's hair.

Several people murmured agreement.

"My father will feed you," Erihan said. "If you want, you can live with the Kalerei."

"Aunt Yashra's nice," Imara piped up. "I want to go wiv *her*!"

Shaiala clenched her fists. If she'd been free, she'd have given the lot of them *Dragonflies,* kicked some sense into them.

Erihan frowned and chewed his lip. "Why do you think they put chains on us?" he said. "If this Singing Palace is supposed to be so wonderful, why did those men put sacks on our heads, throw us all into a dark cellar, and starve us for a week?"

Uneasy mutters. Imara sniffed and hid her face in her sister's hair. "Don't worry, little one. Aunt Yashra will take the chains off soon," Laphie murmured. But she didn't sound as confident as before.

"And what about the ones your precious Aunt Yashra told the men to get rid of?" Erihan went on, with another glance at Shaiala. "What do you suppose that means?"

Some of those Yashra had rejected began to look worried. "They might let us go," a boy said doubtfully.

"Do you know anyone who's made it back to Southport with stories about sacks and cellars and a woman who wanted to hear them sing?"

"No . . ."

"Well then! You've all got heads like empty canyons if you think Greth and his men are just going to let you all go home and tell everyone what they did."

Shaiala couldn't help admiring the way the Two Hoof words rolled off Erihan's tongue. It was a good language for arguing in, more devious than Herd.

"You don't know what they goin' to do to us, either," muttered a boy who up to now hadn't touched his soup. "Laphie's right. You're not one of us. It might be better than bein' on the streets, who knows? I'm willin' to take the risk." He raised the bowl to his lips and took a long swallow.

Erihan shook his head in defeat.

Frustrated, Shaiala sprang from the bench, only to lose her balance when the chain jerked her back. "Yashra bad! I *remember* —" But again the memories evaporated before they could form.

"Calm down," Erihan whispered, putting a hand on her arm. "Fighting among ourselves isn't going to help anyone."

"They *stupid*!"

"They're hungry and confused, that's all. I'll try again next time we're all awake."

"But Yashra say get rid of others, Greth say get rid of I tonight."

Erihan shook his head again. "I think we've got a few days. I overheard Greth's men talking when they were cleaning up. They're planning to keep the ones Yashra doesn't want and sell them in the slave market at Rivermeet. It's not exactly legal but Rivermeet's a long way from anywhere and Father says all sorts of things go on there. They're not likely to get rid of you, or your little blue stone, either, whatever Yashra says. Don't worry, the others will listen better tomorrow night. They won't be as hungry as we will!" He indicated their spilled soup and smiled.

Shaiala didn't smile back. Yashra's voice had stirred the shadows in her head. Dark memories churned just below the surface, trying to get out. She touched her throat where the bluestone used to be. Whatever Erihan said, she knew she dared not fall asleep tonight, nor any other night they spent on this barge.

"Yashra evil," she whispered. "I *know*."

*

The *Wavesong*'s voyage upriver on the trail of Shaiala's bluestone rapidly deteriorated into a tedious, sticky, and fly-infested nightmare. They couldn't travel under full sail because of the heavy traffic and unfamiliar river winds that transformed their beautiful sea-dancing ship into a lumbering, oversized barge. This put the Second Singer in a bad mood, which in turn made the orderlies tense and bad-tempered. Lazim paced the deck, his hand never far from his sword. Frenn rubbed his crooked hand with his good one and gave Renn unsettling stares whenever he thought no one was looking.

To make things worse, Singer Kherron made Renn *listen* for Shaiala's bluestone four times a day. Once before breakfast, once before lunch, once before supper, and once in the middle of the night. He kept asking if the stone was nearer or farther away than the last time, which meant Renn had to keep humming with the echoes hurting his head until he could decide. It wasn't always obvious, but in the end even he realized they were slowly getting left behind. Needless to say, this didn't improve the Second Singer's temper one bit.

Between these listening sessions, when he wasn't catching up on all the sleep he'd missed, Renn tried to stop himself from thinking about Shaiala by questioning the orderlies about where the river led, what it was called, how far they could sail up it, and who lived in the huts they saw on the bank. The answers were grunts. Frenn was the only one who would talk to him, but unfortunately the orderly's knowledge of their surroundings seemed little better than Renn's. The only useful thing he discovered was that the river was known as the River of Sails because of all the sailing barges that plied their trade along it. Eventually, a distracted Lazim advised him to go below where he wouldn't get burned and bitten so much.

On the third evening, when Renn was up on deck enjoying the cooler air and trying not to scratch his sunburn, the orderlies suddenly gathered at the rail to watch something on the south bank. Curious, he shaded his eyes. At first all he could see were rustling purple grasses, shadowy in the dusk, rippling like strange waves across the Plains. Then he, too, spotted the dust cloud on the horizon. The orderlies seemed uneasy. Lazim sent Frenn below to fetch the Second Singer, while the others leaned on the starboard rail whispering among themselves.

Renn crept up behind Lazim and twitched his sleeve. "What's all that dust mean?"

The dark-skinned orderly swung around so fast, one of the little bones in his hair hit Renn on the cheek. He ducked, which was just as well because Lazim's sword was already half out of its scabbard.

The orderly let out a sharp breath and slid the sword back. "Hasn't anyone ever warned you not to creep up behind an armed man?" he snapped. "It's a good way to lose your fingers. What are you still doing up here, anyway? Isn't it time you listened to that bluestone again?"

"S-Singer Kherron hasn't sent for me yet." Renn raised his chin and made himself meet the orderly's gaze. The glint of the sword had scared him more than he liked to admit.

Durall laid a large hand on Lazim's shoulder. "Steady," he said. "We're all too jumpy."

Something passed across Lazim's dark face. "It's only horses, Renn. A tribe on the move, probably." He smiled slightly. "It's said the Horselords are born on horseback. They eat while riding and even sleep tied on to the back of their horses. Some people believe that's where the rumors of centaurs started."

Renn stared at the dust until his eyes watered. "So centaurs aren't real, then? I *knew* Shaiala was making them up! First Singer Graia said —"

"The First Singer doesn't know everything," said an amused voice behind them. "Or we wouldn't be here."

Renn jumped. Lazim's smile vanished.

The Second Singer joined them at the rail and closed his eyes. He was very still for a moment. Then he shook his head. "But in this case Lazim's right," he said. "Those are Horselords, and they're in a hurry."

Farlistening, Renn decided. He wondered how Singer Kherron could tell the difference between a horse's hoofbeats and a centaur's hoofbeats, then mentally kicked himself. Easy. There were no such things as centaur hoofbeats.

Lazim and the Second Singer were conferring in low voices. Something technical about the *Wavesong* not being built for river travel and they might be able to go faster if they hired a barge. Kherron waved the orderly silent with an impatient gesture, exchanged a glance with Frenn, then dropped a hand on Renn's shoulder and steered him down to his cabin.

Renn sighed as Singer Kherron pulled out the bluestone. Resigned to the routine now, he did his breathing exercises, sat cross-legged on one of the Second Singer's cushions, and closed his eyes. He was about to start humming when Kherron's hands closed around his. The Second Singer's calluses scratched his knuckles. "This time I want you to keep listening until I tell you to stop," he said. "I think something's wrong."

Renn looked up in alarm. "But it makes my head hurt —"

The Second Singer hummed *Aushan* under his breath. "You have no idea how important this is, have you? Didn't you listen to a word you were translating back there on the Pentangle? Shaiala knows something about the khiz-crystal! If we lose her now, all my work will be wasted."

Renn stared at the bluestone in confusion, his stomach doing peculiar things. "But I thought we were following her to find out if the centaurs are real."

"Centaurs. Khiz-crystal. Shaiala Two Hoof. Frazhin. Don't you see? They're all connected. And now it looks as if the Horselords might have something to do with this too. Stop asking questions for once and *listen.* I think Shaiala's in trouble."

Renn bit his lip. Maybe because of what the Second Singer had said, it was harder this time to find the echoes. When he did find them, they made his head throb. He didn't know how long he'd be able to keep listening, but he owed it to Shaiala to try.

The bluestone decided for him. Before the Second Singer had a chance to light his lanterns, it suddenly turned ice cold. Renn dropped it with a little scream and watched in dismay as it bounced across the floor.

The Second Singer was on his feet in an instant. "What happened?" he demanded, retrieving the stone and examining it carefully for damage. "What's wrong?"

Renn met the worried green gaze, feeling a bit sick. "It's stopped," he whispered. "Like it died, or something. In the river . . . *underwater.*"

An image flashed behind his eyes — the wild girl lying at the bottom of the river with the bluestone still tied around her neck and her hair swirling across her face like black weeds. He stared at the Second Singer, who stared back.

Kherron closed his fist around the stone. He rested his other hand on Renn's head. "We won't know what's happened until we catch up with it," he said gently. "Go and get some rest, Renn. No point listening again tonight."

8
ESCAPE

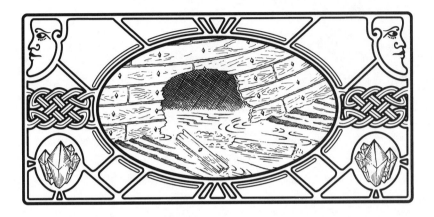

In spite of Shaiala's fears, Greth didn't try to throw anyone overboard that first night, nor the next, nor the next. Though each time the hatch opened, he swaggered up and down the rows of children poking the ones Yashra had rejected and telling them they'd wake up with the fishes. He took special pleasure in dangling the bluestone before Shaiala's eyes and asking if she wanted it back so she'd look pretty lying at the bottom of the river. Shaiala tried to kick him several times, but he was careful to keep out of range. "Have to sleep soon, girlie," he taunted as he took her untouched soup away. "Then I'll come for you."

She bit the backs of her hands to keep herself awake while Erihan used the time to persuade the street children they had to escape. Shaiala, becoming increasingly desperate, said they should kick the soup out of the men's grasp when they brought it down so there would be none left for anyone to eat, whether they wanted to or not. But Erihan said no, that would only make everyone more determined not to listen. "It's like taming a stubborn colt," he explained quietly. "If he feels he's being forced to carry you, he'll buck you off. But if you make him *want* you on his back, he'll be the best horse you ever ride."

Thinking of the way Rafiz Longshadow had offered to carry her when she'd been small and couldn't keep up with the Herd, Shaiala almost burst into tears. She could hardly curb her impatience as Erihan addressed the others in his clear voice.

"My people have a legend," he said, "that tells how the tribes of the Plains once suffered at the hands of wild men from the North who rode down the Great South Trade Route on shaggy ponies, raided their camps, stole their women, and threaded the bones of the men they'd killed into their hair. Everyone was scared. But my people couldn't fight the wild men because they were too busy fighting one another. It wasn't until the Horselords banded together under a temporary truce that they became strong enough to drive the wild men back to the North, and when they did they created such an army that has never been seen in the world, either before or since."

Since they'd all got their supper by this time, Shaiala doubted anyone would take much notice. But Erihan had a way with stories. He didn't even have to raise his voice. One by one, the children Yashra had rejected lowered their bowls to listen.

"Yashra's clever," Erihan went on. "She knows we could easily escape from this barge if we all worked together. So she's made sure we won't help one another by choosing some of us and rejecting others. I'm not suggesting we stick together forever, just that we help one another long enough to escape. Then we can go our own ways. You can hitch a ride on a barge back to Southport. You can come with me and live with the Kalerei. Or you can find your Aunt Yashra and go with her to this Singing Palace, if that's what you really want. But on your own terms. Not chained together like slaves!"

Uneasy whispers greeted these words. The captives hadn't been nearly so eager to eat the soup on the second night, and tonight they were more reluctant still. Even those Yashra had chosen seemed to be considering Erihan's proposal.

Finally, Teggi spoke up. "Erihan's right. They shouldn't have chained us. Even if they're takin' us some place nice, they never asked us, did they? I'd rather starve back on the streets than have a full belly in Yashra's palace!" He turned his bowl upside down.

"Me too!" said the boy next to him, following his lead.

Suddenly, everyone was throwing down their bread, pouring their soup onto the floor, and defiantly stamping on their supper.

Shaiala grinned at Erihan, who grinned back. With Teggi on their side anything seemed possible. Then she sobered. "How us get key?" she whispered.

The prince sucked his lower lip. "I've been thinking about that. It won't be easy. We'll have to pretend to be asleep. Then someone can start screaming, like they're having a nightmare or something. Hopefully, Greth will come down himself to shut them up. When he does, we grab him and —"

"No need," Teggi said, dangling something small and black from one grubby finger.

Shaiala's heart leaped.

The boy's teeth flashed white in the gloom. "Got it off him earlier, when he was givin' us his 'waking-with-the-fishes' line. I haven't served my time on the streets for nothin', yer know!"

*

Tempting as it was to strip off the chains immediately, Erihan suggested they wait until after dark, when at least some of their captors would be asleep and the others wouldn't be expecting trouble. Teggi agreed. Quietly, they trampled the soup and bread into the mess under the bench until no evidence remained. Then they slumped on one another's shoulders.

Once it was fully dark, Greth unbolted the hatch. Through

half-open lashes, Shaiala saw him raise his lantern so the light spilled into the barge. Her heart thumped. What if he'd noticed the key had gone? But after a cursory glance inside, the fat man rebolted the hatch and settled his bulk on the deck outside. The hatch creaked as he leaned against it. Orange light from his lantern flickered through the slit. Almost immediately, he began to snore. Shaiala's heart sank as she realized the flaw in Erihan's plan. But there was no going back now.

They all held their positions as agreed for a count of three hundred, those who couldn't count relying on the others to nudge them when it was safe. Then Teggi silently passed the key down the line, and Shaiala reached over and undid the lock. Her heart thudded the whole time in case it was the wrong key, in case the clink of the chain woke the fat Two Hoof, in case Yashra returned unexpectedly to collect her chosen ones, in case the little ones forgot they were supposed to be quiet. But the key fit and the lock was well oiled. It sprang open without a sound and the chain slid through their shackles as silently as a hunting snake. They all stretched gratefully, then looked expectantly at Erihan.

The prince frowned up at the hatch and its snoring guard.

"I wish I still had my dagger," he said, a note of regret in his voice. "You older boys'll have to be ready to silence him as soon as we get the hatch open."

Teggi made a face. "And how are we supposed to do that, Yer Highness? Ask him nicely not to call for the others? Tell him a story, maybe?"

There were a few snickers.

"It's the only way out of here!" Erihan hissed, glaring at the street boy. "If you've got a better idea, I'd like to hear it."

Teggi pointed to the far end of their prison. "If we can get through there, they won't notice us escapin' till it's too late."

Erihan squeezed past the other captives and put his ear to the wood. He shook his head. "Part of it's below the waterline. And the panel's too solid. We'll never break through without some sort of tool, which will take ages. Even if we do —"

Shaiala had heard enough. There wasn't much room to maneuver inside the barge, but her *Hare* was well aimed. The panel responded with a satisfying splintering sound. She didn't pause to examine her work, but let fly again.

Double Hare.

There was a loud crack. Night rushed through the hole, spangled with stars, fresh and cool. For a heartbeat, no one moved. They held their breath in case someone had heard and stared at Shaiala's feet. There were a few awed whispers. Teggi blinked and said, "How did you *do* that? That'd be real useful in a fight!" Then water started to swirl in, and there was a panicked rush for the hole.

"Careful . . . plenty of time . . . one by one . . . make for the reeds . . . you can hide there." Erihan's voice was hushed and calm. Teggi positioned himself on the other side of the hole. Working together, the two boys quietly thrust children through and into the water.

"You go next, Shai," Erihan whispered. "I'll wait with Teggi till everyone's out."

Shaiala picked a splinter out of her heel and shook her head. Her heart was still thudding and her blood was up.

"I kick Two Hoofs!" she said. "Smash legs! Put Greth with fish!" She gave the edge of the hole a vicious *Snake* to demonstrate. The loose planks exploded into the water with a loud splash.

"Shh!" Teggi hissed.

Too late. Shouts and curses came from the front of the barge where the men slept, followed by feet pounding the deck overhead. Hastily lit lanterns cast fiery ripples across the river, illuminating a line of dark heads and frantically splashing feet.

Then Greth arrived with the barge pole and swung it over the water. There was a frightened scream as the hook encircled someone's neck. Erihan started to climb through the hole to help. But an army of hands reached out of the water, grabbed the pole, and pulled. Greth didn't let go in time and his bulk toppled overboard with a loud splash. Those who had enough breath whistled and cheered. They threw themselves on the fat man in a wild, splashing fury of yells, punches, and kicks.

"Leave him!" Teggi shouted. "Get to the reeds! Quick! Go!"

The stern end of the barge was sinking fast. Teggi and Erihan pushed more children out as rapidly as they could but they were fighting a losing battle. More and more of the river foamed inside until Shaiala had to grab the bench to keep her balance. The cold water swirling around her waist felt like the tentacles of one of Imara's river monsters. The only good thing was that their captors were busy trying to fish their wounded leader out of the river and had given up chasing the escapees.

Afraid she'd be trapped by the rising water, Shaiala began to pull herself toward the hole. A desperate scream from the other end of the barge distracted her. She looked back. Among all the floating bowls and coils of chain, Laphie was trying to persuade her terrified sister to swim. Imara clung to the ladder below the hatch, tears streaming down both cheeks. "We're going to drown!" she screamed. "I can't breathe!"

Fighting her own terror of the enclosed space, Shaiala dragged herself back along the barge and aimed a clumsy *Snake* at the side. Maybe if she could make another hole above the waterline, Imara and the others who were afraid to swim could get out that way. But it wasn't easy to keep her balance waist deep in the swirling debris and the planks held firm. Erihan and Teggi, water swirling around their armpits, yelled at them to hurry. One of Greth's men had swum around to the hole and was trying to climb in. He grabbed Erihan around the neck.

Shaiala saw the prince go under and screamed his name. She started to struggle back down the barge to help, only to find swimming against the inrush of water impossible. The pocket of air under the hatch was growing smaller and smaller as the barge tipped. Real fear gripped her. There were still eight children trapped inside.

Teggi was exchanging punches with Greth's man. They went under and came up again in a sputtering mass of bubbles. Erihan still hadn't surfaced. A chill rippled down Shaiala's back. She didn't know where the strength came from, but somehow she dragged herself down to the hole, which was now almost completely submerged.

"*Erihan!*" She choked on a mouthful of river water as she tried to see him in the murky depths. "Teggi!"

Suddenly, the street boy was there, having disposed of his opponent somewhere underwater. "Don't panic," he said. "I'll get him." He pinched his nose and dived.

Shaiala clung to the edge of the hole, head tipped back and lips brushing the roof, swallowing equal amounts of air and water. For a horrible moment she could see nothing but bubbles and blood.

Twenty desperate heartbeats later, Teggi emerged outside the hole dragging a limp Erihan by the neck of his tunic. "You have to get the hatch open!" he yelled through the last slit of air. "It's the only way if they won't dive!"

Shaiala dragged herself back to the children huddled in the pocket of air under the hatch. Imara was still screaming hysterically, scrabbling at the inside of the hatch and panicking the others.

"Listen to I!" Shaiala shouted, fumbling for the Two Hoof words. "Us not drown if you give I room to kick —" But she didn't have time to outline her plan because at that moment their captors opened the hatch from the outside.

As they gulped the night air, sobbing in relief, a dark head blocked the stars. "All right," he growled. "Out you come! And no more tricks, or we'll lock you back in and let you go down with the boat. You've caused us quite enough trouble for one night."

*

Subdued, shivering, soaked, the trapped children let their captors haul them up one by one onto the roof and from there into a small rowboat, where their ankle shackles were knotted together with a length of soggy rope. Imara kept sniffing, "I'm sorry, I'm sorry," over and over, until even Laphie lost patience and yelled at her to shut up. Shaiala picked at the knots with her nails, but one of the men noticed and clouted her on the side of the head.

"Stop that!" he said. "You're darned lucky you didn't all drown! Didn't any of you stop to think what would happen if you made a hole below the waterline?"

On their way to the bank, they picked up some of the weaker swimmers, who gladly gave up the struggle for freedom in favor of safety and a blanket in the boat. They must have drunk more of the soup than Shaiala had thought. Soon after being hauled aboard and having their ankles roped, they slid to the bottom of the boat and closed their eyes. Of the fat Two Hoof, Greth, there was no sign. Shaiala experienced a flicker of satisfaction. She hoped he'd drowned, even if it meant the loss of her bluestone.

The men made a halfhearted search of the reeds, but their lanterns could not penetrate the tall, thick stems and there were too many places for children to hide. Shaiala eyed the shallow water. One of their captors had a knife. Maybe she could get it off him, cut the rope, and run.

She'd started to edge toward the man when her centaur-trained ears picked up frightened breathing nearby. She stared hard at the spot. At first there were only black reed shadows.

Then the lantern flame reflected in a pair of dark eyes no more than an arm's-length away.

Her heart gave an extra thump. It was Teggi, his arms around a dark, wet bundle she hoped was Erihan. The street boy put a finger to his lips. Shaiala quickly hunched over and started to cough.

"Keep them quiet back there!" said the man who had been peering ahead with his lantern hung over the bows. "I'm trying to listen."

Shaiala coughed harder, choking up the last of the foul water she'd swallowed in the barge.

The man with the lantern cursed and slithered back into the boat. "This is hopeless!" he grumbled to the others. "It's blacker than the Sunless Valley out there! Let's go. We got some of 'em back, at any rate, maybe enough to replace the barge if we handle it right. River monsters'll get the rest, if they haven't drowned already. Stupid kids! They have no idea when they're well off."

Cold shivers worked their way up Shaiala's spine. She wasn't the only one eyeing the reeds uncertainly. She only hoped Teggi had enough sense to get everyone out of the water as soon as the boat was gone.

The men rowed their bedraggled bunch of captives upriver for the rest of the night, keeping in sight of the south bank and taking turns at the oars. One of them was always on watch, a long knife resting across his knees and the end of the rope secured around his waist. Once Shaiala would have kicked him without thought of the consequences, but she knew now how tricky these Two Hoofs could be. She did consider trying to rouse the others and getting them all to pull on the rope so that the guard would fall in. But the sleepers were too drowsy to survive in the river, let alone be much use in a fight, and she didn't want to be dragged under. So she conserved her energy and

made herself watch the bank for landmarks. The most important thing now was to make sure she could remember the way
back to where she'd last seen Teggi and Erihan.

Please let Erihan be alive, she willed fiercely. *Please.*

*

Morning found the Singer party exhausted and bitten half to
death by nocturnal insects. Despite Lazim's protests that the
river was quite dangerous enough when they could see what
they were doing, never mind in the dark, the Second Singer had
urged them on all night. As a result, Renn hadn't slept a wink.
First light revealed a fresh scrape along the port bow of the
Wavesong and showed one of her sails to be tangled around the
mast. Singer Kherron didn't even seem to notice. He was too
busy frowning over the side and muttering to himself.

A barge came downriver under oars. As they passed the
Wavesong, the men on deck shouted and pointed excitedly at the
water. It seemed a barge had gone down in the night. A man had
been found drowned a short way upriver and the wreckage was
fouling people's tillers. Renn peered over the rail and saw a
chunk of splintered wood swirling lazily in the current. Then a
bowl floated past upside down, like a bald head. He stopped
scratching his bites and turned cold. When Lazim dropped a
hand on his shoulder, he jumped.

"Steady," said the orderly, his dark face grave. "Kher wants
you to listen to the bluestone again." And as Renn started to go
below, he added, "No, not in his cabin this time. Up in the bow
where you'll get a better echo."

Renn joined the Second Singer, his stomach churning
uneasily. Kherron did not acknowledge him. In one hand he
held the flat-sided bluestone. His head was tipped to one side.
Farlistening. Renn wondered if he should come back later, but
Lazim gave him an encouraging nod.

He cleared his throat. Singer Kherron whirled. A deep frown
creased his forehead. "Renn," he said, still distracted by whatever

he had heard in the distance. "So, now we know how our blue-stone ended up underwater. Shaiala must have been on the barge that sank. What I need you to do now is find the stone so we can be sure. It should be around here somewhere but I can't seem to get the echoes." He frowned again.

Renn took the bluestone and stared at the swirling river, colder than ever. A note of impatient *Aushan* reminded him the Second Singer was waiting.

He swallowed hard, took a deep breath, and closed trembling fingers around the little bluestone. He closed his eyes. A few bars of *Challa* and . . . He staggered backward in surprise.

"What?" demanded the Second Singer. "What's wrong?"

The orderlies were watching with worried expressions — Lazim and Frenn in front, Durall, Anyan, and Verris trying to see over their shoulders. The sailors who looked after the *Wavesong* when the Singer party went ashore hovered anxiously behind the pentad.

Renn met their eager gazes, his heart leaping in relief. "It's moving again," he reported. "Upriver. Very fast! Only —"

Kherron snatched the stone out of Renn's hand. A look of triumph crossed his face. He spun on his heel in a swirl of gray silk. "Get that sail untangled!" he shouted to the orderlies. "We can't be more than a sunstep behind now. I can hear the echoes myself!"

Renn frowned. He opened his mouth to tell them about the strange echo he'd picked up from the stone as it had left his hand — a single bright word in his head — *Sparkly.* Then he saw the expression on the Second Singer's face and changed his mind.

Probably his imagination. They were surely too far from the sea for him to hear the merlee now.

*

Shaiala and the children who had been recaptured spent an uncomfortable, damp night in the little boat. It was almost a relief when, toward dawn, they nudged through the reeds and put ashore on the south bank. The captives blinked wearily at their surroundings. There were no huts where they might dry off and rest, no sign of civilization at all. The men prodded the sleepers awake and pushed them all out of the boat until they formed a ragged line waist-deep in the purple grass, still linked at the ankle. They paused long enough to drag the boat behind some rocks. Then they marched their captives inland.

Shaiala was third in line with Laphie and Imara ahead of her and, behind her, a skinny boy who'd been rescued from the river. With her sister's help Imara managed to shuffle along well enough, but the boy kept stumbling over Shaiala's heels. Grass seeds made her arms itch. The shackle bruised her ankle every time someone fell out of step, which was more and more often as the captives cut their feet on hidden stones. Even though she'd been used to going barefoot with the herd and had developed tough soles almost like hooves, Shaiala hung her head and stumbled too. Maybe if she pretended to be as weary and dozy as the rest, the Two Hoofs would relax their guard.

But the farther they walked along the riverbank, the more watchful their captors became. They hadn't gone far before one called out and pointed. The others pushed their captives inland through the grass. Suddenly, they were surrounded by low, dark tents sagging in the thin mist that drifted off the river. The remains of a campfire smoked nearby and a half-familiar smell floated downwind.

Shaiala raised her head. Her heart gave a wild leap at the sight of a row of dark rumps and swishing tails. But they were only ordinary horses. Even as her hope faded, four Two Hoofs in dark robes materialized out of the mist. Crimson-and-black-striped sharets hid the lower half of their faces and scimitars swung at their hips. Hard black eyes traveled over the line of children, making Shaiala shudder. She let her hair flop back across her face, a mass of tangles and river weed.

"Where's Greth?" demanded one of the tribesmen.

Their captors glanced at one another. "Couldn't make it," said the one with the knife. "He sent me to collect the payment."

"You're late."

The spokesman walked slowly down the line, peering at each captive in turn. When he reached Shaiala, he lifted her hair with the tip of his scimitar. She stiffened, but he merely shook his head and let the tangles drop again.

"Lady Yashra's gone riding," he told them. "Went to look out for your barge. Strange she missed it."

"Er, I can explain that," said their captor. "We off-loaded this lot into the rowboat. Greth thought we'd be less conspicuous that way. He's busy gettin' rid of the rest like her Ladyship said."

"I see," said the Harai spokesman, oozing suspicion. "Then maybe you'd like to explain to Lady Yashra herself. Here she comes now."

Shaiala felt the hoofbeats before she heard them, drumming through her bare feet and up the bones of her legs. She looked up, more memories tumbling into place. But of course it wasn't a centaur. The woman who'd told them to call her "Aunt Yashra" cantered into the camp on a pretty silver mare and dragged the animal to such an abrupt halt, the poor thing reared in pain. With her tail and legs stained lilac by the dust, the mare was exactly the same color as Kamara Silvermane.

As the captives ducked, Yashra dropped heavily to the ground and passed the reins to one of her men. The mare snorted and plunged. One hoof landed squarely on the man's foot and he jerked the bridle with a curse. Shaiala glimpsed blood at the corners of the mare's tender mouth. Anger knotted her stomach.

Breathing hard, Yashra loosened her sharet and frowned at the bedraggled line of captives. "Where are the rest? What happened?"

"Er . . . nothing, Ma'am. Greth sent us to —"

"Don't give me that! These aren't the ones I chose. Do you really believe you can lie to *me*?"

"No, Ma'am, but —" Their captors glanced uneasily at one another.

"I'll discover the truth one way or another," Yashra went on, staring hard at the man with the knife. "Which way would you prefer?"

The man bowed his head. "We're very sorry, Ma'am. There was an accident. Our barge sank and these were all we could rescue in time. We tried our best but they were chained . . . there was nothing we could do. Greth drowned trying to save the little prince —"

Shaiala bit her tongue to keep the anger inside. Wait, she told herself. Not yet.

But the others weren't so restrained. "Liar!" shouted Laphie. "He'd have been fine if it weren't for fat old Greth trying to hook us all back with his pole!" She turned to Yashra, cheeks flushed. "We don't want to go wiv you to your Singing Palace anymore, so you might as well let us free." She clutched Imara's small hand. The younger girl glared at Yashra with equal fury.

Yashra's expression darkened. She opened one of the mare's saddlebags, then seemed to change her mind and slapped it closed again. To everyone's surprise, she patted Imara on the head and smiled.

"You poor things, all wet and cold. How frightened you must have been! Don't worry, I understand why you say such awful things to me. You'll feel much better after you've changed into some dry clothes and had something to eat. These men will take you into my tent over there and we'll have a nice chat later. All right?"

Eyes flicked sideways to the tent Yashra pointed out. Its flap had been tied back. Inside, golden lantern light flickered off goblets and plates piled with mouthwatering fruit and savories. Bright rugs covered the uneven ground and a brazier smoked in the corner. Laphie licked her lips and lowered her gaze. Imara gave a little shudder. "I'm not hungry," she whispered to the older girl. "I want to go home."

Yashra overheard and smiled again. "I'm sure you do, little one. And we will go home, very soon now. But first, you all need some rest. We have a long way to go, and I intend to look after you poor things a lot better than that horrible old Greth did. I bet you're not sorry he drowned."

There were a couple of nervous giggles. Shaiala ground her teeth. How could they be so *stupid*? Couldn't they see what Yashra was trying to do?

"Where are you taking us?" one of the boys asked suspiciously. "We ain't got no homes. Not real ones, at any rate."

Yashra gave him a radiant smile. "That's why I'm taking you all home with me! There's plenty of room for everyone in my new palace up in the mountains. We call it the Khizalace — that's a nice name, isn't it? It's so beautiful. I'm sure you'll like it there. We built it out of very special crystal so it sparkles in the night. Let me show you. . . ."

She turned back to the saddlebag. While the others stretched their necks curiously, Shaiala turned her attention to the horse lines. Just one guard as far as she could see. Maybe more Harai inside the tents. Four out here with Yashra, but one of those had his hands full with the silver mare. Now that it was clear no one was going to blame them for the loss of the barge, Greth's men had relaxed and were looking around for their fee.

Shaiala studied the horses. They were about twice as tall as a centaur and she'd never ridden anything that needed a bridle before, but it couldn't be all that different. Excitement knotted her stomach. She eased closer to the man with the knife and flexed her free foot — only to be jerked off balance as the others gasped with admiration and crowded forward to see what Yashra was showing them.

"Can I touch it, Aunt Yashra?" Imara whispered.

"Of course you can, little one. There's a lot more of this back at my palace. I'll make sure you get your own special piece, how does that sound?"

"I like the feathers," Laphie said. "They're so soft. . . ."

A dark glitter caught the corner of Shaiala's eye. She froze, the horses forgotten.

Smoothly, with the art of long practice, Yashra slid the thing she'd taken from the saddlebag over her face.

The mask had been fashioned from sheets of black crystal that curled around her ears like dark shells. The eyeholes were crusted with tiny midnight-blue jewels, glittering menacingly in the dawn. A sharp crystal horn protruded from the center of its forehead and long scarlet plumes fluttered in the river breeze like bloodstained hair.

Silence fell as the air around Yashra *blurred*. A chill breathed through the camp, making the Harai pull their robes closer. The horses whinnied and tugged at their picket. Then something exploded in Shaiala's head.

The memory killer.

"No!" she screamed, stumbling backward. The rope attached to her ankle jerked tight. The skinny boy cried a warning as she lost her balance and scrabbled at the dust in panic.

Yashra bent over her until the horn touched Shaiala's forehead. But the voice that issued from behind the mask was not a woman's.

"Silly," it rasped. "You shouldn't have let them use you. Singer games always end in tears, I could have told you that."

For a horrible moment, Shaiala could not move. Like that voice, the eyes that stared down at her through the jeweled holes did not belong to Yashra.

Then her muscles unlocked. She kicked upward with her free foot — a clumsy *Dragonfly* that got tangled in the red feathers.

"Stop that!" rasped the nightmarish voice. "Or you'll never see your friends again."

The final blocks in Shaiala's head fell away. "I you know!" she whispered, fighting fresh panic. "You capture centaur foals! You hobble Kamara Silvermane and Rafiz Longshadow! You steal *herdstones* —" She choked. "You send I to Singer island, where I not remember, not for long time. What you do to friends? Where take they? If you they hurt, I — I —"

"You'll do nothing," rasped the voice, quieter. "It would have been better for all concerned if the Singers had kept you on their island, as they were supposed to, and just sent me the blue-stone. They think to catch me unprepared, forcing you to remember ahead of time. I take it they're following you?" Before Shaiala could reply, he went on. "It doesn't matter. I'm ready for them. As for you, it seems I'm short of children. The Singers gave you your memories back, but I can just as easily take them away again. Next time you see your little blue friends you'll not even know what sort of creature they are, let alone care what happens to them."

"*No!*"

Shaiala flung herself on her back and aimed another kick at Yashra, vaguely aware of the wide-eyed stares of the others. Laphie and Imara were on their knees, clinging to each other. The skinny boy braced his legs and gripped the taut rope with both hands so he wouldn't get dragged any closer. Greth's men hung back, warily eyeing Yashra's mask. The Harai rested their hands on their scimitars.

Then the air *blurred* a second time, and the eyes behind the mask were once again Yashra's own.

"Don't just stand there!" she shouted. "Hold her still, someone!"

Three Harai surged forward as Yashra adjusted the mask. Firm hands pressed Shaiala back in the dust. The second man put his boots on either side of her shackled ankle, treading on the rope, while the third tried to catch her wildly kicking foot. Shaiala gave him a cramped *Dragonfly* that made him leap back but failed to do much damage.

Yashra stared down at her, a flicker of sympathy in her eyes. "You've brought this on yourself," she said. The feathers floated down, suffocating Shaiala in a red mist. She desperately tried to land a decent kick, but Yashra was too close. Any moment now the third man would have her foot captive and the eyes from her nightmare would be staring at her again, and this time —

"Aim for her stomach, Shai!" called a high, clear voice from the edge of the camp.

The grip on her arms shifted as the Harai looked around in alarm. Yashra glanced up. Awkwardly, Shaiala kicked upward. *Snake.*

Her foot sank into soft flesh. It was the wrong place to do any serious harm. Yashra, however, gave an anguished scream and staggered backward with both hands pressed to her belly. Her mask fell off and thudded into the dust. The Harai holding Shaiala let her go and rushed to help their Lady. Others raced across the camp with drawn scimitars, dodging loose horses. They shouted and waved their arms, trying to turn the galloping animals before they reached the tents. The horses panicked, caught their hooves in the guy ropes, and fled, dragging flapping canvas behind them and kicking wildly.

Shaiala sat up and blinked, her head spinning with black stars. A slender, dripping figure darted up and sliced the knots that bound the captives together. He gave Shaiala a quick grin and brandished a lethal-looking carving knife. "Not as pretty as my dagger," he said. "But it works just as well!"

"*Erihan!*" she gasped. "How —"

"No time to explain now. Run!"

The captives scattered. Meanwhile, other small wet figures rushed around the camp, pulling down the remaining tents, throwing lumps of ash from the fire at Yashra's men, dodging scimitars, and yelling at the tops of their voices. If one of them got caught, the others attacked with stones and ash until the Harai had to let go to defend themselves. It was chaos. And it was beautiful.

Only when she and Erihan reached the safety of the reeds, their breath coming in gasps, did Shaiala remember the mask. She looked for Yashra. Bent double between two Harai, the woman was being helped to her tent. The mask lay faceup where it had fallen, its feathers trampled into the dust, its glitter dull. Imara knelt nearby, staring at it. Laphie stood behind her sister, blank-eyed, and offered no resistance when one of Yashra's men took her arm.

Not thinking, Shaiala leaped to her feet. "Why Laphie and Imara not run? Us go back!"

Erihan pulled her down and shook his head. "It's too late. She did something to them with that demon mask of hers. Come on, I said we'd meet Teggi by the big boulder downriver."

"But —"

"You want to go back there and have the same done to you?"

Reluctantly, she allowed Erihan to lead her deeper into the reeds. Behind them, the noise and panic faded as Yashra's men caught the horses and slowly put their camp back in order. They seemed reluctant to leave their injured Lady and chase the runaways. Maybe they realized the futility of trying to find them in these reeds.

Then Shaiala remembered their original captors, who'd made themselves scarce when they saw the mask. "The boat!" she hissed. "Greth's men chase we in boat!"

"That'll be tough," Erihan said with a mischievous grin. "There's a big hole in it. Hurry now, Teggi won't hang around if we take too long."

*

They found the others hidden in a gully where a stream had cut a channel across the Plain on its way to the river. Two battered-looking canoes were drawn up on the bank and those who'd attacked the camp were sorting through piles of spoils. Fruit, nuts, knives, golden goblets, Harai sharets, jeweled belts . . . Shaiala shook her head in wonder. When had they found time to steal all that?

"Only take what you really need," Teggi was telling them. "Food, knives, useful stuff. Hide the rest, an' we'll come back for it when the Horselords have gone."

Erihan snatched up one of the stolen sharets, scowled at it, then turned it inside out so the colors didn't show and savagely wrapped it around his head and mouth. While he paused to look through the collection of knives and daggers, a silver shimmer in the shadows caught Shaiala's eye. "That Yashra's horse!" she said with a surge of sympathy. Her coat darkened by sweat and her mouth covered in blood, the mare reminded her acutely of Kamara Silvermane as she'd last seen her in the canyons. A second horse, charcoal gray with a black mane and tail, was tethered beside the silver one. "Harai come look for horses," she warned.

Teggi grinned and slapped the gray on the rump. "By which time both we and they will be long gone. These good enough for you, Yer Highness?"

Erihan came away from the knife collection looking disappointed. But he brightened when he saw the horses. He turned to Shaiala. "I'm assuming you can ride? We'll transfer the saddle to the gray. He looks the quietest. I should be able to manage the mare bareback all right." Still talking, he reached for her rein.

The mare reared, catching Erihan off balance. He fell flat on his back with a surprised expression. Teggi laughed.

Erihan flushed. "Don't let her go!" he warned, jumping up and tucking his stolen sharet back around his mouth.

Shaiala was already at the mare's head, whispering to her in Herd. At the same time, she felt a bit silly. *It's not a stupid centaur!* she could imagine Renn saying. *How can it possibly understand a word you're saying?* But the mare quieted and let her unfasten the girth and slip the saddle to the ground. Erihan raised an eyebrow but had enough sense to stay clear. He picked up the saddle and expertly transferred it to the gray, then set about knotting the gray's halter into a makeshift bridle.

Still murmuring in Herd, Shaiala slipped the bit out of the mare's mouth and removed the bridle. Before anyone could stop her, she twisted her fingers into the silver mane and jumped as high as she could, pulling herself astride the sweat-darkened back.

Erihan swung around. His eyes widened. "No, Shai! She'll —"

Too late. The mare leaped into a canter, shied at the piles of loot, then put her head between her legs and bucked. Shaiala clung on to the mane, her heart pounding in her ears. Children scattered from their path, shrieking in alarm. The mare's muscles bunched, warm and powerful. With an enormous leap she sprang out of the gully and onto the open Plain. The mare's hooves drummed in time to Shaiala's heart as she stretched her neck in unaccustomed freedom. Grass and boulders blurred at the edges of Shaiala's vision. The wind brought tears to her eyes and stole her breath. For a few wonderful moments she knew what it was like to have four legs like a centaur. So fast! So free!

"Shai!"

Erihan's voice was thin and faint behind her. She turned her head and glimpsed the gray coming after her at full gallop, the prince crouched in the saddle urging him on. "Shai, let go . . . she'll carry you into the river. . . . Jump!"

Shaiala gripped the mane tighter. "Steady, Swift Hoof," she whispered in Herd, a flicker of alarm replacing the excitement. But the mare wasn't stupid. She swerved away from the water and thundered through the waist-high grass. Seeds flew into Shaiala's eyes. A new fear seized her. "Not go back to camp!"

She needn't have worried. The mare had no intention of returning to the place where she'd been treated so cruelly. Neck stretched low, she galloped steadily south across the Purple Plains, her hooves eating the ground. Fingers tangled in the dusty lilac mane and the warm southern wind drying her hair, Shaiala threw back her head and laughed.

9
RIVERMEET

The sun was sinking into a purple haze on the western horizon by the time the mare slowed, first to a trot, then to a weary walk. Shaiala slipped her arms around the steaming neck and whispered, "Stop now, Swift Hoof. I think Erihan try to catch up."

The mare stopped. Shaiala slithered to the ground. It was farther than she thought. Her knees crumpled and she ended up sitting in the dust. The mare lowered her head and huffed at her. Shaiala closed her eyes.

When she opened them, Erihan was staring down at her from the gray's back, his eyes dark and expressionless above his stolen sharet. He said nothing. Simply dismounted, tugged the sharet away from his mouth, and led his horse off to join the mare, who had wandered off to graze beside a small stream. He hobbled both horses, unsaddled the gray, then came back and crouched beside her.

"You're crazy, you know that?" he said. "Whatever possessed you to take the bridle off?" The angry set of his lips softened as he shook his head. "Weren't you scared?"

She smiled. The rustling grass and wide dusky sky brought

more memories of running with the centaur herd. "Swift Hoof more scared than I," she said. "Centaurs not wear bridles."

Erihan's lips tightened again. "Shai, centaurs aren't re —" Seeing her stubborn expression, he changed the subject. "Never mind. You were lucky. She must've stopped when she smelled the water. We've come a long way from the river. I don't recognize this area." He scanned the horizon, a little frown creasing his forehead. "Good thing Teggi thought to pack the saddlebag with food. I was too afraid I'd lose you to worry about anything else. We have plenty to drink, too." He indicated the stream. "With any luck, there'll be a friendly tribe camping somewhere nearby. We can look for their tracks in the morning."

"Not find tribe," Shaiala said firmly.

He stared at her as if she really were crazy. "Be sensible, Shai. Teggi and the others will be halfway back to Southport by now. We can't just wander around on our own out here. We'll starve. . . . Or get attacked by stray Harai . . . or eaten by demons. . . ."

Shaiala laughed. She couldn't help it. Down in the dark cellar, Erihan's stories had possessed power. Out here, surrounded by things she remembered, they seemed silly. "Demons not real!" she said.

A scowl. "Father says all stories are partly true. He says the Harai are half-demon, and you saw what Yashra did to Laphie and Imara back there. She had a demon mask, didn't she? It feeds on people's souls."

At once her laughter died, shadowed by dark memories.

Erihan stared moodily at the southern horizon, where clouds were piling up like mountains. He sighed. "Looks like rain. We'll get soaked tonight with no tent."

Shaiala scrambled up and started toward the stream where the mare's lilac tail swished alongside the gray's darker one.

Erihan sprang after her. "Where are you going now?"

"Find herd."

"What herd?"

"Centaur herd! I last see they in Dancing Canyons. Go there, find tracks, follow. Stallion know what to do."

Erihan gave her that strange look again. He put a firm hand on her shoulder and turned her to face him. He was taller than she'd thought from seeing him crouched in the cellar and chained on the barge. Their eyes were almost level. "Shai," he said with an awkward cough. "Did Yashra ever use her demon mask on *you*?"

Dark shivers. "Once. In Canyons, after she capture foals. . . . Why?"

"Because —" He frowned, took a deep breath and said firmly, "Because centaurs don't exist, that's why! If they did, my people would have seen one before now. Horselords ride the Plains constantly. They know every hoofprint from the Mountains of Midnight to the River of Sails, from the Salt Marshes to the Black River, and I never once heard of anyone seeing a centaur except in a fireside story. Think about it a moment! You admit she used the mask on you. You only have to look at Laphie and Imara to see what it does to people's heads. She made them forget they wanted to escape, wiped it right out of their heads. Couldn't she have just as easily put the centaurs into yours? Made you think you used to live with them?"

Shaiala stared at him, the shivers increasing. It was true. She'd lost her memories and the Singers had returned them to her. But suppose the memories their Songs had found in her head weren't the right ones?

"No!" she whispered fiercely. "Centaurs friends! Kamara Silvermane, Rafiz Longshadow, Marell Storm Temper . . . I live with herd years and years! I remember lots now! They not just dream, they *not* —" She choked. Tears blurred the Plain as she stumbled away from Erihan.

He came after her and quietly put his arms around her.

She sniffed and buried her face in his shoulder. So embarrassing, to cry like a newborn foal! But he held her in the same way Singer Rialle had back on the island. Gently and patiently.

"I know centaur kicks," she whispered. "How I smash barge, if not learn from herd?"

"I don't know. Those kicks of yours are pretty lethal. Maybe you were trained by some secret warrior sect the Horselords don't know about?" He smiled, trying to make a joke of it.

Shaiala shook her head. "Why Yashra make I remember centaurs if herd not exist?"

Erihan looked thoughtful. "She sent you to the Singer Isle, didn't she? And when you told them what you thought you remembered, they came rushing to the Purple Plains. Then you got snatched, and I expect the Singers tried to find you again — they're probably searching for you right now. I know it's a horrible thought, but what if you were just the bait? What if Yashra never wanted you at all? What if she's more interested in the Singers because they have something she wants?"

They stared at each other, suddenly aware of how intimate they were. Erihan flushed and released her, pretending to adjust his sharet. Shaiala chewed her lip and tried to remember her time on the Singer island. It was a confusion of bluestone and sea songs, of flickering blue-shaded lanterns and a spinning stool. Of a sea cave and strange creatures — half fish, half human — who brought black glittering shards out of the depths. . . .

"I see demon crystal on Singer island!" she said. "They call it something . . . Two Hoof word, I not remember. Evil." She shivered again.

Erihan nodded. "Yashra's a Harai, and they're always up to something bad. Father says it's in the blood. It'd be just like her to want something evil."

Shaiala frowned and sat on a boulder. She eased her fingers under the shackle, which had chafed her ankle, and voiced something that had been puzzling her during the ride from the river. "How you know kick in stomach hurt she? She fatter than when I see she in Canyons. If centaur fat, they not feel much."

To her surprise, Erihan laughed. "Yashra's not *fat*, silly. She's pregnant! Pretty far gone, I'd say. I thought you girls knew about that sort of thing."

"Pregnant?" She fumbled over the word, felt her heart stop and start again. "You mean . . . she carry Two Hoof foal?"

Erihan gave her a strange look. "We usually call them babies."

Even after the way Yashra had scared her, Shaiala felt awful. Visions of blue centaur mares, heavy with foals, drifted across the dusky Plain.

"I know it was a horrible thing to do," Erihan said, sober again. "But Father taught me that when you're desperate you should go for an enemy's weakest spot, and it was all I could think of. She was going to mess with your head, remember? Don't worry, she won't lose the baby. Horselord women are tough." He stretched and glanced around. "Come on, it's nearly dark. Let's find some shelter and get some sleep. We can start looking for tracks in the morning."

Shaiala, relieved now that she hadn't been free to deliver a proper kick to Yashra's stomach, set her jaw. "*Centaur* tracks."

A soft sigh. "Shai —"

"Then us know truth!"

Erihan considered her a long moment, his face difficult to see in the gloom. Then his teeth flashed. "All right, I'll come with you as far as the Dancing Canyons. But if we don't find anything, we're both going back to Rivermeet to look for my father. He's got to know about the Harai and what they're doing to the children. No more arguments. Swear."

At that moment, Shaiala would have agreed to anything not to be left alone in the dark. She smiled gratefully at the prince. "Me swear!"

*

Once the *Wavesong* had passed the wreck, the Second Singer took over the chore of listening to the bluestone himself. This left Renn far too much time to sit and worry. He hugged his knees on the stern deck while the flies bit, his sunburn itched and peeled, and his hair bleached ugly brown at the ends. Despite the heat, he was shivery all over.

None of the orderlies had time to talk to him. The sailors were too busy coping with the erratic river winds and avoiding the other traffic, while Lazim kept his pentad exercising on deck at all hours. The clacking of wooden practice swords became as monotonous as the flap of the sail, and although the mock-fights were quite interesting to watch in the beginning, Renn soon grew bored with seeing the pentad dance around one another without ever landing a decent blow. He did notice, though, how Frenn's limp seemed to disappear when he was fighting, as if he'd learned to hide his handicap with a stronger, swifter sword arm than everyone else.

Finally, he worked up the courage to stop Lazim on his way back from one of these training sessions. "Something's wrong, isn't it?" he whispered. "That bluestone was moving much too fast to be on a boat, and I ... er ... thought I heard something, like when I heard the merlee back on the Isle. I don't think Shaiala's still wearing it."

The orderly regarded him with a steady gaze. Still breathing hard, he crouched beside him in the shadow of the sails, wiped his sweaty braids out of his eyes, and said softly, "I won't lie to you, Renn. Kher says the stone's acting very strangely. But he hopes to find out more when we reach Rivermeet. Shouldn't be long now."

"I'm scared," Renn admitted, hugging his knees tighter. "I want to go home."

The orderly rested a sympathetic hand on his shoulder and gazed at the reeds sliding past their starboard bow. "We all do, Renn. But sometimes other things are more important. If it makes you feel any better, you're not the only one who's scared."

Renn frowned. Lazim nodded at the Second Singer, who had been watching the pentad train and was now talking to the men. "Just because someone's grown up doesn't mean they can't sometimes still be afraid," he said.

After that, Renn surreptitiously watched Singer Kherron whenever the Second Singer came on deck to farlisten over the side. He didn't for a moment believe that the Second Singer of the Echorium could be *afraid,* exactly. But Kherron certainly seemed preoccupied and uneasy.

It was a relief to everyone when, on their seventh morning out from Southport, they sailed around a bend in the river into an unexpected cloud of smoke and cooking smells, of neighing horses, colorful stalls, and bright banners snapping in the hot Plains wind. Huts and tents lined both banks, and blocking their way was a solid-looking bridge, much too low to admit the tall-masted *Wavesong.* Downstream from this bridge, a wide basin provided a harbor, tightly packed with ships, barges, and boats of every conceivable shape and size.

Renn joined the pentad in the bows, eyes wide, trying to take in everything at once. "Welcome to Rivermeet," Lazim said, giving him a smile. "It's a trading post, end of the Great South Trade Route. Caravans come down the coast from Silvertown and merchants take the goods on downriver to Southport. Horselords trade here too. See how the river splits farther up?"

He pointed beyond the town, where the waters forked in a swirl of dirty foam and debris. One channel twisted northeast, narrow and choked with weed. The other headed south up a series of foaming weirs.

"Sail traffic stops here. Only canoes go farther by water — and they have to be carried around the falls."

The orderlies fell silent as they approached the basin. Durall and Anyan dropped their hands to their swords. Frenn rested his crooked hand on Renn's shoulder. The reason for their tension soon became clear. The *Wavesong* was being watched in turn by men in dark robes with curved scimitars at their hips, their black eyes hostile above dusty-green sharets.

"Who are those men?" Renn asked, scowling.

"Kalerei," said the Second Singer, coming to join them at the rail. He was in full formal dress and looked grave. "Don't make faces, Renn. Relationships between the Echorium and the Horselords are strained enough already." He exchanged a glance with Lazim, then ordered with a hint of *Aushan,* "Come with me, all of you. We're going ashore, and this place is far too dangerous for a novice to wander around unsupervised."

*

Renn soon forgot the Horselords' hostile stares and even his worry over Shaiala and the strange way the bluestone was behaving. Rivermeet was far too fascinating. His neck ached with twisting his head this way and that in an effort not to miss anything. He wished Singer Kherron would slow down so he could investigate the stalls piled with ripe fruit and unfamiliar smoked meats, the tents stuffed with brightly woven rugs and glittering displays of weapons, and the little, dark shops full of intriguing shadowy items. But every time he hung back for a closer look, one or another of Lazim's pentad prodded him in the back and he had to jog to catch up.

The only time he got half a chance to see anything properly was when Singer Kherron stopped to interrogate the traders. Then he was torn between looking at the goods on the stall and listening to the Second Singer's voice that thrummed with subtle Songs. The traders didn't even seem to realize they were being sung to. While the orderlies examined fruits or trinkets and pretended not to be interested, Renn watched, fascinated, as the traders' hard faces melted and their scarred lips curved into dopey smiles. Men, who a moment before had been bargaining for every last copper, answered the Second Singer's questions without a blink.

"Any suspicious people been seen in town lately?" Singer Kherron asked. "Anyone wearing a mask?" Then, almost as an afterthought, "Any lost children?"

This final question usually resulted in flushed cheeks and stammered replies. The Second Singer grew impatient and resorted to *Aushan,* which made the traders cringe but failed to get him a straight answer. The traders' accents were thick and they tended to babble. By the look of his narrowed eyes, Singer Kherron seemed to be truth-listening. What he discovered, Renn didn't know.

"Ah, Singer?" he whispered, tugging at the Second Singer's sleeve as he strode away from yet another babbling merchant. "Why don't you just ask them about the centaurs?"

Kherron scowled at his hand. "Stay out of this, Renn!" he snapped.

Renn hurriedly let go and made a face at the Second Singer's back. He appealed to Lazim. "I was only trying to help. We might find Shaiala faster if we knew where the stories came from."

The orderly gave him a tight smile and repeated what Frenn had said in Southport after the wild girl ran off. "Kher's got his own way of doing things. Be patient. We'll be moving on soon enough."

All the same, it was mid-afternoon before Singer Kherron eventually stopped questioning people in the town. He led them over the bridge and took the path that climbed beside the weirs. The pentad relaxed a little and loosened the necks of their tunics. Singer Kherron, however, strode as purposefully as ever, his gray robe turning black in the spray, his blue curls clinging to his cheeks. Renn raised his face and closed his eyes, enjoying the cool mist on his sunburned cheeks. He'd never imagined he would miss rain.

Frenn gripped his shoulder and hauled him back from the edge. "Look where you're goin'!" he hissed. "Do you want to end up in that net down there?"

Renn looked down. His heart thudded as he realized how close he'd come to falling in. They'd climbed above the first weir, where white water boiled through a narrow channel. At the narrowest part, someone had strung a net from bank to bank. The holes were much larger than those the Isle fishermen used at home, and its cords were as thick as Renn's wrist. He hated to think what size fish it would catch.

Singer Kherron had noticed the net too. With a thunderous expression, he signaled the pentad to wait with Renn. Then he strode to a small hut at the edge of the weir and disappeared inside. *Aushan* burst from the door, drowning the song of the river. A heartbeat later, a thin man scurried from the hut. He saw the orderlies and skidded to a halt, nervously eyeing their swords.

The Second Singer ducked out after him and jabbed an angry finger at the net. The man stammered something about river monsters and pointed to a nearby pile of rocks, gleaming purple in the spray. Kherron signaled that Lazim should take a look. The orderly crept cautiously behind the rocks, sword in hand. Renn's heart started up again. Then there was a short laugh and Lazim reappeared dragging a second net, this one tangled and torn. The fisherman scurried across and started tugging at the tangles, all the while casting nervous glances at the Second Singer.

"See, Singer?" he stammered. "Chewed to bits, it is! Ruined! We heard the monster from the town in the middle of the night. People thought it was demons. I got a lantern and a couple of men and rushed up here, but we was too late." His voice assumed a wheedling tone. "You can't blame us for protecting our families, Singer. Our women and children were down there, asleep in their beds. If you want my advice, you'll not let the boy wander too close to the river. There's things live up under the Mountains, and I'm not the only one who's seen 'em. A child went missing only last full moon."

Singer Kherron's glare said he did blame the man — though what exactly for, Renn didn't understand. The torn net held his attention. The cords were as thick as those strung across the weir and there was a huge, ragged hole in them. He crept closer and touched one of the severed strands.

Singer Kherron pushed him aside. "Seems your river monster got away," he said to the man. *Kashe.*

The man laughed, a rush of relief. "Yes, Singer! Er, you didn't see it on your way up the River of Sails, by any chance? It must have gone through the town, but no one spotted it."

"Of course no one spotted it." Kherron was still humming *Kashe*. "They weren't looking in the right place, were they? Take another look at that net. See the way the cords are all pulled to one side? Your 'monster' was already downriver, trying to get back up. Fortunately for you it managed to get through, otherwise it'd still be trapped in Rivermeet along with all your women and children. If I were you, I'd take that net down. Just in case." A final note of *Aushan* had the man rushing to obey.

The Second Singer lingered long enough to see one end of the net untied. Then he led them all back down the spray-drenched path to Rivermeet, whistling like a novice.

Renn hurried to take advantage of this rare good mood. "Singer?" he panted out. "What made that hole? What was all that about a missing child? He — he wasn't talking about Sha-iala, was he?"

Singer Kherron sighed. "No, Renn, he wasn't. If you'd been paying attention this morning instead of sightseeing, you'd know that. But it seems we've lost her, anyway. I had my suspicions when the bluestone started acting so strangely. Now we have a decision to make."

He beckoned the orderlies closer so he wouldn't have to

shout above the noise of the weir. "This is what I've learned. There's a boy who's missing from the Kalerei tribe. Favorite son of the Horselord, if I understand rightly. The people of Rivermeet are convinced he's been eaten by a river monster, which they claim breed under the mountains and raid down the Black River when they get hungry. Apparently there have been sightings of such monsters in the River of Sails, too, as far down as the outskirts of Southport. The Horselord claims all this is nonsense, and his boy has been kidnapped by a rival tribe. You saw that net. What do you think?"

The orderlies frowned and glanced uneasily at one another. Renn, forgotten for the moment, eyed the water nervously. Every time the spray touched him he flinched, imagining a tentacle writhing out of the river to drag him in. He hated to think how big the monster's teeth were if they'd done that much damage to the net.

"Cut," Lazim said. "With a crude blade, maybe a sharp stone. Whatever made that hole had human hands."

Renn turned cold, remembering the voice he'd heard in his head when they'd passed the wreck. But the Second Singer didn't seem surprised.

"Stray merlee, perhaps?"

Lazim shrugged. "Don't ask me, Kher. Why don't you ask the boy? Isn't that why you brought him?"

Renn's cheeks burned as every eye turned to him. "I thought we were supposed to be looking for Shaiala," he said stiffly. "Not some missing prince. Anyway, merlee wouldn't come all the way up here. They don't like freshwater, everyone knows that."

This earned him a chuckle from Anyan. "Fresh? The River of Sails? With the rubbish they throw into it at Rivermeet? You obviously haven't swallowed any of it recently!"

Kherron held up a hand. "Quiet. Renn's right. The missing prince isn't our concern, not that the Horselords are likely to welcome the Echorium's help, anyway. They like to settle their disputes in their own fashion. Whatever went through that net, however, *is* our business. My guess is it has taken our bluestone, which means it must have been around when the barge sank. If Shaiala was on that barge, it might be able to tell us which way she went. Our only other option is to go back to the wreck and try to pick up her trail from there. Since she's no longer wearing the stone we'll need a tracker, and unfortunately all the best trackers are Horselords." He frowned. "Considering our current relationship with the tribes, I'm in favor of following the Half Creature."

Renn gazed south, where the mountains the fisherman had mentioned rose ominously out of the plain. To his homesick eyes, they looked like thunderclouds building over the sea. He shivered, thinking of the hole in the net. He didn't want to paddle a small canoe with a creature that size loose in the water.

But after a short, muttered discussion, Singer Kherron got his way as usual. "We'll spend the night on the *Wavesong*," he decided. "It'll be dark soon, and we've got a lot to do if we're heading up the Black River tomorrow."

10
NAGA

The canoes Lazim rented in the morning from a shifty-eyed boatman were designed for two people, only the Second Singer didn't think Renn was capable of paddling and made him sit squeezed in the middle with Durall and Frenn splashing him from each end. Singer Kherron took the front end of the second canoe with his precious chest stowed in the middle and Lazim in the back, while Anyan and Verris paddled a third canoe bringing the rest of their packs. Whenever they had to detour along the bank, however, Renn was suddenly deemed strong enough to help. He got lumbered with the packs while the orderlies tipped the canoes upside down and carried them, dripping, over their heads.

All that day the Black River climbed deceptively, leaving Rivermeet and the plain in a heat haze below. Each time they took to the bank, the Second Singer gazed back the way they had come, frowning. Before they set off again, he made Renn listen to the bluestone. They camped that night near their first real waterfall, its noise keeping Renn awake, then pressed on at first light with the same routine. Meanwhile, the Black River became narrower and its falls more frequent until they were doing a lot more carrying than paddling.

By the end of the second day, Renn's arms and legs were ready to drop off. Even the muscular Durall looked weary. To everyone's relief, Singer Kherron called an early halt and told Lazim to organize a fire. "We'll have to leave the canoes soon," he said, eyeing the foothills ahead of them. "The only way we're going to get up there is on foot." He gave Renn a thoughtful look and pulled out the bluestone again. "Come with me, Renn."

Renn sighed. Every part of him ached. But he followed the Second Singer away from the fire. Get it over with, then he could eat and sleep and dream of the journey back downriver with no paddling or carrying or listening to the bluestone until his head throbbed.

Usually they listened in a sheltered spot. But this time the Second Singer led him over the slippery rocks until they reached the edge of the water where a rocky tongue enclosed a relatively calm pool. He told Renn to kneel.

Nervously, Renn obeyed. In the dusk, unidentified bubbles rose to the surface. From all around came the soft rustles and hoots of unseen animals and birds settling down for the night accompanied by the ever-present song of the river. The crackle of the campfire and the orderlies' voices seemed very far away.

Singer Kherron passed him the bluestone. "Hold it under the water," he ordered. "I think it's time we tried to contact this river monster."

Renn had been dreading this moment ever since the orderlies started to have trouble keeping the canoes going against the current. A shiver crept down his spine as the water closed about his wrist. He wanted nothing more than to be back on the Isle where at least the Half Creatures were friendly. But no one argued with the Second Singer when he was in this mood. He shut his eyes and hummed *Challa*.

Expecting the same vague echo as before, Renn was unprepared for the sheer volume of the response. It came crashing down the mountainside with all the force of the river. With a startled cry, he snatched his hand out of the water.

"Careful! Don't drop it!" Singer Kherron's fist closed around his and forced it back down. Renn's entire body went rigid. He became aware of the Second Singer humming too.

"What do you hear?" Kherron whispered as the river swirled around their clasped fingers.

Renn swallowed. "I — I'm not sure."

"*Listen*, then!" A note of impatience crept into the Second Singer's voice. But the *Challa* continued, soft and calming on the evening air. Gradually, Renn relaxed. The whispers at the edge of his hearing became clearer.

Stone-singer? Want see sparklies?

Renn sucked in his breath. Singer Kherron must have heard something too, for he stopped humming and grew very still.

"Tell it *yes*," he whispered.

Renn shivered again. He felt Singer Kherron's hand tighten and said quickly, "Yes, whoever you are! We'd like to see your sparklies, please!"

At last, the Second Singer allowed him to take his hand out of the water. Renn thankfully gave the bluestone back and breathed on his numb fingers. He hardly dared ask. "W-was that the river monster, Singer?"

"Shh!"

Kherron was staring at the water where it came tumbling over the rocks farther upstream. Renn stared too, eyes and ears straining. Night was almost upon them. Only the foam could be seen clearly, pale in the gloom. Then he caught his breath. Water wasn't the only thing sliding over those rocks. Glints of green and midnight-blue slipped down the rapids as if the river had turned into jewels. As the glints came closer, Renn realized they formed a long, scaled tail twice the length of a canoe.

He scrambled to his feet in terror, but Singer Kherron caught his arm in a fierce grip. The creature surfaced with the sinuous grace of a snake, all rippling blue-and-green shadows. Long weedlike hair clung to a row of glittering spines that ran along its back. It had scaled arms ending in human hands. A green-scaled but recognizably human face swung slowly toward them and studied them with its luminous eyes. Gills opened and closed on its neck as the creature smiled, revealing two rows of tiny sharp teeth.

Renn cringed and shut his eyes. But the Second Singer was still holding him tightly. "Tell it to hand over the bluestone," he ordered. "Then ask it where Shaiala went."

Renn's mouth was too dry to ask anything. He peered up at the creature, which was half out of the water now. Its long tail lashed the river, spraying them with sparkling green-and-blue foam. But it hadn't attacked . . . yet.

He licked his lips. "Singer K-Kherron says . . ." He swallowed and tried again. "C-could we please have our stone back? See, it belongs to the Echorium and —"

The creature made a noise that raised all the hairs on Renn's head. But even as he turned to flee, the monster slipped a green-scaled hand into a pouch where a human stomach would have been and placed three objects on the ledge at their feet, so rapidly its movements were a blur.

Sorry stone-singer angry. Not know sparkly belong to stone-singer. Which sparkly stone-singer want?

All this happened so fast, Renn could do little more than blink at the offerings. Singer Kherron, however, hissed and snatched one off the rock. "Ask where it got *this*!"

Renn took a closer look. One "sparkly" was a handsome dagger, its hilt set with green gems. The second was the flat-sided bluestone Singer Kherron had given to Shaiala back in Southport. The third, which Kherron held like a hot coal, was a shard of black crystal.

The crystal seemed familiar, yet Renn couldn't think. Seeing that bluestone in the creature's hand with a frayed piece of thong still attached made Shaiala's fate real. His throat clenched. Unexpected tears sprang to his eyes.

He rounded on the Second Singer. "Don't you *care*? That's Shaiala's bluestone and all you can do is worry about a stupid piece of crystal! Ask it yourself! And while you're at it, ask what it's done with Shaiala's bones!"

Back in the Echorium, he'd have got *Aushan* for speaking to the Second Singer in such a manner. But he was wet and tired and hungry, stranded in the foothills on the other side of the world with a wild Half Creature that might eat them both at any moment. The tears spilled out. He stumbled away from the river, slipping on the wet rocks in the dark. He avoided the orderlies' fire and plunged into the shadowy crevices that bordered the river course, twisting and turning until he was sure he was alone.

He sank to his knees and pressed his forehead to a boulder. "I'm sorry, Shaiala, I'm so sorry," he sobbed. "I should have tried harder to find you, only I didn't know about those creatures, I swear! Nobody tells me anything! They treat me like a child —" He struck the rock with his fist, then froze.

A soft scrape behind was all the warning he had before a large hand tasting of spices went across his mouth and he was swung around to face a pair of amused black eyes glinting above a green tribal sharet.

"Hush, little Singer boy," said the Horselord, laying a curve of reflected moonlight across his throat. "Or I'll cut that sweet tongue right out of your head."

All Renn could think as that scimitar kissed his throat was how furious Singer Kherron would be with him for running off and getting himself into trouble. Then he glimpsed dark-robed shadows flitting from rock to rock, working their way toward the orderlies' fire, and his blood chilled as he remembered what Kherron had said about relationships between the Horselords and the Echorium. They were going to murder Frenn and Lazim and Durall and Anyan and Verris, and probably the Second Singer, too. Then they'd throw him to the river monster and —

"Stop that," hissed the Horselord. "Behave yourself, and no one need get hurt."

Renn realized he'd been making a noise. A very small squeak — about all he could manage with the hand over his mouth. He took deep breaths through his nose and closed his eyes. When he opened them again, the Horselord had left him in the care of one of his men and gone after the others.

Renn's captor propelled him toward the camp where the clash of metal on metal echoed in the cliffs. They'd clearly been expecting an easy surrender, but Lazim's handpicked pentad was holding its own. Durall laid about himself with furious grunts, keeping three men at bay. Anyan and Verris fought back-to-back, and Frenn threw himself at a line of scimitars in a vain attempt to reach Renn. Lazim leaped the fire, bone-fastened braids flying, and clashed blades with the Horselord, whose eyes lost their amused look as he was forced to fight for his own freedom. When a furious bar of *Aushan* joined the sword strokes, enabling Lazim to disarm his opponent, Renn smiled behind his captor's hand — only to bite his tongue when the man took hold of his hair and thrust him into the firelight. For the second time that night, a scimitar kissed his throat.

"Hold!" called the tribesman, making everyone freeze.

"Singer!" Renn gasped out. "I'm sorry —"

A jerk on his hair brought tears to his eyes. "Quiet!" hissed his captor. "You be quiet, too, Singer. None of your Echorium tricks! Tell your man to let Lord Nahar go."

The Second Singer's face was like a thundercloud lit from

one side by spitting red sparks. His blue curls dripped. He still held the river creature's "sparklies." His gaze flicked briefly to Renn, then back to Lazim. Renn stiffened as Lazim's sword pricked the Horselord's throat.

"Tell *your* man to release the boy," the dark-skinned orderly told his captive. "Or I'll be wearing your fingers in my death-braids, Horselord!"

Lord Nahar's men made angry noises. Frenn tensed. Renn shut his eyes in despair. They were hopelessly outnumbered. Was Lazim trying to get them all killed?

To his surprise, however, Lord Nahar chuckled. "Then my enemies will have to hunt you so they can feed your death-braids to their horses, Karch warrior who rides with Singers! When we saw you in Rivermeet I said to myself, that Singer is on the trail of someone important. Why else does he travel upriver with an armed escort? More to the point, why does he take a boy yet to grow his first beard? Then I heard the boy singing to the river and I realized. I suppose the naga has gone now? I don't suppose you thought to ask it where it found that dagger you're trying to slide up your sleeve, Singer?"

Singer Kherron's hum was dangerous. Low and dark, almost *Yehn*.

"Shh!" warned Renn's captor. "Or the boy suffers."

Kherron clenched his fists. "What do you want, Lord Nahar? Why did you follow us? We're on an important mission." No Song in that, though Renn sensed the frustrated *Aushan* hovering beneath the surface.

Again, the Horselord chuckled. "Let's say I might be able to help you. That is, if you'll do something for me in return."

Lazim prodded him with his sword. "Do what?"

Unruffled, Lord Nahar gestured with his chin. "That dagger belongs — belonged — to a son of mine. It meant a lot to him and he wouldn't trade it willingly. He went missing a few weeks back. If you can tell me where the naga found it, we'll be on our way and let you continue on yours. Far be it for the Kalerei to interfere with Echorium business."

Renn tried to think, except thinking straight with a scimitar at your throat isn't easy. The missing prince, he remembered. The one the fisherman at the weir had mentioned. The one who was supposed to have been eaten by the river monster. What had Lord Nahar called it? Naga? He shuddered.

"I've heard a rumor Singers can communicate with Half Creatures," Lord Nahar was saying. "If you can find out where my son lost his dagger, I'll tell you something about where you're headed that just might save all your lives."

The Second Singer frowned. "You'll tell us, anyway, if I decide to ask."

The Horselord smiled. "Ah-ah. No singing, that's the deal."

The scimitar moved under Renn's chin, making his knees wobble. In a moment he'd slide to the ground and slice his own throat on the way — save Lord Nahar's man the trouble.

Now Lazim was frowning, too. "He might know something useful, Kher."

The fire snapped and crackled as everyone waited for the Second Singer's next move.

"I think, Horselord," Singer Kherron said slowly, "that we ought to talk."

The night breathed again. Warily, Lazim lowered his sword. Lord Nahar rubbed his throat and nodded. His man let go of Renn's hair and gave him a small push. As Renn staggered to his knees and Frenn rushed forward to catch him, the Horselord loosened his sharet revealing a long scar that split his left cheek.

"That's what I've been saying all along, Singer," he said, retrieving his scimitar with a smile that banished the tension as effectively as *Challa*.

From the safety of Frenn's arms, Renn watched, fascinated, as the scar on the Horselord's cheek folded and unfolded like a fan.

*

Once all weapons were safely sheathed, the orderlies hurried to rescue their supper and finish erecting the tents, while the Kalerei vanished downriver and returned with their horses. They strung a picket safely away from the river and started to rub down the animals. Lazim put his hands in his pockets and strolled across, whistling softly through his teeth.

Despite the unpromising beginning, it was the best night of the whole journey so far. After they'd all eaten, Nahar's men brought a large leather flask and a bundle of hollow reeds to the fireside. They balanced the flask on a flat rock and handed out the reeds. Then Lord Nahar showed everyone how to drink by pushing their reed through one of the small holes in the leather, putting their lips around the end, and sucking up the contents.

This was fun. After the first stream of fire that, much to the amusement of the Kalerei, sent the younger orderlies rolling on their backs sputtering and coughing, Renn found himself involved in a contest to see who could swallow the most times while holding his nose.

At first, Frenn tried to stop Nahar's men from passing Renn the reeds, but Durall slapped him on the back and said, "Why not let the boy have some fun?" Then he winked at Frenn and muttered something about how it might help him sleep after his scare. Since Singer Kherron and Lord Nahar had retired to the Second Singer's tent by this time and the others were getting rather merry themselves, Renn had little difficulty sneaking a reed into the flask when no one was looking. His Echorium breathing exercises gave him a distinct advantage, and he quickly swallowed considerably more of the flask's contents than anyone realized. So much, in fact, that the rocks began to swim around him, the stars blurred and swirled in the sky, and his head felt large enough to hold the entire River of Sails. Soon he forgot all about the naga that must have eaten Shaiala and quite probably Lord Nahar's son as well.

In the Second Singer's tent, two looming shadows on the canvas showed the men examining something. Renn let his reed slip from his lips and lay back on the rock with a sigh. No, he didn't want to be a Singer. Too serious by far. He cushioned his head on his arms and stared at the stars, delightfully dreamy. It was like having *Challa*, only better, because whatever had been in that flask tasted a lot nicer than Song Potion. On the other side of the fire, the Kalerei were laughing over a game Lazim was trying to teach them that seemed to involve the bones from the ends of Lazim's braids and handfuls of pebbles. Durall kept thumping people on the back. Anyan and Verris were giggling like First Years. Frenn had gone into the rocks to relieve himself. A horse snorted in the picket. The river splashed in the background. Random words from the Second Singer's tent floated into the night.

". . . naga . . . Half Creatures . . . centaurs . . . Harai . . . khiz . . . mines . . . treasure . . . Pass of Silence . . ."

Feeling guilty, Renn made an effort to focus his thoughts. It wasn't easy. They kept drifting back to Alaira and Geran in the Echorium, to the way the stars made patterns in the sky, to what it would be like to live with a tribe on the Plains, free as the wind. He shook his head. Must concentrate.

"Tell me more about these Harai," Singer Kherron was saying.

Lord Nahar made an angry sound. "They were the only tribe that didn't join the Plains army back when the Karchmen attacked us from the north, and that created bad feelings among the other Horselords. They're loners, always picking fights with someone or another, but they've never directly challenged the Kalerei before. If they've hurt my son, I won't rest until I've fed every last Harai bone to my horses."

Kherron sighed. "It sounds as if your son isn't the only youngster to have disappeared lately. The merchants of South-port reported a drop in the number of urchins begging on the streets — they thought they'd gone upriver, say it happens every summer. Yet no one in Rivermeet noticed any extra mouths. They think some of *their* homeless children must have gone downriver to Southport. Then there's our girl, Shaiala." He paused, then said very softly, "Do you think it's possible these Harai could be snatching children to mine the treasure in this fabled Sunless Valley of yours?"

Lord Nahar's shadow leaped to its feet and the side of the tent bulged. Renn watched with a curious detachment as Lazim and two of the Kalerei scrambled up in alarm. But the Second Singer's shadow calmed the other, and everyone relaxed as the two sat once more.

The bone game had been abandoned in favor of talk about horses. Boring. Renn trained his ears back on the tent.

"I'd like to know where my son lost his dagger," Lord Nahar was saying.

"We'll have to ask the naga again." Singer Kherron. "I'm afraid you interrupted things last time."

"Now?"

"If the men have drunk as much of that *fohl* of yours as it sounds like they have, I think we'd better wait until tomorrow morning, don't you? I thought I saw Renn sneak a couple of sips, too."

At this, Lord Nahar laughed. A full-throated bellow that disturbed the horses, making them stamp and snort. Renn's cheeks went hot. He started to push himself to his feet, meaning to tell the Second Singer he could sing to the naga anytime they wanted, he felt just fine. But the ground seemed to move under him every time he pushed, and somehow he couldn't make it beyond his knees.

The next thing he knew, Frenn was standing over him shaking his head. A blanket folded around him like a dark wing. He did not dream.

*

Morning found the Kalerei and the orderlies standing on the west bank below the falls, their hair and clothes damp after the night by the river, awaiting the sun's first rays.

Fortunately for all of them, sunrise was much later in the steep-sided valley than it would have been out on the Plains. Renn nervously joined the Second Singer on the ledge from which he'd fled yesterday and tried to ignore his thumping headache. And to think he'd almost volunteered to do this last night! The fact that Singer Kherron thought Shaiala and the Kalerei prince were still alive didn't reassure him in the slightest. Just because the naga hadn't eaten them didn't mean it wouldn't eat someone else, particularly if it was hungry as most creatures tended to be before breakfast.

"Are you sure you're up to this?" Singer Kherron asked in a pallet-whisper, giving Lord Nahar a quick glance.

Renn straightened his shoulders. "Of course!"

"Your head hurt?"

"A little," Renn admitted.

Kherron sighed. He, too, seemed subdued this morning. The dark rings around his eyes made Renn wonder how long the two men had talked after he'd fallen asleep.

"I could sing you some *Challa*," Kherron offered. "But it'd probably just send you back to sleep and Lord Nahar's an impatient man. Do your best, Renn. I wouldn't ask if it weren't important. We'll rest later before we tackle the Pass."

"Er — Singer?" Renn meant to ask about Shaiala. But what came out was, "Is there really treasure in the Sunless Valley?"

Singer Kherron gave him a sharp look. "So you were listening last night, were you? Forget the treasure and concentrate on the naga. You're quite clear what I want you to ask?"

"Yes, Singer."

"Tell me again."

Renn's blood rose. As if he were some First Year prone to forgetting his lessons. But he closed his eyes and repeated what the

Second Singer had told him. "I'm to ask where it found the dagger and where it found the khiz-crystal. Then I'm to ask if it knows another way into the place where the sun doesn't shine."

"Black crystal," Kherron corrected. "It won't know what khiz is." But he seemed pleased. "And don't let it leave until it answers all three questions."

Renn nodded and eyed the river. The sun had cleared the far cliff and a mist hung above the water. "Er — Singer?"

"What now?"

"What if the naga doesn't come — with the Kalerei here?"

Singer Kherron smiled. "Leave that to me. Ready?"

Renn swallowed and managed another nod, though he'd never felt less ready for anything. His head throbbed like a rhythm drum. Echoes, why had he drunk so much of that stupid *fohl*?

The Second Singer hitched up his long robe and waded waist-deep into the river. He faced upstream. Head flung back and both arms raised to the falls, he began to sing.

The Kalerei whispered uneasily. Lazim hushed them. Frenn gave Renn an encouraging wink. Worried that the naga might spook the horses, they'd left them picketed back at the camp, but they heard the Second Singer's Song and whinnied.

With the first sun, the naga slipped down the falls. Blue-and-green scales glittering, it looked even more magnificent than it had last night. Renn's throat clenched as it swam around the Second Singer. Its tail was long enough to coil three times around Kherron's waist. Its human half surfaced and took something from the Second Singer's hand, which it stowed safely in its pouch before staring at the men on the bank. Kherron did not flinch. He allowed his song to fade and nodded to Renn. "Ask it," he whispered.

Renn licked his lips and asked first about the dagger.

The naga blinked at him. *Bottom of human river under boats that catch wind with stone-singer's sparkly.*

"The River of Sails where it found our bluestone!" Renn shouted, making the creature rear in alarm. Rainbows flashed as its tail lashed the water.

Kherron's Song calmed it, though his expression warned trouble for Renn later. On the bank, Lord Nahar's scimitar whispered out of its scabbard. Renn bit his lip and quickly asked about the khiz-crystal.

High place where river jumps from mountain and children are born.

He reported this straight, unable to work out what it meant, except it obviously wasn't the same place Shaiala had lost the bluestone. Lord Nahar frowned and whispered something to his men. Renn strained to hear. Between this and his throbbing head, which the naga's inside-speech had done nothing to ease, he forgot Singer Kherron's third and final question.

"Renn!" snapped the Second Singer. "Quickly!"

His attention jerked back to the river. The naga was already halfway up the falls, using its hands to pull its glittering body over the rocks. Strong, he thought in admiration.

"Wake up, boy!" Singer Kherron began to wade toward the bank, swinging his arms to push the water aside.

Renn stiffened. "Is there another way into the place where the sun doesn't shine?" he called after the retreating blue-and-green glitter. But the naga obviously didn't hear.

Singer Kherron climbed out of the river, his face flushed. He wrung out his robe and shook his head at Renn. "I don't dare call it again. I promised it one of its sparklies back if it helped us, and I can't give it the dagger or the bluestone. Why didn't you ask sooner?"

Tears sprang to Renn's eyes. He blinked them away. "My head hurts," he mumbled. "I asked about the other things. It's not my fault it went so soon. You shouldn't have given it the sparkly till after."

Kherron took a furious stride toward him. Renn became aware of Lazim hovering nearby and of Frenn's frown. He tensed, expecting *Aushan* at least. But Kherron stopped and stared at him. Quite unexpectedly, he laughed.

"Shouldn't have paid it until I'd got everything I wanted, huh? You'll make a good Second Singer one day, Renn! Come on, let's get that head of yours sorted out, then maybe we can get moving again. It probably wouldn't have helped us much, anyway. Where the river jumps from the mountain and children are born? Typical Half Creature, can't give a straight answer to anything. Brrr, but that water was *cold*."

"She means her own children," Renn whispered. But the Second Singer had ducked into his tent to change out of his wet robes, and the orderlies were lighting the fire to brew something hot and sweet for their sore heads, so no one heard.

*

Now that he knew where the naga had found the dagger, Lord Nahar was anxious to continue the search for his son. The Kalerei held a fierce discussion at the edge of camp that resulted in a decision to return to Rivermeet where they'd left the rest of their tribe and gather reinforcements before picking up the Harai trail. To Renn, this sounded infinitely more sensible than the Second Singer's plan to press on into the mountains and attempt something called the Pass of Silence in search of the source of the khiz-crystal.

But when he asked why they weren't going back to look for Shaiala now that they'd spoken to the naga, Lazim merely told him to go and pack. "And leave out anything you don't really need!" the orderly called after him. "We're heading away from the river soon. It'll be steep terrain farther up."

Head still too fuzzy from the *fohl* to argue, Renn pushed a few clothes into his pack. Then his eye fell on the horselines, where the Kalerei were mounting amid clouds of breath, snorts, and flashing bridles. A wild idea seized him.

He'd made it as far as the picket when the Second Singer's

warning hum stopped him in his tracks. One foot in the stirrup
of a spirited black stallion, Lord Nahar looked around.

"Where do you think you're going, Renn?" Kherron said.

Renn stood his ground. "You don't need me anymore, so I'm
going with Lord Nahar to look for Shaiala."

A frown. "Don't be so foolish! The Kalerei haven't time to
look out for an untrained boy."

"I'm nearly a Final Year," Renn said. "I can look after myself."
All the same, he wished he dared ask Frenn or one of the other
orderlies to come with him. But Lazim would never split the
pentad, and it wouldn't be right to leave the Second Singer of
the Echorium unprotected. "Besides," he added, the Horselord's
presence making him bold, "if Singer Graia knew you were
chasing after khiz-crystal instead of doing what you were supposed to, she'd be angry —"

Aushan, low and dangerous, made the orderlies look around.
Renn cringed inside. But Lord Nahar passed his horse's reins to
one of his men and stepped between them.

"I know you're worried about your friend," he said in a reasonable tone, glancing at Kherron. "But the Singer's right. These
are dangerous parts, and there'll be fighting when we catch up
with the Harai. I promise I'll keep my eye open for your girl.
Once we've dealt with the Harai, she'll be fine."

"No she won't!" Renn eyed the snorting, stamping horses
and thought of the dream he'd had in Southport. "You don't
know her. She's looking for centaurs and she's crazy! She won't
stop till she finds them, and they're supposed to be in some sort
of trouble —"

The Horselord and the Second Singer exchanged another
glance. Lord Nahar smiled, reached under his robe, and brought
out his son's dagger. The jewels flashed in the river light, green
as Singer Kherron's eyes. He offered it to Renn, hilt first. "Here,
Singer boy. A token of my promise. If I don't bring your girl back

safe, you can keep it. In the meantime, it might be more use than Songs where you're going."

As Renn fingered his unexpected gift, trying to work out what the Horselord meant, Lord Nahar patted him on the head. "Try not to worry too much about your friend. We were talking about this last night. She'll have a hard time finding the trouble she's looking for because centaurs are just a story invented long ago by my people to while away the long nights. Horselords know all the Half Creatures in these parts, and you can take it from me — centaurs don't exist."

11
HERDSTONES

It took Shaiala and Erihan six days to find the Dancing Canyons. During this time they came to know each other a lot better than was entirely comfortable. More than once, Shaiala was ready to ride off and leave the boy to run to his father, or whatever else Two Hoof foals did when they were scared, but it seemed a Kalerei prince did not go back on his word as easily as that. Each time, Erihan came after her and in his quiet persuasive way made everything right again.

One of their arguments was over food. When their supplies ran out, Erihan wanted to hunt in the way of his tribe — on horseback, wasting valuable energy galloping after hares in the wrong direction. When Shaiala showed him the centaur way — standing still until the hares lost their fear, then stunning them with a single kick — he got very quiet. She tried explaining how the centaur kicks were named after the creatures who shared the Plains with them, but he ignored her. That was until she tried to eat the hare raw. With a look of disgust he snatched it from her, expertly skinned the carcass with his stolen knife, and insisted on cooking it sprinkled with freshly picked herbs that, despite her impatience to eat, made Shaiala's mouth water.

Then there was the trouble over the mare's bridle. Shaiala flatly refused to put a bit back into that torn mouth. Equally stubborn, Erihan insisted a bridle was the only way to control a horse, and if the stupid mare put her leg down a burrow and broke both their necks, who'd help her precious centaurs then? She could see his point about the burrows, and the wild ride from the river had proved she didn't have much control. So in the end they compromised. Erihan put the bridle on the gray, while Shaiala knotted the halter around the mare's muzzle in a way that wouldn't hurt her mouth however hard she pulled on the reins.

Night was the best time, when they built a small fire of dried grass and huddled close to the flames safe from the vast Plains dark. Then Erihan would tell her the stories of his people. And on the fifth night she finally discovered what he'd been doing in Southport when he'd been captured.

As he told his own story, the prince drew squiggles in the dust with his knife. "It was really silly," he said, avoiding her gaze. "Father has lots of wives; all Horselords do. He and my mother had a terrible fight one morning and she stormed out of the camp. Rode away to Southport, taking two of his best mares with her. She'd always been his favorite. But when he found out where she'd gone, Father just laughed. He said if she wanted to live in that dung pile of a town, it was up to her, and if she thought he was going to chase after her and beg her to come home then she could think again."

The knife moved faster.

"So I rode to Rivermeet and paid someone to take me down-river, meaning to find Mother and ask her to come home myself. Only the man I'd paid waited till I was asleep then stole every-thing I had except my dagger, which I'd hidden in my boot, and threw me overboard. I managed to find another barge willing to take me the rest of the way if I helped them load and unload cargo. But when I reached Southport, I had no idea where to start looking and no coins or jewels left to pay anyone to look for me. Of course I realize now I should have hidden everything and pretended to be poor but by then it was too late. I was searching the warehouse district when they snatched me and the next thing I knew I was in that awful cellar without my dagger or my boots. They didn't know I was a prince. In Southport, I was no one at all."

Erihan's story haunted Shaiala all the way to the Canyons. He hadn't found his mother. As the black cliffs rose around them, she started to wonder what she'd do if they couldn't find the herd. Nothing seemed familiar. What if she really had dreamed it all?

Thrusting the doubt firmly out of her head, she led the way up a steep, twisting trail. Maybe if she could find the ledge where she'd crouched in her nightmare, she'd remember more. She wished Erihan would say something. But he didn't speak until the silver mare stumbled, sending a shower of stones over the edge.

"This is stupid," he grumbled. "This path's too narrow and steep for horses. It's obvious your centaurs aren't up here. Let's go back to the canyon floor before we all break our necks."

"No." Shaiala clutched the mare's halter rope. "Foals come this way to reach place where herdstones buried." She gave the mare a firm kick past the landslide and pressed on.

Erihan shook his head but followed. She could hear him muttering to himself as he fought to keep the gray on the path. In this way they reached a ledge open to the sky, where time stood still.

Kamara Silvermane and Rafiz Longshadow rearing in the moonlight, teasing each other about who would find their herdstone first.

The image was so real, she could almost reach out and touch her friends. She reined the mare to a stop, a lump in her throat. After what Erihan had said about the demon crystal, she'd been terrified that she'd remember nothing at all.

"This is place," she said, slipping down and gazing around for more clues. The wind stirred her hair, bringing bitter odors. The mare sniffed at a pile of dung, raised her head, and curled her upper lip.

Shaiala's heart leaped. She fell to her knees, jammed a handful to her nose, and inhaled.

Herd.

"Uck!" Erihan exclaimed. "What are you *doing*?" His disgust trailed off when he saw her face.

Shaiala blinked back tears. She wiped her hand on her Singer tunic. "They here! Dung stale, but they here!"

Erihan shook his head. "Looks like an ordinary horse dropping to me."

"You say path too narrow for riding."

He frowned at the centaur spoor. "We managed it, didn't we? Maybe there's another way up. . . ." His voice trailed off as both horses suddenly flung up their heads and stared across the ledge, ears pricked and nostrils flared. The mare nickered softly. Shaiala's heart gave an extra thump.

"This way," she whispered, leading the mare forward.

Erihan shook his head again but dismounted and followed.

They came to a precipice overlooking a wide canyon, where yet another memory flashed into being. *Two Hoofs creeping through the shadows, scimitars glittering at their hips.* Shaiala blinked, took a deep breath, and looked down.

Empty.

Beside her, Erihan sighed. "Satisfied now?" He touched her shoulder and added more softly, "I'm not surprised the horses are seeing things. It's pretty spooky up here with all these shadows."

"Shh!"

Faint sounds carried up the cliff. The scrape of a hoof. The frightened murmur of voices. Hardly daring to believe, Shaiala knelt on the edge and peered over. So difficult to see.

Then she glimpsed a glimmer of green light. And, haloed by that light, a horse's ear.

She clutched the cliff edge with trembling fingers and leaned forward. She hardly felt Erihan's alarmed grip on her shoulder. As she stared harder, more details shimmered into view. A dappled rump. The swish of a blue tail. A stern, bearded face with a long nose staring up the cliff straight at her, ears laid flat in suspicion.

"It me!" she shouted, leaping to her feet and waving her arms. The mare danced backward with a surprised snort. Erihan staggered as the gray tugged him off balance. The face began to fade.

In her excitement, she'd forgotten centaurs didn't understand Human. Quickly, she changed to Herd. "It I! Shaiala Two Hoof! And this Prince Erihan of Kalerei! Not be afraid, him horse friend. And this Swift Hoof, and other horse The Gray. Us rescue they from Two Hoofs."

The bearded face disappeared as if it had slipped sideways into a different part of the air. Then an amazing thing happened. A centaur stallion trotted out of nowhere. Green stars sparkled briefly around him, then vanished with little twinkles. He stood beneath the ledge, very solid and very real, staring up at Shaiala and Erihan and swishing his magnificent blue tail in agitation.

For a long moment, he didn't speak. Then he stamped a fore-hoof and called in his ringing stallion voice, "Come down here, Shaiala Two Hoof! Herd want speak to you."

*

By the time they reached the canyon floor, the mares were visible, too, and the eerie green glimmer had gone. Erihan was very quiet. He led the gray carefully down the trail, his eyes fixed on the centaurs as if he were afraid they might vanish again the moment he blinked. Shaiala resisted an urge to say, "I told you so," and gave him an encouraging smile.

"Not be scared," she whispered. "They not you hurt."

Erihan shook himself. "I'm sorry," he said gravely. "I had no idea." He shook his head again and clasped the gray's reins tighter. "But where did they come from? There's nowhere for that many of them to hide down here."

Shaiala had been wondering the same thing. That green light . . . it seemed familiar. Yet when she tried to remember, the darkness returned. She let it go. The memory would come, she was sure now. Only one thing mattered, filling her head and her heart until she thought they would burst with joy.

The centaurs were real.

Real, real, real.

"They're much smaller than I thought," Erihan whispered as they drew closer. "I can't imagine you riding one. Your feet would drag on the ground."

"Centaurs stronger than look," Shaiala said proudly. "And grow quicker than Two Hoofs. When I little, Rafiz Longshadow carry I easy. He big, like stallion. . . ." She thrust away an unlooked-for memory of the dark colt hobbled and beaten, his head hanging, the fire gone from his eyes. "We leave horses here?"

Their Harai mounts were balking, snorting as they caught the centaur smell. Erihan nodded. They looped the horses' reins around their forelegs and left them to pick at the weeds that sprouted from cracks in the rock. Then they went to meet the herd.

The older mares clustered around them, giving one another sly *Dragonflies* as they vied for position. Shaiala looked at them carefully, searching for her foster mother. But the stallion didn't allow them time for reunions. Shouldering the mares aside, he trotted up to Erihan and stared intently down his long nose at the prince. Because the stallion was so tall for a centaur, their eyes were almost level. Erihan bore the scrutiny well.

"Welcome, Horse Friend," the stallion said at last.

The prince's blank look jolted Shaiala out of her memories. She translated quickly and Erihan smiled. "Thank you, Centaur."

There were more formal greetings between Erihan and the lead mare, then all the other mares in order of decreasing rank. Shaiala fidgeted from foot to foot. The centaurs were frightened, she could tell. Their fear seeped out of them in patches of dark sweat. They kept the younger foals huddled together, shielded by adult bodies. She kept seeing green glimmers out of the corner of her eye. If this went on much longer the whole herd might vanish again.

"Herd Stallion!" she blurted out. "Us help rescue Kamara Silvermane and other foals. Two Hoofs take they to evil place called Singing Palace."

The green glimmers brightened. Scuffles broke out at the edges of the herd. The press of centaur bodies suddenly seemed threatening. Her hand crept into Erihan's. He returned her squeeze.

"Herd can no longer hear foals," said the stallion, swishing his tail again. "Foals gone to place of great power and endless shadow. When Herd try follow, tracks enter narrow place where mountains spit rocks. Very bad for hooves. Three mares break legs before Herd get out again."

When Shaiala translated this, Erihan bit his lip. "It makes a sort of sense," he said. "The place of endless shadow sounds like our valley of the demons where the sun never shines. That would make the narrow place where mountains spit rocks the Pass of Silence. It's supposed to be the only way into the valley and the slightest noise triggers an avalanche. The sound of centaur hooves would have brought the rocks down. The Harai probably muffled the foals' feet before they took them through."

The stallion tweaked a lock of Shaiala's hair. "What Horse Friend say?"

When Shaiala told him, the stallion thoughtfully stroked his beard. The nearest mares passed the whisper back through the herd. More green glimmers teased the edges of Shaiala's vision as the centaurs uneasily fingered their herdstones.

The stallion's ears flicked back and forth. "Foals need herd-stones. Herdstones bend light, hide centaurs from Two Hoofs. No herdstone, no protection."

Shaiala stared at the glimmers. As had happened on the Singers' pentangle, a barrier in her head slid aside and memory blazed.

She seized Erihan's arm in excitement. "They use stones to make herd invisible! That why us not see they before. I remember now! Whenever there be danger, centaurs put we foals in middle and mares stay on edges to bend light with herdstones. That why your people never find they!" She thought quickly. "If us take herdstones to foals, they can bend light and be invisible too. Escape easy!"

Erihan looked gloomy. "If Yashra's built her palace in the Sunless Valley, the Pass is bound to be watched. Even if there's enough light in there for anyone to bend, they're hardly going to let us through with a sack of enchanted stones."

"It not matter! Centaurs make we invisible!" She turned excitedly to the stallion. "You wrap hooves, so not set off avalanche. Us cut The Gray's saddle blanket to make hoof-wrappings, mares braid cords from tail hair to tie they on. . . . How many centaurs to bend light? How many centaurs to hide I and Prince Erihan? How much light herdstones need? If us leave some mares outside Pass, then maybe —"

The stallion snorted. "Not gallop before can walk, Shaiala Two Hoof! Herdstones bend faintest light from stars, but not work unless hooves in contact with ground. Need special echoes. Foals would learn this after night in Dancing Canyons. Now too late."

Shaiala's heart sank as she passed this on to Erihan.

The stallion shook his mane.

But the lead mare pushed closer. "There another way into place of endless shadow," she ventured. "Underground way guarded by centaur friends, not enemies."

The stallion gave the mare a gentle *Dragonfly*. "Centaurs not pass through wet naga places."

Shaiala's hopes lifted again. "Can Two Hoofs pass through wet naga places?"

A slow nod. "Perhaps."

"Then us take they! Erihan and I! Where foal herdstones? Where naga way? Us hurry!"

The stallion caught her arm in a strong centaur fist. "Shaiala Two Hoof, always so impatient!" But his lips curled up at one corner, softening the rebuke. "Foals been gone two moons, can wait till morning. Horses need rest. Also Erihan Horse Friend tired, big shock to find stories true."

When Erihan tried to deny this, the stallion chuckled and patted him on the shoulder. Then he glanced at their ankles, where the shackles had rubbed their skin raw, and his eyes darkened.

"Two Hoofs cruel," he said. "Even hobble own foals."

12
PASS OF SILENCE

The weather closed in as the Singer party prepared to leave the river. After striking camp, they sorted through their belongings and stored the bigger items beneath the upturned canoes to collect on their return. The essentials, including several bluestone pendants from the Second Singer's chest, were divided between the orderlies' packs. Renn watched uneasily as the packs got heavier and heavier.

"I can carry something," he said.

Singer Kherron gave him an impatient glance. "You concentrate on where you're putting your feet. You heard what Lord Nahar said."

Before they parted, the Horselord had given the Second Singer hurried directions and advice about the Pass. As far as Renn could make out, this consisted of dark warnings about noise and avalanches and not talking above a whisper and preferably not even that. "I'm not stupid," he muttered under his breath. But when he saw Anyan stagger as he heaved the pack on his shoulder, he felt rather relieved they hadn't taken him up on his offer.

For the next two days, they climbed higher and farther than he'd thought possible. Jagged crags reared up on all sides and disappeared into low clouds. Soon they were in the clouds as well. Renn's spirits sank with every step. The mist soaked through his goat-hair cloak and chilled his sweat. He scowled at the Second Singer's back, wishing more than ever that he'd gone with Lord Nahar.

Toward mid-afternoon of the second day, just when he was thinking they were certainly lost and things couldn't get any worse, Singer Kherron held up a hand. "Quiet," he whispered. "I think this must be it."

The orderlies shrugged off their packs and set them down quietly. They rubbed their shoulders and stretched. Lazim joined the Second Singer. Renn tried to hear what the two men were saying, but they were using pallet-whispers. Their bodies blocked the narrow opening in the cliffs ahead so he couldn't see what lay beyond.

Durall, Anyan, and Verris loosened their swords in their scabbards and began to whisper among themselves. Frenn walked off a few paces and stared up at the cliffs, rubbing his crooked hand the way he did when he was nervous. Frustrated, Renn plunked himself on a nearby boulder, scooped up a handful of dark gray flints, and skimmed them at a flat rock on the opposite side of the path. Tiredness must have affected his aim. He'd thrown six times before a flint skittered across its target, trailing sparks in the mist.

The Second Singer's head snapped around. His hum — furious *Aushan* — was followed by an ominous rumble from the pass ahead. Frenn seized Renn's wrist and snatched the remaining flints out of his hand. "Are you crazy?" he hissed.

Renn bit his tongue. The echoes of that rockfall were making his stomach churn too. "I'm sorry. I didn't think it would matter out here."

"Then you'd better start thinkin'! You heard what the

Horselord said. Any noise at all in that Pass, and the whole lot comes down on our heads." He glanced at the Second Singer and added more gently, almost in a pallet-whisper, "You know what his temper's like. Don't antagonize him."

With a grave expression, Singer Kherron ordered them all to take off their boots. He frowned at the flint-strewn path, then told the orderlies to cut strips off the hems of their cloaks to wrap around their feet. When these were tied at the ankle, the resulting little gray bags looked so funny, Renn couldn't help a giggle.

Lazim frowned as he jerked the final tie tight. "This isn't a joke, Renn," he warned. "Not a squeak until we get to the other side and the Second Singer says it's safe, understand? If you slip or twist an ankle, stuff your fist in your mouth and bite hard until someone reaches you."

The giggle died in Renn's throat. He nodded, a chill going down his back. "If it's so dangerous, why don't we go one at a time?" he whispered. "Then if someone gets buried, the others can dig him out."

Lazim and Frenn glanced at each other. "It's a good idea, Renn," Lazim said. "But we dare not split the pentad, not here. Anyone guarding this Pass would be quick to take advantage of the ones waiting at the other end. Kher thinks there's less risk if we stick together."

The Second Singer had paused in the mouth of the Pass, his sandals clutched in one hand, the mist swirling around his gray robes. He looked as if he were about to step off the edge of the world. A sudden gust whipped his curls around his face and moaned in the rocks ahead. Pebbles rattled in response.

The orderlies glanced uneasily at one another. "Even the wind could bury us," breathed Frenn, going pale.

"Shh," Lazim warned, dropping a hand on Renn's shoulder. "Keep close together. Walk quickly but don't run. It doesn't look far. Don't worry, we'll be safe on the other side well before dark."

Renn's mouth dried as they entered the Pass. Dark cliffs pressed on each side, ghostly in the mist. The air was completely still, as if they'd entered a windowless room. Renn's wrapped feet felt clumsy, like trying to walk in boots full of soft sand. To make things worse, the path was littered with debris. They had to keep stopping to climb one at a time over each pile of rocks, everyone holding their breath in case the climber dislodged a loose stone. Once, Renn put his hand on a human skull and opened his mouth to scream. Remembering just in time, he crammed his fist between his teeth and bit hard until the scream went away. Lazim gave his shoulder a sympathetic squeeze. Renn managed a weak grin. Now that he was looking for them, he realized there were bones scattered all over the pass. It was only too obvious how their owners had died.

They were about three-quarters of the way through. As Renn waited his turn to climb over another pile of debris he stared upward, trying to work out how much rock hung unseen in the mist above them. A glint in the rocks caught his eye. A dark-robed figure was gliding silently down the cliff, a scimitar glittering between its teeth.

Renn's stomach clenched. Before he'd thought, the warning burst free. "BEHIND YOU, SINGER —"

He slammed a hand to his mouth as large rocks, dislodged by his yell, came thundering down the cliff. Taking advantage of the panic, more of the sinister figures rushed out of the mist. A boulder knocked Durall off the path in front of Renn and bounced high into the air before slamming into the base of the opposite cliff. Echoes rolled alarmingly, bringing down yet more rocks. Renn glimpsed Singer Kherron, Anyan, and Verris whirling to face their attackers in a cloud of black dust. Then hands tugged him backward out of the path of the avalanche.

He struggled in terror before he realized the hands belonged to Lazim. "Hide!" the orderly hissed, pushing him off the path.

Unable to see in all the choking black dust, Renn stumbled

around boulders. He couldn't find anything large or stable enough to crouch behind. The rocks were everywhere, crashing down like enormous hailstones. Then Frenn's arms closed around him, pushed him to the ground, and held him there, shielding him with his own body. Trembling violently, Renn thrust his knuckles into his mouth and squeezed his eyes shut. *We're all going to die,* he thought. *Why did I have to yell like that?*

After what seemed like several sunsteps but could only have been a few heartbeats, the avalanche rattled to a stop and the dust settled. Silence returned to the Pass. Eventually, Renn's shaking subsided. He risked opening one eye. From where he lay beneath Frenn's arm, he couldn't see the Second Singer or Lazim. A pile of fresh boulders blocked the path. Durall lay in a ditch nearby, frighteningly still. Blood pooled around his head and his leg was twisted at a strange angle. As Renn stared at the dead man, feeling sick and small and helpless, he became aware of a lump digging into his hip. The prince's dagger. He wriggled out from under Frenn's arm, drew himself carefully into a crouch, and turned to whisper to the orderly.

"Do you think Lazim —"

He broke off in dismay. Frenn's face was turned toward him and his eyes were open. But they stared past Renn to a different place, wide and blue in the mist. Blood trickled from a tiny wound on his temple.

Tears blurred Renn's vision. He clenched his fist on the jeweled hilt of the dagger and rushed toward the debris, but sense caught up with him before he could scramble over. He crouched behind a large boulder and listened. His heart was thumping too loudly to tell who had won, but it sounded as if the fighting had stopped.

He took his hand from the dagger and wiped his eyes. Cautiously, he peered over the boulder. Robed figures, their faces hidden behind crimson-and-black-striped sharets, surrounded what was left of the Singer party with glittering scimitars. The Second Singer stood motionless, glaring at the blades, his green eyes blazing. Lazim, Anyan, and Verris flanked him with drawn swords, but they were hopelessly outnumbered and seemed reluctant to fight. Remembering the noise their clashing blades had made back at the river camp, Renn thought he knew why.

His numbed brain had barely registered all this when the robed figures disarmed the three surviving orderlies and forced them to lie facedown on the ground. One of the tribesmen produced a small, silk-wrapped package from under his robe and carefully unwrapped it to reveal a glittering black crystal. This, he touched to the back of each captive's skull. First Lazim, then the other two slumped like limp seaweed. All this was done in eerie silence while the Second Singer stood helpless inside that ring of scimitars.

"*No!*" Renn whispered, and quickly jammed his fist back into his mouth. He felt for the dagger with a trembling hand. Why didn't Singer Kherron *do* something?

Almost lazily, the leader swaggered silently up to the Second Singer and showed him the little khiz-crystal. Kherron's jaw clenched in fury. He jabbed a finger at the prone orderlies. The leader smiled and waved a hand at the cliffs, miming a fall of rocks. Kherron opened his mouth, but the leader put a finger to his lips. A curt wave of his hand brought two of the robed figures closer. They held the Second Singer's arms as the leader jammed the khiz-crystal between Kherron's teeth, pushing it deep into his throat. He bound it in place with the silk, and the other two tied Kherron's wrists behind him. The Second Singer's face twisted in pain.

Renn gripped the dagger tighter in an effort to stop his hands from shaking. An image flashed behind his eyes — himself running up behind the nearest robed figure and sinking the dagger into his back. Just as quickly, it was replaced by one of him getting caught and knocked out like Lazim and the others. He remained behind his boulder, biting his knuckles, as the robed figures checked the motionless orderlies and made a cursory search of the immediate debris. Then the leader turned and stared straight at Renn's hiding place. His lips curved into a cold smile.

Renn ducked. His hands began to sweat and he almost dropped the dagger. But no one came to drag him out. When he next plucked up the courage to look, the robed figures were escorting their captive out of the Pass.

He waited until the last bright sharet had vanished into the mist, then made himself count to a hundred. Only after this did he dare climb the debris and hurry to Lazim's side.

"Wake up!" he hissed in a pallet-whisper, shaking him. "Lazim! Wake *up*! They've made Singer Kherron swallow a piece of the khiz-crystal and taken him prisoner. Please, Lazim! I don't know what to do."

He choked on a sob. The orderly lay as if dead, his skin sickly gray. Renn had to put an ear to his mouth to check that he was still breathing. He tried shaking the other two. "Anyan! Verris! Wake up!" But they were just the same.

He didn't think things could get much worse. But no sooner had he settled beside Lazim and resigned himself to a long wait, than a terrible cacophony of clanging metal sounded from the far end of the Pass where the robed figures had taken Singer Kherron. He leaped to his feet and stared up the cliffs in alarm as a second avalanche came tumbling out of the mist.

There was no time to think. With Frenn's and Durall's deaths still sharp in his mind, he grabbed the shoulders of Lazim's tunic and, gasping with the effort, dragged the orderly into a crevice between two large boulders where an overhang protected them from above. The first pebbles were already bouncing across the path. He hurried out, seized the unconscious

Anyan, and dragged him into the crevice, too. Verris was farther away and heavier and he almost left him. Then he remembered how it had been his yell that had started the first avalanche and dashed back, dodging the falling rocks. With the third orderly folded into the small space, there was barely room to squeeze himself in. For once in his life, Renn was thankful he didn't have a physique like Geran's. He burrowed under Lazim's limp arm and closed his eyes as boulders the size of barges thundered harmlessly overhead and the black dust came down.

*

Finally, it was over. Thick, misty silence descended on the Pass. Renn moved cautiously, spilling layers of dust and small stones, testing each limb in turn. Everything seemed to work. He muffled a cough, eyes watering, then realized he wasn't the only one coughing.

"Lazim!" he squeaked, only just remembering to use a pallet-whisper. "You're alive!"

The orderly unfolded himself from the crevice, shook the dust from his hair, and blinked up at the overhang. His sober gaze settled on Renn. "Thanks to you, it seems," he whispered back. "That was quick thinking, Renn. Well done."

The other two were sitting up now as well, wiping their eyes, and rubbing the backs of their necks. Verris had a graze on his arm where a flint had scraped him, but other than that they appeared unharmed. Lazim looked around, frowning.

Renn bit his lip. "I couldn't . . . Durall's dead. Frenn tried to protect me and a stone hit his head. Only a small one, but I think he's dead, too. Then the tribesmen knocked you out and took Singer Kherron prisoner! I couldn't do anything, I'm sorry —" It all caught up with him at once. He started to tremble again. Although he tried to choke them back, several loud sobs burst free. "Oh, Lazim, I was so afraid! It was all my stupid fault!"

Lazim's arms went around him. He sent the other two order-lies to check on Durall and Frenn, then pressed Renn's face to his chest, muffling the noise. "Shh," he whispered. "Shh, don't blame yourself, Renn. You were very clever and brave just now. And you couldn't have done anything to help Singer Kherron with your one little dagger. There were too many of them and they had us trapped. Even my pentad couldn't do anything — if we'd fought, the rocks would have killed us more surely than a scimitar. If it's anyone's fault, it's mine. I didn't think they'd dare use the Pass of Silence that way." He paused, staring at the debris. "At least Kher's still alive. Don't worry, we'll find him."

Renn sniffed, feeling slightly calmer now that Lazim was back in charge. He pushed himself away from the orderly, cheeks hot with embarrassment. "Why did they take Singer Kherron?" he whispered. "Were they Lord Nahar's men? I thought he was our friend. He gave me his son's dagger —" He pulled out the little weapon and stared at it, ready to cast the thing away in disgust.

Lazim dropped a gentle hand on his. "Not Lord Nahar's, no. Didn't you see their tribal colors? The Kalerei wear green, remember. From what Nahar told us, I think those men were probably Harai. As to why they've taken Kher, let's say I have my suspicions. It's all to do with the Khiz and the man who used to wield it. I could tell you some tales about him, but not here. Let's get out of this Pass before any more of it falls down, shall we?"

Anyan and Verris had by now collected their boots and what they could recover from their split packs and were waiting nearby. Their faces were grimed with black dust, their tunics torn, and they had blood on their hands. But they had found their swords and Lazim's, which Anyan presented to their leader. "We piled rocks on the bodies," he whispered. "So the crows don't get them." Lazim smiled grimly as he accepted the weapon and checked it over. He dropped a hand on Renn's shoulder.

"They've made their first mistake," he whispered back. "Thinking the boy would just sit there like a limp salad. It's time we showed these Harai the Echorium is made of sterner stuff than that!"

Renn jammed the dagger back into his belt, picked up his boots, and straightened his shoulders. He ached all over and no doubt looked as filthy and blood-spattered as the orderlies. Yet he felt stronger and more alive than ever before. When they caught up with the Harai this time, he'd *fight*.

*

At the far end of the Pass, they discovered the apparatus responsible for the second avalanche. Two enormous gongs of beaten black metal swung eerily in the mist beneath archways of rock, one on each side of the path. The wind moaned through the ropes and chains that supported the gongs, teasing a faint song out of the metal that made Renn's skin prickle. Under each gong waited a pile of stones, each the size of a man's fist. Other stones lay scattered among the rocks beyond. Two of the Harai were busy picking these up and returning them to the piles. Renn heard their quiet laughter and clenched his fists.

"Quick," Lazim whispered. "While they still think we're dead. I expect they have orders to go in and check once they've finished tidying up out here."

With the mist to hide them and their feet still wrapped from the Pass, it wasn't difficult to creep past the guards, who weren't expecting trouble so soon after the avalanche. Lazim led them off the path and up the shadowed side of the mountain. Once they were sure they were out of earshot of the guards, they stopped to put on their boots. Then they continued to climb until it was too dark to see where they were going. At last, Lazim let them stop and unroll their sleeping pads. He wouldn't allow a fire because the flames would have made the mist glow. So the four of them huddled together for warmth and shared the dried fish and fruit they'd managed to salvage from the Pass. There wasn't much and Renn was still hungry afterward. Thirsty too. He tried squeezing the moisture from his own tunic, but it tasted foul.

Then Lazim began to tell them the story of the Khiz, and Renn forgot how hungry and thirsty he was as the importance of their mission finally became real.

Lazim had been born in the northlands in a place called the Karch where the priests had all the real power because their chief, Frazhin the Khizpriest, wielded a spear of black crystal that could control people's thoughts. "If ever a Karchholder stepped out of line," he told them darkly, "they'd vanish into the priests' levels and never be heard from again. People were so scared of the priests, they even turned a blind eye to the fact that the Khizpriest was slowly killing their young Karchlord by feeding him poisoned merlee eggs." Lazim paused. "But Frazhin hadn't bargained on Kher."

"Was Kherron the Second Singer back then, too?" Renn asked, impressed, trying to work out how old that would make Singer Kherron. "Was he sent to punish the Khizpriest?"

Lazim smiled. "No. It was in Second Singer Toharo's day. Kher wasn't in the Singer party at all, not officially. But Rialle was."

Renn stared, a lot of things falling into place. "Singer Rialle who lives in the cave? My . . . mother?"

A sober nod. "The same. Frazhin tried to use the Khiz to force her to teach him our Songs of Power, which he then tried to use against the Echorium. But Rialle defied him long enough for Kher to heal the Karchlord, who then sailed with his army to the Singers' aid. That was the Battle of the Merlee, which you should know about if Singer Ollaron's been doing his job."

Renn nodded, thinking furiously. "So the secret weapon the priests used against the Isle was Frazhin's mind-controlling spear?"

"Exactly," Lazim said. "You saw the shards the merlee found. Singer Graia and Kher spent time fitting them together. There's no question they came from the original Khiz that Frazhin had wielded in the Karch."

"And Singer Rialle . . ." Renn bit his lip, remembering his mother's dark words. *Things were done to me*. "That's why she's crazy, isn't it? Because of what Frazhin did to her?"

Lazim sighed. "What's so crazy? Living where she can be near her friends? Some would say we're the crazy ones. Leagues from home, hiding up here in the dark. Three parts of a pentad and a half-trained Singer planning a raid on Frazhin's stronghold!"

Once Renn would have contested the "half-trained." Yet it was all too true. "So where did Frazhin go after the battle?" he asked to take his mind off the "raid" part.

"Ah," Lazim said. "As to that, no one really knows. But soon after First Singer Eliya's death a delegation was sent out under the command of a new Second Singer called Parrien. He was wise and experienced but rather old. The Echorium was in a bit of confusion, you understand, losing both its First and Second Singers within such a short space of time. I don't suppose Parrien was the best choice for the job. But he went to the mainland and checked on all the people who'd been given *Yehn,* confirmed their deaths, and took back their Trust-Gifts. He reported all this to Singer Graia through the bluestone. Then he sailed north on the trail of the Khizpriest, and that was the last anyone saw or heard of Singer Parrien, his escort, or the original *Wavesong*. The Echorium had to have another ship built."

Anyan and Verris shifted uncomfortably on the dark mountainside. Renn shuddered, glad he hadn't heard this story before they'd set sail.

"That was when Kher started telling everyone Frazhin wasn't dead," Lazim went on. "But shortly afterward the merlee began bringing Rialle shards of the shattered Khiz, and Singer Graia decided that even if Frazhin had somehow survived, he was of no threat without his Khiz-spear. She promptly appointed another Second Singer, this one younger and more suited to the job. Lirill lasted ten years, by which time Kher had gained enough experience to be considered for the position." Another smile. "I don't think Singer Graia was too keen to appoint him at first, but you know Kher. If he wants something badly enough, he gets it. One way or another."

Renn was having difficulty thinking of the Second Singer as an untried novice, but there were more important things to think about now. "You said you thought you knew why the Harai had captured Singer Kherron?"

Lazim was immediately serious again. "Kher outwitted Frazhin, back in the Karch. Frazhin wouldn't forget a thing like that. If he's found more khiz-crystal, then he'll have his powers back. I expect he wants Kher somewhere he can't use his Songs so he can have his revenge. The Harai must be working for him."

Renn scrambled to his feet and drew his dagger. "Then what are we waiting for? We've got to go after them!"

The orderly's dark hand enclosed his wrist. "Sit down, Renn. We go stumbling around up here in this weather in the dark, and we'll all end up at the bottom of the next crevasse. Then we won't be any use to anyone. If I know Kher, he'll find some way to turn the tables on his captors. In the meantime, I didn't just bring you up here for a history lesson."

He rummaged in his depleted pack and extracted a small bluestone pendant on a silver chain, which he held out to Renn. "We need to contact the Isle. Kher brought this along as a Trust Gift, but it should work all right. See if you can contact the First Singer. I don't suppose you'll be able to communicate both ways like Kher can, but if you can tell her what's happened that'll be a help. At least then she'll know what to do if we — Well, she ought to know, anyway."

Goose bumps erupted on Renn's arms. The undercurrents in Lazim's words were only too clear. *If we don't come back.*

He fingered the chain and stared miserably into the dark. The mist was thinning. A crimson moon broke through the clouds, staining the far side of the valley the color of blood. Just because he'd been able to follow Shaiala's stone didn't mean he could contact the Isle, all that distance away. He opened his mouth to tell Lazim so, then saw the hope on the faces of the other orderlies and closed it again. The least he could do was try.

He cupped the little pendant in his palms, closed his eyes, and hummed softly. *Challa. Shh, calm.* He didn't expect to hear anything, except maybe a vague echo of the Echorium, far across the sea to the northwest. He must have unconsciously tuned his thoughts that way. When dark echoes slammed into him from the southeast, it was like a blow to the back.

He staggered and the pendant leaped from his hand. His head whirled, his ears rang. The crimson moon turned black.

He must have fainted. He opened his eyes to find himself in Lazim's arms. "Wh-what happened?" he whispered.

The concern in the orderly's eyes changed to relief. "Thank the echoes! You gave us quite a scare. What happened? Did you reach Singer Graia?"

"No," Renn managed. "No, not the Isle . . . something else, something dark . . . like a shadow." Now that it was gone, he couldn't explain. He fought free of the orderly, stumbled three steps into the drifting, crimson mist, and *listened,* every muscle tense. But whatever he'd picked up from the bluestone had vanished when he dropped it. He shook his head, feeling foolish, and gave Lazim a weak smile. "I'm sorry, I couldn't reach her."

Lazim sighed and ruffled his hair. "Never mind. She couldn't have done anything to help us, anyway. I suppose it is a bit much to expect you to do the Second Singer's job when you haven't even started your Final Year!"

The other two chuckled.

"But —" Renn began, annoyed that they were treating him like a child again. The three orderlies were already discussing tactics for tomorrow, excluding him.

He hugged his knees and stared into the night, trying to fit Lord Nahar's tales of treasure and Singer Kherron's theories of khiz-crystal with what had happened when he'd tried to contact the Isle.

"There's something out there," he whispered, shuddering. "I heard its echoes. Something *huge*."

13
SUNLESS VALLEY

After a dark and windy night in the Dancing Canyons, the centaurs led Shaiala and Erihan along secret paths into the mountains, the mares taking turns to bend the light. They didn't stop when the sun went down but continued at the same ground-eating trot. Although both centaurs and horses had good night vision, it was unsettling to feel the wind howl up an invisible precipice and know there was nothing to stop them from falling if a misplaced hoof slipped over the edge.

It grew noticeably colder on the second day. Shaiala shivered and buried her hands under the silver mare's mane. Erihan pulled his stolen sharet over his ears. Toward midnight, a strange roaring noise replaced the howl of the wind, so loud that Shaiala could no longer hear the herd's hoofbeats. She tightened one hand on the mare's halter rope, clutched the sack containing the foals' herdstones with the other, and stared into the darkness until her eyes hurt. Only when she felt spray on her cheek did she realize —

"Water!" she called in relief.

Erihan's saddle creaked as he shifted his weight. "We must be near the start of the Black River," he shouted back. "It's supposed to come out of the mountain and drop for ages before it hits rock! My people call it the Fall of Clouds. Hardly anyone's actually seen it." His head twisted in excitement. But in the dark all they could make out were faint green bubbles where the herdstones' glow reflected off foam.

Further conversation was out of the question as the water filled their senses, soaked their hair and clothes, bubbled up their noses and streamed into their eyes. Then the stallion led them behind the thunderous wall of water and the noise receded as they followed a tunnel into a large cavern. The exhausted mares stood with drooping shoulders and bedraggled tails, making puddles on the floor. Although they had stopped bending the light when they entered the cave, their herdstones gave off a soft green glow that reflected on the wet rock. At the back of the cavern glimmered a pool that reminded Shaiala of the sea cave back on the Singer island.

Erihan dismounted and gazed around in wonder. "I've heard of these caves," he said in an awed whisper. "The whole of the Mountains of Midnight are supposed to be riddled with them. No one's ever found a way in before."

Neck prickling, Shaiala dismounted, too. A centaur took the mare's halter and led her to one side. Another took the gray from Erihan. When the horses were safe, the stallion raised a forehoof and splashed the surface of the pool.

Shaiala's heart lurched. Something was moving beneath the dark water. Scales glittered green where they caught the glow from the herdstones. Then the creature surfaced. The horses shied, dragging their centaur handlers back through the tunnel in a panicked rattle of hooves. Shaiala crept closer, still thinking of the sea cave. Although this creature had a partly human body, it was no merlee. Midnight-blue-and-green scales rippled from its head to its rather beautiful snakelike tail. Dark green hair was tangled around the little spines along its back, and it glowed a faint blue in the shadows.

The centaur stallion pawed the rock, shook his mane, and made a deep sound in his throat. In answer, the creature rippled around the pool, its luminous eyes fixed on Shaiala and Erihan. The stallion beckoned them closer and reached into the bag Shaiala carried. He extracted one of the herdstones and showed it to the creature. It stroked the stone reverently, then flicked its tail and disappeared into the depths.

Shaiala let out her breath. "Naga?" she asked.

The stallion nodded. "Her say Two Hoofs travel wet naga way, but must not breathe until reach other end. Else, Two Hoofs sleep with children under mountain forever."

When Shaiala translated, Erihan's eyes widened. "There must be an underwater tunnel that leads right through to the Sunless Valley!" His excitement faded and he gave her an uncertain look. "How long can you hold your breath?"

Shaiala turned to the stallion, uneasy. "How long is naga way?"

"Centaurs not know. Never travel this way."

She bit her lip as Erihan tied the bag of herdstones more securely to her shoulders. "I wish you'd let me carry some of these," he whispered.

"They not be so heavy underwater," she said, hoping it was true. For such small stones, the sack had given her a lot of trouble during the ride from the Canyons.

When they were ready, Erihan gave her a weak grin. "Don't worry, this should be easy after the barge. See you at the other end!" He pinched his nose, took a deep breath, and dived after the naga.

Wishing he hadn't chosen to remind her of the bungled escape, Shaiala followed.

Her greatest fear was that it would be dark. But Erihan's bare feet kicked like pale fish ahead of her, illuminated by thousands of little glowing blue pebbles that littered the bottom. The pebbles gave off enough light to show the twists and turns of the flooded passage quite clearly. Shaiala reached down and scooped a few into her hand. She brought them close to her eyes and stared in surprise. They were not stone, after all, but transparent shells. The light came from the tiny, perfect nagas curled inside sucking their miniature thumbs.

"Ohhh!" The exclamation escaped in a stream of bubbles. Only then did she see that many of the eggs were dark and dull, the tiny nagas inside already dead. At first she didn't understand. Then she realized. Scattered all over the breeding ground were Two Hoof jewels and, mixed in with this treasure, the sinister glitter of black demon crystal.

She pressed herself to the rock, felt the herdstones dig into her back, was blinded by bubbles . . .

Erihan's hand knocked the naga eggs out of Shaiala's hand and grasped her wrist. Sharet swirling around him, his feet stirring a cloud of mud, jewels, and eggs from the bottom, he pointed urgently along the tunnel. Shaiala shook her head in terror. Something huge and dark blocked the light ahead. *Demon. Come to steal our memories.*

A cold, scaled hand grasped her other arm and the next thing she knew she was being dragged through the tunnel, bumping against the rocky ceiling. She fought a fatal urge to scream. The speed blinded her. She had a vague impression of Erihan being dragged along too. Then the tunnel twisted and they were rising toward a circle of red light. Her ears popped, her lungs burned. They exploded into chill night air and suddenly she could breathe again.

She sputtered and coughed up water. Nearby, she heard Erihan coughing too. Satisfied they were still alive, the naga vanished into her underwater domain. Shaiala became aware of clouds boiling across a crimson moon, of cliffs so high and sheer that birds could not nest in them, of a vast expanse of water as black as the rocks it reflected — and, glittering in the shadows at its shore, a beach of the demon crystal.

She trod water and stared in dismay. Above the beach, four-legged silhouettes moved slowly and painfully across the dark landscape with oversized baskets strapped to their backs. From time to time, one of these weary silhouettes would lift a hoof to break off a piece of crystal and reach down with its hands to add the shard to its own load. The distant sound of shattering crystal was echoed by the faint cracks of Two Hoof whips. Fortunately, they were too far away to see details, but Shaiala glimpsed a pale shape working among the darker ones. "Kamara Silvermane," she whispered, and something pierced her heart.

Erihan splashed across to help her with the waterlogged sack. "Come on," he said in a tight voice. "Let's get these herdstones up there before the moon sets."

*

The mine was a huge open wound in the side of the valley. Where the crystal had been exposed to the air, jagged ridges pierced the sky like sheets of black glass. Navigating by sound alone, Shaiala and Erihan crept through the maze, their clothes and hair dripping. They kept out of the crimson moonlight and flattened themselves to the rock whenever they heard feet approaching.

The Two Hoofs weren't the only danger. As they worked their way agonizingly slowly past the guards toward the centaurs, a dark crystal song whispered from all sides, making them both jittery. Shaiala wanted to leap up and shout to her friends to come and collect their herdstones. But Erihan said that would only alert the guards to their presence, and the more herdstones they could get in centaur hands before then, the better.

At last, they heard the labored breathing of a foal approaching. "Try it," Erihan whispered. Carefully, Shaiala reached into the sack and extracted a herdstone. She left it glowing like a green star at the bottom of the crevasse, and she and Erihan crept behind a boulder to see what would happen.

A centaur colt scrambled up the ridge and skidded down the other side, hooves sliding on the sheer crystal. He lifted a foreleg and gave the mountainside an unenthusiastic but efficient *Snake*. A small shard of crystal broke loose and skittered across the rock. Listlessly, the colt fumbled with bleeding fingers and added the shard to the load in his baskets. Then he saw the herdstone.

He froze, one forehoof raised. His blue ears flickered back and forth as he peered over his shoulder. Hesitantly, as if he thought it were a cruel illusion, his crystal-scarred fingers reached for the stone. As his hand closed around the green light, he gave a huge shudder. Then he twisted his torso and frowned at the baskets. An angry spark lit his eye and he bucked, sending a shower of crystal over his head. He trotted off along the crevasse, shaking his head and swishing his tail.

Shaiala's heart lifted.

"It works!" Erihan hissed. "Quick, let's find another one."

It took them the rest of the night to empty the sack in this manner, leaving herdstones where the centaurs would come across them as they worked. When they found Rafiz Longshadow, Shaiala nearly leaped out of hiding, desperate to throw her arms around her friend. But again, Erihan held her back. "No," he whispered. "Not yet." And since they hadn't found Kamara Silvermane yet, she let him pull her on through the dark maze.

The sack became lighter as the night wore on, though by dawn Shaiala was so weary it might as well have been full again. The dark song wouldn't leave her alone. She stumbled often, bruising her shackled ankle, unable to think straight. Erihan couldn't have been in a much better state. When the first shouts and whip cracks echoed in the cliffs, fatal moments passed before either of them realized what was happening.

They broke into a stumbling run. The guards had rounded up most of the centaurs and penned them into a natural corral above the lake. It seemed this was a daily ritual so they could collect the crystal mined during the night and feed and water the foals before sending them out with empty baskets for a fresh load. The guards obviously weren't expecting trouble. But this morning some of the centaurs had herdstones. A filly laid back her ears and reared as the Two Hoofs tried to unload her. Other guards hurried across to help, whips cracking. The filly swung her hindquarters on them and kicked. *Double Hare.* Crystal showered from her baskets and shattered all around. The other foals with herdstones joined in, kicking the guards until they retreated from the corral and slammed stout poles into place across the narrow entrance.

"All right, that's it!" one of them yelled, rubbing his knee. "No food or water for any of you until you calm down."

The filly led a charge on the poles, but the guards whipped her back. Some of the foals without herdstones lay down and stared longingly at the lake, too listless even to unload their own baskets. Meanwhile, more centaurs were being driven down from the mine and pushed into the corral one by one with much whip cracking. No one got out.

Shaiala shook off her exhaustion and scrambled onto a ledge above the corral. "Fight!" she shouted. "You not Two Hoof slaves! Fight they!"

Centaurs and guards alike looked up in alarm as she emptied out the remaining herdstones and started to throw them down to the foals. She'd spoken in Herd, but Erihan realized what she was trying to do and joined her, throwing the stones as rapidly as he could into the corral. Some of the foals caught them in midair. Others let them fall, stared at them stupidly for a moment, then scrambled for the precious stones among the spilled crystal. Each herdstone worked the same miracle Shaiala and Erihan had witnessed on the first colt. Soon the corral was a blur of blue tails and flying crystal as the centaurs unloaded their baskets the quickest way they knew. The guards retreated to a safer distance. A few dropped their whips and fled.

As Erihan threw the last of his stones, Shaiala kept one clutched to her heart and searched the skyline. If they were too late, if her friend had already succumbed to the demon song — Then she glimpsed a pale shape trotting down from the mine and her heart leaped.

"Kamara Silvermane!" she called. "Catch!"

The lilac filly snatched the stone out of the air. Her hands and elbows were bleeding and fresh stripes on her haunches showed where she'd borne more than her fair share of the whip. But as soon as the herdstone touched her fingers, fire blazed in her eyes. "Bend light!" she shouted. "Quick, everyone! Bend light like mares do!"

Close behind Kamara Silvermane, Rafiz Longshadow swished his dark tail and gave the first guard to try whipping Kamara Silvermane into submission a swift *Hare* in the gut. Now that most of the trapped foals had herdstones, they rallied to his cry and renewed their attack on the poles. Wood splintered under their hooves. In a wild fury, they kicked the whips out of their captors' hands. Soon the last of the guards were fleeing for the lake, some clutching broken arms.

Shaiala wished she had the energy to give chase. Green glimmers below showed where Kamara Silvermane had organized some of the fillies to practice bending the light. Erihan had slithered into the corral and was in the thick of the herd, thrusting the final few herdstones into eager centaur hands. He flashed Shaiala a grin. The foals helped one another unstrap the hated baskets, then they threw them down and stamped on them. A few hotheaded colts started after the guards but returned when Rafiz Longshadow called them back. Shaiala scanned the valley, wondering where the Pass of Silence might be.

Even as she was worrying how they would get fifty excited centaur foals out through it alive, a voice she remembered all too well jolted her back.

"Two Hoof traitor!"

She looked down. Marell Storm Temper, his herdstone clutched in one stocky fist, was glaring up at her with hostile eyes. The other foals gathered around the colt, muttering uneasily.

Shaiala opened her mouth to give him a piece of her mind. But before she could speak, Rafiz Longshadow shouldered his way through the herd. "Not be stupid, Marell! Shaiala not traitor. Her bring herdstones!"

Marell Storm Temper snorted like a horse. "Then why her not work in mine under Two Hoof whips? It trick. Us give she good kicking, get truth out of she!"

A few of the foals stamped their hooves in agreement. Shaiala curled her toes in exasperation. If anyone needed a good kicking, it was Marell Storm Temper.

Kamara Silvermane trotted forward, a green halo glimmering around her pale coat. "Pick on someone with same number of hooves, Marell," she said.

There were a few snickers.

The colt's expression darkened. "Why her with Two Hoof same color as those who carry whips? Ask she that!"

"Prince Erihan horse friend!" Shaiala shouted, suddenly fearing for Erihan who was fighting his way through the press of now hostile centaur bodies. "Him Kalerei, not Harai!"

Marell Storm Temper scowled. "All Two Hoofs same. All lie, all cheat."

Uneasy whispers. Tails swished. More hooves stamped.

"Not be fool, Marell!" Rafiz Longshadow snapped. "Shaiala help we." He gave her a tight smile. "Which way out of Two Hoof valley?"

Shaiala licked her lips. "Us go through Pass of Silence," she said. "It dangerous —"

"See!" Marell interrupted. "She kill we!"

Erihan struggled through at last and scrambled up the cliff to join her. "Translate my words," he whispered. He gave her hand a squeeze and smiled down at the scowling colt.

Shaiala felt her strength returning. Her legs might even be good for exchanging a few kicks with Marell Storm Temper, if it came to that. But Erihan spoke in the same quiet tone he'd used on the street children in the barge. And it had the same effect. Though they couldn't have understood a word, the centaurs crowded closer to hear, shushing one another.

Haltingly, she translated as the prince told them the story of how they had been captured, kept in the dark with no food, chained in the barge, and taken to Yashra's camp. The centaurs listened in sympathetic silence. Even Marell Storm Temper didn't interrupt, though he glowered at Shaiala the entire time.

"Centaurs aren't the only slaves in the Sunless Valley," Erihan concluded. "I've worked it out. Yashra's built her Singing Palace out of the crystal you've been mining for her, and she's imprisoned the Two Hoof children there. We don't know what she's doing to them. But it's not Two Hoofs against centaurs. It's grown-ups against children."

Uneasy whispers greeted Shaiala's translation. The crystal hummed eerily in response to her voice. Green glimmers from the herdstones reflected in the lake as the fillies fidgeted.

Marell's jaw worked. "*Two Hoof* grown-ups," he insisted.

Erihan nodded sadly.

To Shaiala's surprise, Marell Storm Temper grinned. "Then us fight together! Give Two Hoofs good kicking, like I say!" He wheeled on his powerful haunches and punched the air with his fist. "Who help I?"

Several colts whooped and raised their herdstones. Marell Storm Temper started to push his way out of the corral, but Rafiz Longshadow caught his elbow and said in a low voice, "You forget something."

The purple colt scowled at him.

"You owe Shaiala Two Hoof big apology."

"It all right. . . ." Shaiala started to say, noting the way Marell swished his storm-colored tail. But Rafiz Longshadow and Kamara Silvermane closed on each side of the colt, and Erihan — obviously understanding a lot more centaur speech than he let on — folded his arms and nodded.

Marell Storm Temper gave in. "Sorry," he mumbled. "You not bad . . . for Two Hoof!"

Before anyone could make him apologize any better, he was out of the corral and galloping toward the lake, green light spilling from his fingers. Four hotheaded colts wheeled and followed. Kamara Silvermane rolled her eyes and led her fillies after them to bend the light before they ran into any Two Hoofs. Rafiz Longshadow gave Shaiala and Erihan a wry grin. "Marell Storm Temper never change," he said. "That best you get."

Shaiala grinned back. "I expect *Flying Snake*! But him go wrong way."

Rafiz Longshadow nodded. "Us go after he. This not good time to split herd." He caught the arm of a tall colt called Grall Thunderleg and had a quick word in his ear. The two sidled close to the cliff. "Jump on, Shaiala Two Hoof and Prince Erihan Horse Friend! Tuck up feet and hold tight. Us show you *real* ride!"

*

Shouts echoing in the cliffs woke Renn from a fitful doze. For a moment he couldn't remember where he was, nor why he was so damp and cold. Then the events of the previous day came back in a rush. He sat up and rubbed his eyes.

During the night the mist had lifted, and the Sunless Valley lay at his feet in all its dark glory. Directly below was the narrow entrance to the Pass of Silence with its twin gongs swinging in the wind. The guards were on their feet, pointing at the Pass. Their shouts carried faintly up the mountainside, but Renn had a feeling they weren't the same shouts that had woken him.

He looked in the other direction. Water blacker than the dark of the moon gleamed in the widest part of the valley. Around the lake, jagged blades of black crystal leaped from the rock in a futile attempt to reach the sun. Something was going on down there. Tiny glimmers of green light. Renn squinted but couldn't make it out. Then a footstep sounded behind him. He scrambled to his feet, fumbling for his dagger, the strange lights forgotten.

"Keep your head down," Lazim whispered, drawing him behind a rock. "Looks like someone's coming through the Pass. The guards aren't using their gongs, so whoever it is must be expected. They seem worked up about something, though."

Renn's heart thumped. He peered at the gongs. The guards had positioned themselves near the stones, clearly anxious. There was a pause. Then out of the narrow gap burst a monster with a face of black khiz-crystal trailing scarlet feathers that glowed like little fires in the Sunless Valley.

A scream escaped before Renn could stop it. Lazim clamped a hand over his mouth and hissed, "Shh, silly. It's only a mask."

Renn sat down again, feeling rather foolish. A group of dark-robed tribesmen followed the masked leader, dragging in their midst two ragged, barefoot girls. The girls had been gagged with crimson-and-black sharets, their left ankles were shackled, and their wrists were roped together. The leader puffed up to the guards and pointed urgently back at the Pass.

"What are they doing with those poor girls?" Renn whispered.

"Shh!" Lazim said. "Someone must be chasing them."

Even as he spoke, another robed man burst from the Pass and locked scimitars with one of the guards. The masked figure waved imperiously at the gongs and the other guards scurried to grasp stones. The Harai who'd come through the Pass with the masked leader were still pulling on their boots when the first clang echoed in the cliffs. Renn's stomach clenched in sympathy as he heard the answering rumble.

Lazim leaped to his feet. "Quick!" he hissed to Anyan and Verris. "We've got to disable those gongs!" He vaulted over a boulder and leaped down the mountainside, calling back almost as an afterthought, "Stay where you are, Renn! Keep out of sight. If anything happens to us, wait until the mist comes down again and creep back through the Pass. Find Lord Nahar's people. They'll know what to do."

Renn opened his mouth to say he could fight too, but the orderlies had already gone. He worked his way down the mountain after them until he found a hiding place with a good view of the path. He chewed his nails as he watched Lazim and the orderlies hurry toward the gongs. Surely the three of them weren't going to take on the masked leader and all those men?

But the orderlies worked their way around the cliff until they were above the rock arches that supported the gongs. They waited for Lazim's signal, then dropped silently on to the tops of the arches — Anyan on the left arch, Verris on the right. Swords in their teeth, they slithered on their bellies until they were close enough to saw through the thick ropes that secured the chains to the arches. The guards were so busy throwing stones, they didn't notice the danger until too late. At a chopping motion from Lazim, Anyan and Verris severed the final strands.

Despite his fear, Renn grinned. It was beautiful. In perfect synchronization, the two enormous metal disks dropped to the ground, bounced once with great booms that echoed in the Pass, then slowly toppled and settled across the path with a terrible clattering and clanging. The air filled with the thunder of a huge avalanche and a cloud of dust issued from the mouth of the Pass. The guards scattered, yelling in alarm. One slipped and screamed as a gong settled on his legs, another was struck on the head by a stray boulder, another ran the wrong way into the Pass and didn't reappear. The Harai who had been hiding farther up the trail leaped out with drawn scimitars and plunged into the dust cloud, from which came wild yells, the clash of metal, and men's dying screams. The orderlies took advantage of the confusion to retreat up the cliff. The noise of the fighting grew more furious, and as the dust began to settle, it revealed the path to be choked with struggling men in dark robes. Only when Renn saw the green sharets around the faces of the newcomers did he understand.

"Lord Nahar," he whispered. *"Yes!"*

Lazim and the other two had been forced to join the fight, their retreat cut off by Harai who'd scaled the cliff to get ahead of them. Renn bit his tongue, drew his dagger, and started to make his way closer to the battle. He had to detour around some debris that had escaped the Pass, so he was the only one who saw the masked leader and four of the Harai detach themselves from the fighting and hustle their two small captives farther into the Valley. He ducked as they drew level.

The girls' gags had been removed now that they were safely through the Pass, but they stumbled and sobbed with fear as they were dragged past Renn's hiding place. The older girl planted herself and they clung together while the men struggled to pull them apart.

"Oh, for the Khiz's sake!" The leader raised the mask and a dark fall of hair tumbled out.

Renn stared. The last face he'd expected to see behind the mask was that of a pretty young woman.

Her voice, however, was sharp with impatience. "First there was that trouble at the river. Then we get chased through the Pass by the Kalerei, only to learn that in my absence a Singer has been captured trying to reach the Khizalace. And now four grown men can't control two small girls! Pick them up and carry them! Need I remind you, enemies are in the Valley? If they harm Frazhin before I get there, I'll shackle you all to lumps of crystal and throw you into the Black Lake for the monsters to finish off."

Frazhin. The name tickled Renn's memory. Then he had it. *The man who hurt my mother.*

He crouched lower, heart pounding, as the Harai forced the girls apart, picked them up like sacks, and flung them over their shoulders. The smaller one screamed and kicked, but to no avail. Renn looked desperately for Lazim and the others. But all three orderlies were in the thick of the fighting, their Echorium swords dripping blood.

He hesitated only a moment. Remembering what the Harai had done to them in the Pass, a cold, hard determination lodged itself in his gut. Keeping to the darkest shadows, he followed the woman and her captives along the shore of the black lake.

There was plenty of cover and the Harai were in a hurry. By the time they reached the place where Renn had seen the green light, he was starting to think he made a good spy. But he'd forgotten to watch his back. With a sudden rattle of loose flints, a man stumbled down the mountainside, barged past Renn, and fell to his knees before the woman with the mask, jabbering incoherently and clutching his right arm. The woman snapped a question and the man pointed up the slope. Straight at the ridge where Renn crouched.

He ducked, cursing his stupidity. Then he realized the man hadn't been pointing at him, but *past* him. Under the woman's sharp questions, his words slowed and started to make sense. ". . . centaurs gone crazy . . . green stones . . . Half Creature magic . . . escaped children . . ."

"Children?" snapped the woman. "From the Khizalace?"

The man mumbled something else. The woman cursed. With an impatient gesture, she waved two of the Harai up the slope. Renn shut his eyes as their boots crunched closer. Quietly, with trembling hand, he drew his dagger. The boots stopped on the other side of the ridge. The Harai's low voices carried clearly on the still air.

"Told you there'd be trouble in that mine, didn't I?" said one. "Those centaurs were a mistake. Lady Yashra should've used human slaves and built her palace out of stone like normal people. Can't see why she has to use so much crystal, anyway. It might look pretty, but it gives me the creeps and I'm not the only one."

"Shh! She'll hear."

"I don't care. I'm not climbing all the way up there just to get kicked by some wild centaur. Come on, let's go back. If any of those poor things have escaped, the mine's the last place they'll be hiding."

Renn's heart slowed slightly as the boots crunched away. He wiped the back of his hand across his forehead. Then the worst happened. The dagger, its hilt slippery with sweat, slipped from his fingers and went clattering down the slope toward the lake. He stared after it in dismay.

The Harai looked around.

"It came from up there!" the woman shouted, picking up the dagger and frowning at it. "Behind that ridge!"

The boots started back up. Renn drew a desperate breath and did the only thing he could think of. He hummed *Aushan*.

Aushan makes you scream.

Both Harai froze. "It's a demon!" cried one.

"Don't be so stupid!" the woman called. "I know Kalerei craft when I see it. One of them must have followed us from the Pass. Kill him!"

The mention of their ancient enemy spurred the Harai on. Renn sprang from his hiding place and made a desperate dash up the slope.

He might have made it, too, if the crystal debris hadn't avalanched under his boots. He couldn't get a handhold because it was too sharp and slipped back in a cloud of glittering dust. A hand closed around his ankle. He kicked frantically, singing *Aushan* with what little breath he had left after the dust and fear between them had stolen his voice. A Harai bent over him, scimitar raised. Renn shut his eyes in terror.

"No!" called the woman. "It's only a boy. Bring him here."

The Harai glanced at each other, then shrugged and sheathed their weapons. They seized an arm each and carried Renn, limp with fear, down to the lake. The girls twisted their heads but the hope in their eyes died when it became obvious Renn was alone.

"So," said the woman, thoughtfully turning the dagger. "You've got a good voice, don't you, Kalerei boy? What were you doing up there all on your own? What was that song you were singing just now?"

Renn raised his chin. His feet were still off the ground and the Harai's fingers dug painfully into his armpits. But he looked the woman in the eye. "*Aushan!*" he said. "And I'm not Kalerei, I'm a Singer! If you don't let me go, I'll sing *Yehn* and kill you all!"

She stared at him. A slow smile spread across her face. "So you think you can kill Yashra of the Harai with a song, do you? The guards at the Pass said something about a boy with the Echorium party, but they told me you'd perished in the avalanche. I'm so glad you survived. Your sweet voice should please my Frazhin greatly." Her tone hardened. "Tie his hands and bring him."

Renn finally started to think. He couldn't hope to fight trained, armed men with his one little dagger, even if he somehow managed to get it back from Yashra. But he could use his voice. It had almost worked when he'd been scared and out of breath. All he had to do was wait for the right opportunity. The First Singer would surely understand this was an emergency.

As the Harai bound his wrists, he forced himself to take deep, calming breaths. He began with a gentle hum. Shh, *Challa*, calm . . .

But Yashra was too clever for that. Taking her sharet from around her neck, she twisted it into a knot and smiled coldly. "Open your mouth, young Singer," she said. "We don't want you wasting any of those pretty songs out here, do we?"

Renn let her have a burst of *Aushan*, but too late. While the Harai held him firmly, she moved behind him and stuffed the knotted cloth into his mouth, tying it tightly behind his head. She trapped a strand of his hair in the knot. Renn's eyes watered.

"Mmmm!" he protested as one of the Harai heaved him up onto his shoulder. "Mmmm mmm!"

Yashra patted his cheek. "A surprise gift for my Frazhin," she said.

Renn glared at her. Then he froze. Beyond Yashra's head, something green had glimmered high on the mountainside.

He stared in disbelief, and what remained of his world turned upside down.

Just for an instant, their manes and tails streaming against the sky, four blue centaurs led by a purple one galloped across his line of vision before vanishing into that green light.

*

Riding a centaur at full gallop down those treacherous crystal slopes was the craziest thing Shaiala had ever done. After she'd got over her initial terror of being thrown onto the sharp spikes and ridges, she relaxed her grip on Rafiz Longshadow's mane and laughed, trusting the colts to carry them both safely to the valley floor. The wind whipped her hair and brought stinging tears to her eyes. Her knees ached with keeping her feet off the ground. Grall Thunderleg matched Rafiz Longshadow stride for stride, carrying a rather flushed Kalerei prince with his fingers twisted in the tangled blue mane and his feet braced against the colt's withers. Behind them, in a great rattle of loose crystal, came the rest of the herd.

From Erihan's torn cry, it seemed the prince had never ridden quite like this, either. Belatedly, Shaiala remembered his obsession with bridles and twisted her head, worried. But Erihan had enough sense not to interfere with his mount. They plunged into cold shadow beside the lake and raced along the shore, following Marell Storm Temper's prints. The path curved around the end of the lake, climbed a steep ridge, and plunged steeply into shadow. In the sunken end of the valley something huge, black, and humanmade glittered ominously. A group of Two Hoofs wearing familiar crimson-striped sharets and carrying what looked like sacks over their shoulders had just been swallowed by those vast dark gates.

"Stop!" Shaiala screamed, jerking on Rafiz Longshadow's mane. "It trap! Stop!"

Erihan immediately dropped his feet, put his arms around his mount's neck, and leaned back, using his weight to slow the colt and his feet as brakes. Grall Thunderleg slapped at Erihan's hands. "Crazy Two Hoof!" he sputtered. "You try st-strangle me?" Then he saw the building too. His eyes widened. He slithered to a halt, forelegs splayed, leaving a trail of sparks across the rock.

Rafiz Longshadow reared to a halt and Shaiala slipped off over his tail. A short way ahead, green glimmers showed where the fillies had stopped as well. But Marell Storm Temper and his hotheaded friends were already hurtling down the final twists of shadowed path toward that monstrous palace, yelling threats at the tops of their voices and waving their fists. They didn't seem to realize they were visible.

"Wait!" Rafiz Longshadow bellowed, his deep voice echoing from the rocks.

It was no use. The colts' blood was up. They either didn't hear or didn't care.

Shaking green light off their tails, Kamara Silvermane led her fillies back to join the others. They were panting from the effort of using their herdstones and at the same time chasing Marell Storm Temper. Everyone looked at Rafiz Longshadow.

"Us follow," he decided. "But stay together, inside bent light. Tread quietly. No talk. If you see a Two Hoof, freeze. When us catch up with Marell, us decide what to do next."

"Like give Marell Storm Temper good kick where it hurts!" a filly who'd been in the chasing group called.

There were a couple of nervous giggles.

"This not game!" Rafiz Longshadow said sternly, sweeping the foals with his dark centaur gaze. "Us work together! Kicking matches must wait. I go first. Grall Thunderleg come next. Shaiala Two Hoof and Erihan Horse Friend keep in middle. Kamara Silvermane stay at back, check no one step outside herdstone light. Ready?"

The tense, determined centaur faces hardly seemed to belong to the same foals who had entered the Canyons on the night of the Dancing Moon. No longer teasing or play-kicking, colts and fillies clustered together, their coats brightened by green haloes, dwarfed by the black cliffs. Kamara Silvermane raised her herdstone and nodded. The Kalerei prince pulled out his knife.

Shaiala stared at Yashra's palace and shuddered, suddenly overcome by an overpowering fear that once they descended into that darkness, none of them would ever come out again.

14
KHIZALACE

Yashra's stronghold was a maze of black rock and darkly glittering crystal that seemed to have grown from the mountain itself. As the Harai carried their captives under the rock arches that linked the cliffs like a broken tunnel, Renn had an upside-down view of full-sized horses with stiff-backed riders standing sentinel in the shadows, watching the captives with their cold black eyes. He shuddered.

They passed through a gateway high and wide enough to take ten ships under full sail. Immediately, the air turned chill. No daylight reached through the thick purple clouds. Black khiz-crystal glittered on all sides, pressing at Renn's thoughts and confusing his senses. As if from a great distance, he heard someone mention the centaurs they'd seen on the mountain. Yashra laughed and told the men to leave the gates open. Then the Harai party split up.

The two girls were carried off toward a tall windowless tower, while Yashra led the man carrying Renn to a trapdoor in the darkest corner of the yard. She opened it, causing a shower of rust. Steps led down into darkness. Faint moans like those of a wounded animal escaped into the air.

Renn closed his eyes in terror as they descended. They seemed to go down forever, his captor's shoulder lurching into his stomach. There was a grinding noise followed by the sharp stench of urine and sweat. Then the Harai dropped him on cold, damp stone.

Renn instinctively curled into a ball. Now they would lock the door and leave him here in the dark. Unable to sing, unable even to breathe properly through his gag. But maybe, once they'd gone, he could work his hands free.

Yashra's boots came into view. "Get up," she said, hauling him to his feet and turning him around. "Stop whimpering. That's no way to greet an old friend, is it?"

A terrible coldness stole over Renn. A single flickering torch revealed black walls that glistened with running water. The sparse straw on the floor was saturated with mold. And in the center of the cell, chained by ankle and wrist to a huge slab of black crystal, lay the Second Singer of the Echorium.

Renn stared in horror. Kherron's once-blue curls were stuck to his cheeks with blood and dried sweat. His Singer robe had been torn in several places, revealing a mass of bruises beneath. He was still gagged with the same piece of silk Renn had seen the Harai apply in the Pass and the crystal must still have been in his throat, for fresh blood trickled from the corners of his mouth. Yet despite the lines of pain on his face, the green eyes glittered with all the force of the Second Singer's legendary temper.

"See?" Yashra said softly. "He recognizes you."

Then she raised her voice. "Frazhin, my love, I think your gift might prove even more useful than we thought."

Renn's heart missed a beat. Yashra's fingers tightened on his arms, and the man who'd carried him into the dungeon took a step backward.

The shadows in the far corner of the cell had moved.

As Renn stared, unable to look away, the shadows formed themselves into a twisted shape that scraped its way slowly around the slab, swathed in darkness. Frazhin wore a crystal mask that was an exact replica of Yashra's but without the feathers. His robe writhed with strange spirals and symbols worked in crimson thread. Although it had voluminous sleeves and reached the floor, it couldn't hide the fact that Frazhin's legs were crooked and his left arm was missing below the elbow. He leaned heavily on a pair of crystal crutches.

For what seemed like an eternity, eyes blacker than the dark side of the moon studied Renn through the mask. Then Frazhin turned to his prisoner and said in a voice that sounded like fingernails scraping across dry rock, "Is she right, Singer? Is it possible you care for the boy?"

The Second Singer's eyes flashed furiously. Yashra pushed Renn forward and thrust him to his knees beside the slab. Though he hadn't the strength to get up, let alone run, she kept one hand on his shoulder.

Frazhin scraped closer, still watching his prisoner with the same intense interest shown by an eagle tracking its prey.

"I've heard these Singers don't care all that much for their children," he rasped. "I've heard they give them into the care of wet nurses until they're old enough to start school and the poor things are brought up never knowing who their parents are. A few weeks in the Tower with the Khiz, and he'll forget the Echorium and be as biddable as the rest. It'd be a waste to carve him up. After all, our guest has proved remarkably stubborn so far. Why should the suffering of an insignificant novice persuade him when even the crippling of his Songs has failed?"

The Second Singer rattled his chains and made a furious sound through his gag. Almost, but not quite, *Aushan*.

Frazhin laughed coldly. "On the other hand, Singers are flesh and blood like the rest of us. They make mistakes, otherwise we wouldn't have the pleasure of our guest down here at all. Maybe this particular Singer made an even bigger mistake than underestimating our men in the Pass of Silence? I understand his capture was rather easy. I have to say I expected more of a fight from the Second Singer of the Echorium."

He leaned over the slab until the horn of his mask was touching Kherron's forehead and stared into his prisoner's eyes. "The first Harai in the Pass were quite prepared to die. They had strict instructions to shield you with their bodies if the Pass avalanched. There were others standing by to dig you out and bring you here. But you didn't sing, did you? Not a note. That's been puzzling me. All right, so you had others with you. But surely a handful of Echorium orderlies are replaceable enough? So who were you protecting back there in the Pass? It wasn't until my faithful Yashra contacted me at the lake and showed me her gift that I began to understand. At first, I couldn't think why you'd bring a half-trained novice into such danger. Then I started to suspect that perhaps even a Singer could be illogical where his own son is concerned."

The Second Singer went very still. He refused to look at Renn.

Behind the mask, Frazhin's eyes glittered. He reached down and gently eased the gag out of Renn's mouth. "Let's test our theory, shall we?"

At first, Renn didn't understand. He was too busy staring at the Second Singer, Frazhin's words crashing around his head. He barely registered the fact that his voice was free again. Then it was too late. In a single swift motion, Yashra slipped her mask from the top of her head and slammed it over his face.

Black lightning flashed, driving from his head every Song he'd ever learned. For a terrible instant, he had a glimpse of Frazhin's thoughts. A bottomless pit of wild, thundering darkness that threatened to suck him in and tear him apart. Then —

Pain!

His scream echoed around the cell and escaped through the tunnels. On his slab, the Second Singer made a small strangled sound.

The mask lifted, letting light and air rush back. As suddenly as it had come, the pain died. Renn slid to the floor in a little heap, shivering and whimpering. He could hardly remember who or where he was, let alone what he'd been planning to do when they removed his gag.

"So, Singer," rasped Frazhin. "In return for the boy's well-being, will you agree to teach your Songs of Power to our children?"

There was a scrape. It must have been Kherron nodding, for Yashra clapped her hands in delight.

Frazhin, however, laid one of his crutches on Renn's shoulder. Renn shrank from the touch. If the pain came again, he knew he'd die.

"Don't think you can trick us, Singer," rasped that nightmarish voice. "When you're not giving lessons, the khiz fragment will be replaced in your throat to ensure your cooperation. And if you even think about trying to use your voice on any of our people when you're supposed to be teaching, I'll cut a small piece off the boy and put that down your throat, too. Of course, the longer the khiz remains in your mouth, the less use your voice will be. But by the time it has destroyed your Songs completely, your pupils will be grown and the Khizalace will rival the Echorium. We'll no longer need Singers, here or anywhere else in the world. The power of the Khiz will rule supreme and our child will wield it!"

He rested his good hand on the curve of Yashra's belly. The Harai woman's lips curved into a strangely vulnerable smile.

Still reeling with the echoes of that terrible pain, Renn could only blink at this new revelation. He found it difficult to imagine Frazhin as a father, yet Yashra's smile confirmed it. But they were both Crazies if they thought the Second Singer would ever betray the Echorium.

The crutch lifted from his shoulder. Frazhin scraped out of the cell and away down the tunnel. As the Harai who'd brought him down here dragged him away from the slab, Renn finally found his voice. He braced his feet against the door frame. "Singer Kherron!" he choked out. "Don't do it! I won't let them use me. I'll . . . I'll escape!"

He willed the Second Singer to look at him. He needed to know if that other thing Frazhin had said, the impossible thing, was true. But the Second Singer lay unmoving on his slab of crystal, eyes closed.

Yashra chuckled and slapped Renn's ankles until he lost his grip. "Escape, huh? And how are you going to do that, Singer boy? Your voice doesn't work so well in my palace, does it?" She patted his cheek and addressed the Harai. "Take him up to the Tower and secure him on a pallet. We'll see how defiant he is in the morning after a night with the Khiz. Meanwhile, Frazhin and I have some centaurs to deal with."

*

The centaurs' steps grew slower and slower as they neared the walls of Yashra's palace. They stopped outside the vast gateway. Everyone stared in silence at the windowless black tower that rose from the center of the courtyard and disappeared into drifting purple clouds. The massive gates stood open, unguarded. Strange echoes moaned around the walls. There was no sign of the Two Hoofs they'd seen, nor of Marell Storm Temper and his friends.

Rafiz Longshadow peered into the shadows, ears pricked, every muscle tense. "You think it Two Hoof trap?" he whispered.

Shaiala shivered in new fear. Every instinct screamed at her not to step through that gate. Erihan fingered his knife and frowned up at the walls.

"Listen," Kamara Silvermane whispered. "What that noise?"

They all held their breath as a dark song crept out of the Khizalace. It sang of shadows, of night, and of death. Shaiala edged a little closer to Erihan. But apparently that wasn't the noise Kamara had heard. Ears swiveling nervously, she ventured alone through the gate and raised a delicate hand. Now Shaiala heard it too. The faint sound of splintering crystal, muffled shouts, and screams.

Rafiz Longshadow made the decision for them. "Us go in."

The foals picked their way carefully across a courtyard inlaid with fragments of polished crystal. The mosaic was sharp and cold under Shaiala's bare feet. Although Kamara Silvermane directed the fillies to keep everyone invisible, the centaurs' hooves echoed alarmingly. Still, nobody challenged them.

A strong smell of manure came from a stable block near the gate. As the centaurs trotted across the courtyard, the horses caught their scent and whinnied nervously. Rafiz Longshadow pointed to a doorway and led them into a polished black corridor wide enough for five centaurs to walk abreast. There was less crystal here and the noise of the battle was louder. "This way!" Rafiz Longshadow said, and the foals broke into an excited trot. Shaiala and Erihan had to run to avoid being trampled by those behind.

Shaiala hoped they'd find Marell Storm Temper quickly and get out again before anyone noticed them. But sounds were confusing inside the Khizalace, and its corridors were a maze of unexpected reflections and turns. One moment the battle seemed to be just around the next corner. Then it was behind them. Then on all sides at once. Also, it was difficult for the fillies to hide everyone in the narrower places. All too often, they had to break cover while they squeezed through doorways or scrambled up flights of stairs designed for Two Hoofs. The centaurs slipped on the polished surfaces and their ears flattened in growing agitation.

They were negotiating one of the upper corridors when a group of Harai in flapping black robes rushed around the corner, struggling to fasten scabbards to their hips. Quickly, Rafiz Longshadow herded the foals into an empty room. Shaiala stayed outside to shut the door but there was no time. The prince dragged her behind a statue. Her heart thudded wildly lest a filly should flick her tail at the wrong time. But the Harai clattered past without noticing anything amiss.

Erihan cautiously peered out. "It's clear," he whispered. "Only —"

"What?" Shaiala leaped to the door with visions of her friends sliced to ribbons by Harai scimitars. But the room was quiet. She frowned at the prince. Then she realized.

Too quiet.

She ran into the middle of the space, hands outstretched, feeling for warm centaur bodies that were not there. A second door stood open at the far side of the room. "Kamara Silvermane!" she cried, rushing toward it. "Rafiz Longshadow! No, not leave me again!"

For a horrible moment, her head went completely dark. Then Erihan's arms were around her. "Shh," he said. "Shh, Shaiala, someone'll hear you. We'll find them again, don't worry. You don't lose a herd of centaurs that easily! Look, scratches — they must have gone this way."

As they followed the scratches deeper into the palace, the noise of the fighting ceased, replaced by the dark crystal song they'd heard before. It stopped all conversation. Shaiala stared at the floor until her eyes hurt, not sure anymore that the marks they were following had been made by centaur hooves. They were too even, too deep. But she wanted to believe Erihan, so she said nothing.

They went up again. Wide, curving steps lit by torches with shadowy landings between, winding endlessly skyward. With a shiver, she realized they must be climbing the tower they'd seen from the gates.

Finally, even Erihan stopped pretending. "I think we've gone the wrong way," he whispered, kneeling to examine the marks in the edges of the steps. He scraped his knife in one of the grooves and frowned. "Would centaurs be able to climb so many stairs?"

Shaiala glanced over her shoulder, searching for the human words to say that they should try to find their way back down to the courtyard. Then she froze, her skin prickling all over. *Something* was shuffling up the tower behind them. It sounded like a naga out of water.

"Quick! Hide!" Erihan pushed her behind another statue.

Shaiala's stomach clenched as the noise approached the landing. It was going to be something bad, she knew. The dark song that throbbed and moaned all around said so. But even though they'd known a terrible fate awaited the children Yashra captured, and it was obvious their barge hadn't been the first to make that journey upriver, they were unprepared for what came around the bend in the stair.

A double line of children, barefoot, their heads shaved, shuffled past their hiding place and continued up the next set of steps. Boys and girls were dressed exactly alike in crimson tunics and black leggings. They walked in perfect step, their blank eyes staring straight ahead, their pale hands clasping small black crystals that hung from their necks on black chains. Before she could stop him, Erihan had followed them.

The children halted at the top of the tower before a pair of solid crystal doors carved with strange symbols that made Shaiala's skin crawl. The leading pair — a boy and a girl, though without their hair it was difficult to tell them apart — pressed their crystals against two of the symbols. There was a soft tone and the doors swung open. Crimson light spilled like blood down the stairwell. The dark song, which had been growing louder as they climbed, rose to a crescendo.

Shaiala covered her ears. *No!* she wanted to shout. *Don't go in there!* But the children entered silently, dwarfed by the doorway. Inside, the boys shuffled to the left and the girls to the right. When the final pair had been swallowed by that crimson light, the doors swung shut again, cutting off the song.

Her ears rang with the sudden quiet. Erihan pulled her to the top of the final staircase and pushed at the doors. They didn't move. He slid the blade of his knife into the crack between them and wriggled it up and down. He frowned. "They're locked," he whispered. "The crystals must work like keys. I don't suppose you can repeat that trick you did with the barge?"

We should run, Shaiala thought. *As far from this place as possible.* But the prince was watching her expectantly. She clenched her fists and forced the dark song out of her head. Trying not to think what dreadful things they might find beyond, she pushed Erihan out of the way, flexed her leg muscles, and took a run at the door.

Double Hare.

The resulting crack echoed alarmingly down the stairwell. She landed, twisted on the ball of her foot, and struck again.

Snake. Flying Snake.

The doors shattered. Shaiala and Erihan burst through, the prince brandishing his knife, Shaiala balanced on the balls of her feet, both of them tense enough to attack the first thing that moved.

Gleaming crimson floor . . . torches on the walls . . . strange sweet smell . . . deep grooves leading to a black wall . . . more doors to the left and the right . . . a pair of life-size Two Hoof statues, heads turning to look at them —

"Look out!" Erihan shouted. "Harai!"

Fortunately, the guards seemed as surprised as they were. For a heartbeat, they stared at the two children as if trying to work out how they could be on the wrong side of the doors. Then their scimitars left their scabbards in a hiss of bright sparks.

Shaiala was already in the air. A *Flying Snake* took care of one guard, snapping his right arm and knocking him backward. His head cracked against the wall, and he slipped to the floor, unconscious. His scimitar skidded across the landing and rattled down the stair. The other guard made a wild slash at her, but she leaped over the blade and slammed the side of her foot into his ankle. *Dragonfly.* He screamed as the bone shattered and crumpled in a heap of pain. Shaiala stamped on his wrist and sent his scimitar sliding after the other with a flick of her toe. Erihan leaped on top of the captive and pressed the point of his knife to the man's throat.

"What have you done to the children who came in here?" he demanded.

The Harai's eyes clouded. "Nothing."

"What's behind that wall?"

"The power to make the Harai the greatest tribe of the Purple Plains. The Khiz."

"You're lying," Erihan said, pressing harder. "It's a demon crystal, isn't it? You dragged it up here so it could swallow their souls! How does it work?"

The Harai let out a choked laugh. "Think *she* trusts us with her secrets? Why don't you put that knife down and let me take you to the others? The Khiz will help you relax. After a while, you'll feel much better."

"No!" Erihan's jaw clenched. "You're going to tell us how to free the children, or I'll . . . I'll carve your eyes out one by one."

Shaiala saw blood well under the knife. "Careful!" she said. "He —"

Too late. The Harai heaved upward and pierced his own throat on Erihan's blade. The young prince staggered back, a look of horror on his face.

Shaiala stepped off the Harai's limp wrist. Erihan was still staring at his bloody blade, shaking his head. "I just wanted to scare him," he whispered.

"Maybe you scare he too much."

Erihan's lips tightened. "Maybe. But the way they treated us on that barge . . . worse than the Kalerei treat their enemies." The color returned to his cheeks. He pushed back his shoulders, wiped the knife on his tunic, and glanced at the unconscious guard. "Come on. Let's get everyone out before he wakes up."

He put his eye to the crack between the set of doors on the right and frowned. "The girls are all asleep. There's a lot of smoke, but I can't see any more guards. There's something glittering . . . I can't quite see . . ." He shifted position and went very still.

"What?" Shaiala demanded, though she knew. That dark song, the scratches on the stairs, the grooves in the floor, her own unreasoning terror.

"It's demon crystal," Erihan whispered, confirming her fears. "Absolutely huge! It must fill the whole upper level! I bet the boys' room is the same. Can't see anyone too close to the doors. Do you think you can kick them open?"

Shaiala's feet were sore and her head throbbed. But she bit her lip and took care of both sets of doors with well-aimed *Hares*. The children whimpered in their sleep.

The dormitories curved like crescent moons around the huge crystal. Torches set in their outer walls gave off a sickly scent that made Shaiala's eyes water. At the far end of the girls' dormitory, in the thickest smoke, two small figures with freshly shaven scalps had been tied to their pallets. They were writhing in their bonds and moaning as if trapped in a nightmare. "There's Laphie and Imara!" Erihan said, his tone cold. "Maybe I should have gouged that Harai's eyes out, after all."

"I help they." Shaiala worked her way through the pallets, coughing as the smoke got into her throat.

"Don't breathe it in!" Erihan warned, drawing his sharet over his nose and wafting smoke through the broken door. "I'm going to see if I can wake the boys. Here — use this!" He tossed her his knife.

As the air cleared, some of the girls sat up and blinked blearily at Shaiala. In the boys' dormitory, Erihan was snatching off crystal pendants, pulling the boys from their pallets, and shoving them toward the door, shaking and slapping them when they refused to get up. "Wake up!" he shouted. "Run down to the courtyard! Go on! Take your crystals off — they're making you ill, can't you see?"

Shaiala sank to her knees beside Laphie's pallet. Her face was a funny color. When Shaiala cut her bonds and shook her, the girl's eyes rolled up frighteningly in her head. She tugged off Laphie's crystal and flung the thing as far as she could, then did the same for Imara. The smaller girl clung to her, sobbing about dungeons.

"This is no good!" Erihan shouted from the door. "They keep going back to sleep! This smoke's not helping anyone. We've got to get rid of the torches."

He seized one and smashed the burning end against the wall. Sparks flew across the pallets. The children they landed on whimpered in their sleep, but still didn't wake. The tower darkened. Shaiala's eyelids began to droop.

The Khizalace is a good place, breathed the demon crystal. *Aunt Yashra is your friend. This is your home. Relax, dream, forget.*

She sighed. The knife slipped from her fingers and clattered to the floor.

"*Shai!*" Erihan yelled, appearing back in the doorway with one of the boys slumped on his shoulder. "Fight it! You've got to fight!" He shook the boy in frustration. "Oh, this is hopeless! I can't carry everyone! Shai, *please* wake up. We have to break the demon crystal. It's the only way."

With an effort, Shaiala pulled herself together. Imara was still clinging to her neck. She prized the girl off and climbed wearily to her feet.

She eyed the huge crystal that formed the entire inner wall of the girls' dormitory. The room was too narrow for much of a run, but she dragged two pallets out of the way and sprang off the far wall.

She tried every kick she knew. But the crystal was just too big and too solid, her stupid Two Hoof kicks not powerful enough. It was as hopeless as when she'd tried to break out of the ship on her way to the Singer island.

Give up, lie down, sang the crystal, mocking her efforts.

Erihan tried to help, jamming his knife into a tiny crack between crystal and floor. He only succeeded in snapping the blade. Imara cowered against the wall with her hands over her ears. "Don't," she sobbed. "Don't, or Aunt Yashra will put you in the dungeon."

Frustrated tears pricked Shaiala's eyes. She turned and gave the crystal a vicious *Snake* that hurt her foot. "Shut up!" she screamed. "Shut *up!*"

With all the noise and confusion, no one noticed the unconscious guard come to. He staggered to his feet, took one look at the wild girl kicking the Khiz, and hurried down the Tower to raise the alarm.

*

When Yashra had gone, the Harai set Renn on his feet and gave him a shove toward a shadowy stair. "You can walk. I'm not carrying you all the way up there." He seized a torch and gave Renn a blow across the shoulders. "Get climbing! I'm right behind you."

Renn started up the stair, plans forming sluggishly in his head where Frazhin's black lightning had struck. But it wasn't easy to climb with his hands tied, and he kept stumbling on the dark steps. Even when they left the dungeon level and the steps opened out into a well-lit spiral staircase with landings between flights, he couldn't motivate himself to escape. That same dark song he'd heard when he'd tried to contact the Echorium trickled down the stairwell and wound itself like invisible threads around his thoughts. Soon his legs were trembling, and he was gasping for breath as if . . . as if . . . as if he'd tried to run all the way up the Five Thousand Steps back on the Isle!

His head cleared and all of a sudden he knew what the Harai was up to. Just like Geran and Alaira. Drive him to the limit of his strength until he was too weak even to think of escape. He'd played that game before.

He allowed his knees to give way and collapsed on the next landing. "I c-can't," he gasped. "Too steep. My hands —"

The Harai swiped at his head with the torch, showering sparks. "Get up, you little imp! I'm not untying you, if that's what you think. If it weren't for you, I'd be bathed and changed and have a full belly by now."

"Please," Renn whispered, hardly having to force the tears. The *Shi* was difficult. But if he listened carefully, he found he could squeeze his hum between the dark whispers. "My wrists hurt."

The Harai frowned at him.

"I won't run away," Renn sniffed, squeezing out another tear. *Shi, Shi makes you cry*. "Please sir, Yashra will never know. She —"

"Oh, stop your sniveling! You're not a baby." But the Harai leaned his torch against a statue and bent to untie the rope binding Renn's wrists.

Renn tensed. But as he felt the knots begin to loosen and was about to duck under his captor's arm and flee back down the stairs, a great clattering came from below. A company of Harai came running around the spiral, scimitars flashing in the torchlight. The leader tripped over Renn's captor and almost fell. The others piled up behind.

"What the Khiz are you doing, blocking the stairs?" the leader yelled. "Haven't you heard? There's trouble in the Tower! Some nonsense about a girl who kicks like a centaur and smashes doors. It's probably as tall as that story about invisible warriors who throw bolts of green lightning — but you know Frazhin! He'll have the lot of us thrown in the lake if the children escape. If we're lucky, we'll catch 'em before they get too far from the Khiz." His eye fell on Renn, crouched in the shadows behind the statue. "Hey, is that one of 'em? Look out! Get a hold of him!"

Renn dragged off the rope and threw it at the leader. There was only an instant to think. At least twenty armed Harai were on the flight below. He sprang past his captor and raced on up the tower, heart pounding, legs wobbly, humming desperately under his breath to stop the dark song from getting into his head.

A girl who "kicks like a centaur"?

His spirits lifted. He scrambled up the final stairs on all fours, the Harai clattering at his heels.

15
BATTLE

When the first crack appeared in the Khiz, no one realized what had happened. Shaiala's foot vibrated strangely, Erihan's broken blade went in a little deeper, and the noise in the Tower changed somehow. They glanced at each other in confusion. Then a slender, gray-eyed boy came staggering out of the smoke, coughing and sputtering, and . . . *singing*.

Shaiala stared in disbelief.

"Look out!" the boy gasped. "The Harai are right behind me! Run!"

"We've got to smash the demon crystal first to wake everyone up," Erihan said, obviously mistaking Renn for one of the captives in spite of the fact that he had hair. "Quick, find something sharp and see if you can jam it into this crack —"

Renn took one look at the crystal, then pressed both hands against the glittering wall and closed his eyes. Ignoring Erihan's advice, he carried on singing.

"Out of way!" Shaiala gave the Singer boy a shove that sent him staggering over a pallet. "Or you get kicked!" She couldn't think how Renn came to be in Yashra's tower, but she wasn't going to let him ruin things this time.

To her surprise Renn picked himself up and planted himself between her and the crystal, a determined look in his eye. "You can't break it that way! It's not just crystal anymore. It's been enchanted like Frazhin's old spear and Yashra's mask. Only Echorium Songs have the power to smash it now."

"Not true! *I* crack it!"

"You couldn't have!"

"Look! What that, then?"

They were still yelling at each other when the first Harai reached the top of the stairs. Imara cowered in her corner. Erihan clutched his broken knife and dropped into a defensive crouch.

But the men didn't attack. An awed hush fell as they gathered in the doorway and pointed at the crack in the Khiz. They muttered uneasily. Shaiala was suddenly aware of her breathing, rapid and harsh. Renn's wrists were bleeding, she noticed, and there were strange burn marks on his face.

"If you'd just stop kicking things for once, I might be able to hear what note it's making and sing something to help us," he said.

She shook herself. "Not be silly! You only novice."

They glared at each other again. The Harai took advantage of this to venture into the dormitory. Stepping over the sleeping girls, they warily worked their way toward the Khiz.

It was Erihan who figured it out. He'd been frowning at the crack. His face suddenly lit up. "It was *both of you*!" he said excitedly. "You kick, Shai, while your friend sings. Both at once! Go on, try it!"

The Harai leaped forward to stop them, but Renn took a deep breath and let out a hum that made the entire Tower vibrate. The Harai stopped in their tracks. Not really believing it would work, Shaiala gave the Khiz another *Snake*.

A huge black crack zigzagged up the inner wall. The Khiz screamed. Black rain tinkled from the roof. It was better than any of them could have imagined. The sleepers sat up, clutched their heads, and stared about them in terror.

"Yes!" Erihan said, shaking glittering shards from his hair. "Do it again! I'll get everyone out."

Shaiala's heart leaped with the fierce joy of success. This time, she put all her strength into a two-legged kick. *Flying Snake.* A sheet of crystal the size of a small barge slid down the wall and shattered across five abandoned pallets. The Harai staggered backward, their arms over their heads. Imara ducked through their legs and ran to Laphie, who hugged her tightly. The other girls, urged on by Erihan, charged the door yelling and screaming at the tops of their voices.

"Get Lady Yashra!" called the Harai leader, marshaling his men at the top of the stairs. "We'll hold them in here as long as we can. But if the Khiz shatters, the whole Khizalace will come apart!"

The man he'd chosen to be messenger hesitated. "She's with Frazhin. They're doing something to the gates."

"Idiot! What use will gates be if the Tower collapses? Fetch her up here right now!"

Renn's song was growing stronger and more confident — a pure, powerful note that made Shaiala's hair stand on end. She gritted her teeth and attacked the Khiz with a wild flurry of *Dragonflies.* The scream of shattering crystal was deafening. "That for scaring I!" she yelled, delivering a perfectly aimed *Double Hare.* Her feet were bleeding but she didn't care. "And that for Laphie! And that for Imara! And *this* for centaurs!"

By now, many of the captives were on their feet. Broken knife in hand, Erihan led them in a stampede at the stairs. The Harai didn't stand a chance. Boys and girls alike followed Shaiala's example, kicking shins and ankles then ducking under the men's blades while they were distracted by the pain. The Harai didn't seem to know whether to try to recapture the children, kill them, or flee. They shouted down the stairs for reinforcements. Meanwhile, more and more children were rousing from their Khiz-induced sleep and joining the fight. By sheer weight of numbers, they swept the Harai aside and raced down the stairs, yelling and cheering, their heads glittering with black shards.

"Head for the courtyard!" Erihan shouted after them. "Stay together! We'll finish up here and come and find you."

Then they realized their mistake. With the captives gone, they were only three against twenty armed men. The Harai recovered fast and advanced through the pallets with drawn scimitars.

"You can stop your tricks right now!" snapped the leader, raising his blade in a threatening manner. "Or I swear we'll cut you down where you stand! You've done more than enough damage to merit it. Who are you, anyway?" His eye fell on Erihan's sharet, which had been pulled loose in the struggle and was showing both sides of the material. "Hey — aren't those Harai colors?"

Erihan's eyes flashed. He snatched off the sharet and threw it on the floor. "I'm Prince Erihan of the Kalerei! You touch me, and my father won't rest until he's fed every Harai bone to his horses!"

The leader drew in a sharp breath. Then he smiled coldly. "A Kalerei brat. I should have guessed. And where exactly is your father now, my little *prince*? Last I saw of him, he was trapped in the Pass of Silence with rocks falling on his head."

"That's a lie! Lord Nahar would never allow the Kalerei to be trapped anywhere!" But Erihan had gone pale. His knife hand lowered and he glanced at the stairs. On a signal from the leader, the Harai rushed him.

Shaiala whirled, only to find herself facing a ring of scimitars. Then Renn, whom no one seemed to consider a threat, stepped forward. "Leave him alone!" he snapped.

Shaiala noticed his hands were trembling but his voice emerged steady and pure. It brimmed with Songs that reminded her of cool bluestone and salt spray, of faraway echoes and ships.

"I was there when Lord Nahar came through the Pass," Renn went on, staring challengingly at the Harai leader. "And the last *I* saw, the Kalerei were winning. I expect they're storming your gates at this very moment."

The light returned to Erihan's eyes. The Harai glanced around uncertainly and began to retreat toward the stairs. The leader swung his scimitar in a bright arc. "Stand firm! The boy's lying, for Khiz's sake! Secure them on the pallets, then get out there and start rounding up the runaways. Need I remind you what Frazhin will do to you, and your families, if they escape? What are you afraid of? Look, the Khiz has stopped cracking now."

He spoke too soon.

Renn let the air out of his lungs, and the dark note he'd picked up from the Khiz swelled to the size of a mountain.

The Harai's hands flew to their ears. Horror showed in their faces as that note became louder and purer, was echoed by the crystal and the walls, the pallets and the domed roof, traveled deep beneath their feet and spread through the dark layers and glittering mosaics of the Khizalace, out from the Tower to the very cliffs of the Sunless Valley and beyond.

"Stop singing!" the leader yelled at Renn. "You don't know what you're doing! Stop!"

But the damage was done. Even when Renn's breath ran out, the terrible dark note continued. The floor shuddered beneath their feet. Lumps of crystal broke off the ceiling and rained down like dark knives. One speared the Harai leader in the shoulder. He clutched at the wound with a surprised expression. His men covered their heads and fled, yelling as they went. "I'm getting out of here!" . . . "I've never liked this place. Give me a tent on the Plains, a good horse beneath me, and the wind in my hair any day!" . . . "Lady Yashra's gone as crazy as that cripple she worships." . . . "It's time for the Harai to choose a new leader."

The three children followed close on the Harai's heels, taking the stairs two at a time and skidding around the landings. Shaiala's legs wobbled, but her blood sang in her veins. They were almost at the bottom of the Tower before she realized Renn was trying to say something.

"Second Singer . . . dungeon." He grabbed her sleeve and pointed at some shadowy steps that led behind a statue and plunged underground.

Shaiala shuddered and shrugged him off.

"The centaurs are in the courtyard, Shai!" Erihan called, peering through a narrow window.

Her heart leaped. Eagerly, she sprang across. But Renn had more power than she'd thought.

"*Shaiala!*" Now that he'd got his breath back, his voice was like an invisible chain tightening around her throat. "We have to rescue Singer Kherron! I need you."

She cast an anguished look at the centaurs.

"*Please*, Shaiala! I'm sorry, all right? Everything you said was true, I know that now. But you've got to help me. I can't do it alone."

This time there was no Song in his voice. Renn stood at the top of the shadowy steps with the crystal falling all around him, pleading with his strange gray eyes. Erihan looked from one to the other of them but held his tongue. Like Renn, he must have sensed he couldn't force her into the dungeon if she didn't want to go.

Shaiala sighed. "Quick, then!" she hissed in Herd, giving the Singer boy a shove toward the steps. "Before roof collapse!"

*

The dungeon was the last place Renn wanted to revisit. He forced himself into the darkness one step at a time, breaking into a fresh sweat at every turn. They soon left the noise of shattering crystal behind, but as they descended, the black rock shuddered ominously around them and the roof supports creaked. Torches cast smoky red light into side passages that echoed with the screams of prisoners. He bit his lip, desperately trying to get his bearings. Shaiala hadn't spoken since they'd parted with the Kalerei prince at the bottom of the Tower, for which he was glad because he had no idea what to say to her. It was a miracle she'd come at all. He hesitated as he recognized the dripping tunnel with its row of locked doors.

"What wrong?" Shaiala hissed.

"Nothing," Renn said, shaking off his doubts. "It's down here."

She was limping, which worried him. Had she hurt her feet cracking the Khiz? Would either of them be able to fight if they ran into Harai guards down here? His mouth felt dry and sore. When he tried to hum *Challa* to calm them both, the Song died in his throat.

But what they'd begun up in the Tower had already overtaken them. By the time they reached the Second Singer's cell, black dust was showering from the tunnel roof and cracks were appearing in the walls. Any guards had long gone.

Renn pulled Shaiala to a halt before the Second Singer's cell and tried the door without much hope. "It's locked."

Without a word, Shaiala pushed him out of the way. Her heel slammed into the metal just below the keyhole. The lock cracked and Renn used his shoulder to break it open. He fell into pitch blackness and picked himself up, shivering.

So cold. Not a sound. What if — ?

Shaiala grabbed a torch from the tunnel and brought it into the cell. The flame flickered across the slab of crystal, the dark links of chain, the Second Singer's body splayed helplessly just as Renn remembered. Kherron's eyes were closed and he didn't seem to be breathing.

"We're too late," Renn whispered, despair flooding through him. Was everyone he knew going to die?

Shaiala's fingers digging into his arm reminded him they'd die, too, if they didn't get out of here soon. But, instead of dragging him out of the cell, she tugged him toward the slab.

"Take gag out," she ordered. "Him breathe better. I see to chains."

Renn rushed forward in wild relief as Singer Kherron's bruised flesh stirred. With shaking fingers, Renn tugged at the gag. At last, the knot loosened and he was able to ease the chewed silk free. The Second Singer moaned but did not wake.

Shaiala frowned at the chains. "I can break they," she said softly in Herd. "But might hurt Second Singer if I miss."

Renn could see what she meant. The links were very short. He quickly searched the shadows in the slim hope that Singer Kherron's guards may have left the key to his shackles somewhere in the cell, then realized that even if they did get him free they'd have another problem. How were they going to get an unconscious man out of the dungeon and through enemy territory without Singer help?

"It better if Second Singer awake," Shaiala said, looking at him expectantly. "To keep chain taut when I kick."

Renn shook himself. "Do you mean — Oh no, I can't . . . I've never —"

"You nearly Singer. Crack Khiz!" She grinned.

Renn hugged himself. He thought of the *Aushan* he'd tried by the lake and the *Shi* he'd used on the Harai who'd taken him up the Tower. But those Songs had been directed at enemies. It hadn't mattered if they went wrong. He looked at Singer Kherron's bruised eyes and sunken cheeks. What choice did he have?

Trying to look more confident than he felt, he straightened

his shoulders and took deep breaths to clear his lungs of the black dust. Softly, gently, he began to hum, pouring all his need into the Song.

Challa, shh, calm, Challa makes you dream. . . .

The Second Singer's low moaning stopped. His breathing grew easier. He snuggled into the crystal slab as if it were a cushioned pallet.

"Not sleep-song!" Shaiala said, breaking the spell. "Wake!"

Renn scowled at her. But she was right. They didn't have time to heal Kherron now, and, anyway, proper therapy needed five Singers on the points of a pentangle. Quickly, he changed to *Kashe. Kashe makes you laugh.*

He wondered if it would work without the pentangle. But after a few moments, Kherron's eyelids fluttered. His hands clenched in their shackles. Then, with a great rasping breath, he heaved upward, choking and spitting blood. One last cough, and something flew across his cell, tinkling when it hit the floor. It was the small khiz-crystal the Harai had put down his throat in the Pass. Renn stared at it in horror. Though no larger than his thumb, the crystal had hundreds of glittering edges sharp as blades. More blood followed, then a trickle of bile. Finally, the Second Singer managed a cracked smile.

"Thank you, Renn," he rasped. "It's a strange thing . . . I sang my first real Song in the heart of an enemy stronghold, too." He laughed in a terrible, grating croak.

Shaiala shouldered Renn aside and frowned at the Second Singer. "Not laugh! Not funny! Need break chains. You stretch they. Stay very still."

The shadows returned to Singer Kherron's face. "I understand, Shaiala Two Hoof. Do what you have to. If you break one of my bones, it'll soon heal — unlike other things." A bleakness whispered through his words.

Renn listened in growing dismay to the Second Singer's voice. Where were all his Songs?

More black dust showered from the roof, settling on the Second Singer's body. "Hurry!" he snapped with something of his old strength.

Shaiala glanced at Renn. He saw the uncertainty in her eyes and bit his lip. "We can't leave him here," he whispered. "He'll help the centaurs once he's free." He didn't see how Singer Kherron could help anyone now the Khiz had destroyed his Songs, but he dared not mention that to Shaiala. Would Kherron's voice recover now the crystal was out? It *had* to recover.

He held the torch while Shaiala kicked the links that fastened the Second Singer's ankles to the slab. She used the side of her foot, leaping into the air and striking as she landed. The block cracked and the chain rattled free. The Second Singer smiled, slithered sideways off the slab, and crouched awkwardly so she could kick the chains securing his wrists. He never moved as her heel whistled past his ear. Again, the block cracked in exactly the right place. Renn wanted to cheer, but it was too soon to start celebrating.

Singer Kherron rose stiffly and wiped his mouth with his tattered robe. Without a word, he took charge of the torch and led them quickly from the cell.

*

With all the noise above, it was rather a surprise to find the tunnels still passable. Other prisoners were wailing in fear behind locked doors, but Singer Kherron wouldn't stop.

"If we get trapped down here, it'll help no one," he said in his rough, broken voice. "The roof's well supported, and there's no crystal in the other cells to set off avalanches inside. We'll free them later. The important thing now is to find Yashra and Frazhin."

Shaiala seemed relieved not to have to kick down any more doors. Her limp had grown worse, and her feet left bloody prints in the dust. Renn would have lent her his boots, except there wasn't time to stop and change, and she probably wouldn't have worn them, anyway. As they hurried toward the trapdoor that led up to the courtyard, Singer Kherron interrogated them about what had happened since his capture in the Pass. When Renn told him of the second avalanche and the orderlies they'd left beneath piles of rock, he closed his eyes in pain. Then he squeezed Renn's shoulder and urged them onward with a dark, dangerous expression.

The tunnel took a turn, and they found themselves at the bottom of a flight of steps leading up into stormy purple light. Above them, shouts, screams, and the clash of scimitars mingled with the background hiss of shattering crystal. Before anyone could stop her, Shaiala darted past the Second Singer and raced up the steps. "Kamara Silvermane!" she shouted. "Rafiz Long-shadow! Wait for I!"

The Second Singer's lips tightened. "She never learns, does she? Sounds like the Harai have their hands full. Stay close to me, Renn. I might need your voice."

Need his voice! The Second Singer!

Renn almost asked — it was on the tip of his tongue — *Are you really my father?* Then they were out of the dungeon and plunged into the midst of the battle. There was no time for questions of any sort.

The courtyard was crammed with struggling bodies, the sky thick with falling crystal and dangerously large lumps of black stone. In the midst of the destruction, Lord Nahar and his men were engaged in furious duels with the Harai, who had fled their collapsing palace only to find their ancient enemy waiting for them outside. Their clashing scimitars reflected the storm light in purple glints that ended with spine-chilling death screams. The centaurs were in the thick of it, too, hooves flying and blue coats splattered with blood. There seemed to be a lot more of them than Renn had seen on the mountainside, though every time he tried to count the creatures a glimmer of green distracted him and the next time he looked the same centaur was fighting on the opposite side of the courtyard. His heart lifted as he spotted Lazim clinging to a statue with one arm, wrenching Harai scimitars from their hands with expert twists of his Echorium sword. The orderly's braids with their bone fastenings flew against the stormy sky, and his eyes gleamed. A short way off, Anyan and Verris were fighting back-to-back as they had at the river camp. The children from the Khiz Training Tower dodged hooves and blades to snatch up fallen stones and shards of crystal that they threw at the Harai with furious yells. The ground shook; hailstones joined the crystal rain. With a noise like a thunderclap, a huge crack opened across one corner of the yard, swallowing three statues and a company of Harai hurrying from the stables to join the battle. A centaur leaped the chasm, scrabbled precariously on the far side, then galloped toward the open gates, yelling something in Half Creature speech. He was followed by several loose, panic-crazed horses. More Harai were trampled as they tried to get out of the way.

Renn's heart was beating so fast he thought it would burst. He looked for Shaiala but could see no sign of her. How anyone might survive such carnage, he couldn't think. The dungeons with their deserted tunnels and supporting props suddenly seemed very appealing. But the Second Singer caught his arm, pulled his tattered robe over both their heads, and started to drag him through the battle toward the gates.

At first, Renn thought they were abandoning the others and pulled back in protest. Then he saw the furious set of Kherron's jaw and the way his green eyes were fixed on a patch of darkness at the foot of one of the gate towers. He turned cold all over as he glimpsed the glitter of a black crystal mask in the shadows.

Unnoticed by those fighting in the courtyard, a small company of Harai had slipped away from the battle and formed two lines outside the walls. Under Frazhin's command, they were slowly pushing the heavy gates shut.

"He's trying to trap us in the yard!" Singer Kherron warned. "Translate for me, Renn!"

He caught the nearest centaur by the arm and shouted into its ear. "You have to call your people together! Break the gates so they can't close them. All of you at once! Do you understand?"

The filly gave the Second Singer a wild-eyed look. Before Renn was halfway through the translation, she'd wrenched herself free and vanished in a flare of green light. Kherron swore as the metal links still dangling from his wrist whipped back and hit him in the eye. Renn bit his lip. If the whole thing hadn't been so terrifying, it would have been funny.

"Stupid Half Creatures!" Singer Kherron raged, grabbing Renn's wrist again. "Come on! We'll have to stop him ourselves."

But, even as they ducked through the falling crystal toward the gate tower, four Harai detached themselves from the group outside and barred their way with flashing scimitars. The Second Singer thrust Renn behind him and raised his chin. "Let us through!" he commanded in his rough voice, adding, "*Aushan, Renn! Now!*"

Renn's Song, though breathless with fear, was enough to make the Harai throw down their weapons and cover their ears. The Second Singer dragged him past. But it was already too late. Their view of the valley and the sky narrowed as the massive gates of black crystal creaked shut. As they closed the Singers caught a glimpse of Frazhin's mask glittering triumphantly through the crack. A dull boom shook the ground and the air suddenly turned cold. Renn shivered as a new darkness settled over the courtyard.

Kherron placed his palm across the place where the gates met and tipped his head to one side, *listening*. Then he slammed his fist into the crystal.

"They're locked with Khiz-power," he said. "I don't know how we're going to open them now."

*

Shaiala had raced through a struggling knot of Two Hoofs and ducked a badly aimed scimitar before she realized the danger she was in. She didn't think she had a scrap of energy left, but the sight of Kamara Silvermane being attacked by four Harai at once lent her strength. Three *Flying Snakes* and a *Double Hare* brought her to the filly's side.

"What happen?" she panted out. "Where you find Marell Storm Temper?"

Kamara grinned. "Good kicking, Shaiala Two Hoof! I *say* you not dead! Us find Marell Storm Temper in armory. Him smash Harai weapons. Do good job, but stupid colts not know herd-stone skill. Two Hoofs trap they inside building. Us arrive just in time, make everyone invisible — Look out!" Kamara Silvermane flattened her pretty lilac ears and dispatched a yelling Harai with a skillful *Hare*. "Rafiz Longshadow over there! Him say work our way toward gate, leave Two Hoof palace quick as possible."

Shaiala couldn't have agreed more. As they fought their way toward the gates, she made a quick count of centaur heads. Miraculously, no one seemed to be missing. Rafiz Longshadow was trying to organize the foals into a group so the fillies could use their herdstones to hide them all. Untethered horses added to the confusion, racing this way and that in panic, kicking out at imagined demons. Led by Laphie and Imara and waving pitchforks and brooms, a crowd of yelling children chased the last of the horses from the stables. But the rain of crystal seemed to be easing, and Shaiala began to believe they might get out alive.

Then the gates slammed shut.

The centaurs let out a collective moan. Something dark pierced Shaiala's head in the place where her memories lived. She clutched Kamara Silvermane's arm in dismay as a plump figure appeared on the arch above the gates, her mask glittering in the storm light, its scarlet feathers torn by the wind.

"Lord Nahar!" Yashra called. "The gates are sealed. You are trapped and cannot win! You might have cracked the Khiz, but not even a Singer can hold a note continuously all day and all night. The crystal is now back under our control. My lord Frazhin suggests I give you a small demonstration."

She pointed to the Kalerei who was whispering into Lord Nahar's ear. There was a hissing sound and, suddenly, a spear of black crystal was protruding from the man's chest. He stared at it in surprise, then slowly toppled facedown at his lord's feet. Lord Nahar took an alarmed step backward. The other Kalerei rushed to surround him as he knelt to examine his man. The scar on his cheek jumped. Breathing hard, he glared up at Yashra.

"Surrender your weapons and hand over the Singer," she continued, "and we'll be merciful. The centaurs will return to the mine. The children will be cared for in our Khizalace. And we'll escort you and your men to the Pass of Silence so you can return to your families."

Kamara Silvermane made a noise of disgust in her throat. Rafiz Longshadow and Marell Storm Temper swished their tails and scraped the cracked mosaic with their hooves. The Kalerei scowled. "Let me climb up there and cut the lying Harai tongue from her head, Lord!" one muttered. "Does she think the Kalerei are stupid? As soon as we set foot in that Pass, she'll send an avalanche down on our heads! That spear was an accident. She's not controlling the crystal, nor anybody else!"

Yashra must have heard or guessed the gist of this. "Killing everyone would be counterproductive," she said. "Maybe someone closer to your heart will help persuade you?" Casually, she reached behind her, pulled a dazed captive into view, and set her scimitar across his throat.

Shaiala's heart sank. It was Erihan!

*

The fighting in the courtyard stopped as if someone had melted the men's weapons in their hands. Kalerei muttering rose to an angry roar. The trapped Harai backed away and called to their comrades behind the gates to let them out. Another slab of crystal fell from the Tower and shattered like spray from a huge dark wave. The Kalerei robes parted and Lord Nahar stepped out. His scar writhed in fury as he answered Yashra in a dangerous voice.

"You've betrayed your people!" he called. "You've imprisoned their spirits behind walls where they cannot reach the Great Sky Plain. Two-thirds of the Harai horses are riderless and your palace is destroyed! My stallion is tethered on the other side of the Pass. Even if you spill every last drop of Kalerei blood in this valley, the Horselords will not rest until you are fed to him, Lady. Bone by bone."

Yashra grabbed Erihan's hair, dragged his head back, and pressed with her blade until a line of scarlet appeared across his neck. If she thought to force a scream from him, she was disappointed. The prince bit his lip and made no sound.

"A Horselord does not bargain with those who have abandoned the ancient ways," Lord Nahar said coldly. "All my sons know this. If you mean to kill him, do it."

Shaiala held her breath. An intense hush descended over the courtyard.

"You are a fool, Nahar!" Yashra said. "Now your son will die, and you and your men, too!" Her scimitar rose in an angry arc. Erihan flinched, but bravely raised his chin and stared his father in the eye as the air above the courtyard once more filled with lethal crystal shards.

"I think not," said a cracked voice accompanied by a faraway

Song that cut through the destruction like a cool stream trick-
ling across the summer plain. The crystal spears fell short and
shattered harmlessly into the rubble.

Everyone uncovered their heads and looked around. Whispering excitedly, the Kalerei parted to allow a blue-haired Two
Hoof through. The Second Singer — bruised, bleeding, and still
wearing his chains — carried himself like a lord. Flanking him,
came three weary orderlies with proud looks on their faces. At
his side walked Renn, singing that beautiful Song.

"Let the boy go, Yashra!" commanded the Second Singer, and
Renn's Song changed.

The Harai trapped in the courtyard cast desperate looks at the
walls. A few attempted to climb but slipped back. Yashra's mask
glittered as its eyeholes turned toward the Second Singer. A
spear of crystal flew at him but turned aside as if it had hit an
invisible shield. Renn ducked and missed a note.

The air above the arch *blurred*. A nightmarish laugh rang out
across the courtyard and Yashra's voice was replaced by one that
scraped like hooves on rock. "Your Echorium magic doesn't
work on me, Singer! You tried to use your Songs to destroy me
once before, remember? But you didn't succeed, did you? I
found a way to stop you. I killed your First Singer in the heart
of your precious Echorium, and if you don't tell your young one
to stop singing right now I'll do the same to him. The Khiz has
power. It can turn your Songs."

Shaiala turned cold all over. But the Second Singer's expression did not change. Standing directly beneath the gates, he
stared straight at Yashra's mask and smiled.

"Is that so? Then how come you're too afraid to confront
me yourself, Frazhin? Your Khiz is shattering as we speak, yet
you leave your woman to do your dirty work for you. Show
yourself!"

After a moment's hesitation, Renn's Song changed yet again,

becoming deeper and darker. Yashra let out a little cry and snatched off the mask as if it had burned her.

"Where's Frazhin hiding?" the Second Singer went on smoothly. "Why isn't he at your side?"

The Harai woman glared at him. "You know he can't climb up here! You Singers made sure of that, didn't you? He doesn't need to be here in person. He sees everything he needs to through my mask. He's right outside the gate listening to every word we're saying and watching every move you make. The moment your boy stops singing he'll put a spear of crystal in his throat."

"Are you sure?"

Uncertainty flickered across her face. "What do you mean?"

"Do those masks of yours work both ways? Can you see through Frazhin's eyes as he sees through yours?"

Shaiala edged closer to Kamara Silvermane, and the filly put an arm around her. The warm centaur smell helped keep the darkness out of her head.

Yashra's expression was terrifying. She replaced the mask over her face and scanned the courtyard, the stables, the roofless Tower, the crumbling walls of her palace. Then she turned to look across the Valley. She went rigid. "No, my love," she whispered. "Oh no, they're not ready —"

Erihan saw his chance. While Yashra was distracted by whatever she'd seen, he twisted out of her grip, grabbed the mask from her face, and without a moment's hesitation leaped from the arch into the courtyard.

It was a leap that would have broken a centaur's legs. But Erihan crumpled upon landing, rolled several times while the Kalerei leaped clear, then picked himself up. He staggered slightly and shook his head, the mask clasped to his chest. Lord Nahar raced across, snatched the thing from his hands, and hugged him hard. Erihan flushed.

Yashra remained on the arch, her hands pressed to her naked cheeks, a look of confusion and loss in her eyes.

"See how Frazhin abandons you in your time of need?" the Second Singer continued mercilessly. "He doesn't deserve anyone's love. Even as he did twenty years ago, he flees the battle when all is lost and leaves you to die in his place." The Harai began muttering and called again for their comrades to open the gates.

Yashra shook her head. "You don't understand! If he gets to the lake, everything's finished. Let me have the mask back. I'll see what I can do for you all, just let me have my mask. Please."

Lord Nahar stared at her in disbelief. "You would have killed my son, yet you expect us to give you back your demon powers? I'm going to make sure no one ever wears this thing again." Before anyone could stop him, he took a firm grip of the scarlet feathers and swung the mask as hard as he could at the gates.

"NO!" shouted the Second Singer.

But his broken voice had little effect on Nahar's fury. The mask struck the gates with an earsplitting shriek and disintegrated into millions of tiny needlelike shards. That horrible note rose to a crescendo, making everyone cover their ears. Yashra screamed and flung herself off the far side of the arch. There was a faint rattle of hooves outside. Then someone shouted, "Look out! It's coming down!" And everyone flung themselves at the gates in panic as the Tower swayed, wobbled like a pillar of water, and slowly began to topple toward them.

Shaiala clung to Kamara Silvermane, the darkness in her head spreading. Then, through all the terror and screams, she thought she heard a voice calling her name.

"Small Two Hoof want something," Kamara Silvermane said.

All at once, Shaiala realized the Second Singer and Lord Nahar were pushing everyone away from the gates. Renn, standing small and alone in the shadow of the black crystal, was calling to her. She saw his frantic gestures and understood.

"KICK!" she shouted. "Centaurs kick gates! Renn sing!"

The few moments it took the Singer boy to get the right note gave Rafiz Longshadow a chance to get the herd in position with their rumps turned on the gates. A line of perfectly coordinated *Double Hares* combined with Renn's Song silenced the horrible shriek. There was a hush. They all looked at one another, desperately hoping it had worked. Then, with a sound like the air popping, Frazhin's seal broke. Lord Nahar's men flung the gates wide, releasing a roar of cheers. People and centaurs streamed through the open gates as the Tower crashed down behind them, destroying the last undamaged part of the Khizalace.

The Second Singer stared up the valley where dust kicked up by galloping hooves hung in the air. "Yashra's heading for the lake," he said, and exchanged a dark glance with Lord Nahar. "I think we'd better go after her, don't you?"

16
TRUST-GIFT

Lord Nahar wanted to go after Yashra and Frazhin immediately, taking a party of warriors on foot. But the Second Singer counseled caution. "Frazhin's still got his mask," he reminded them. "Just because we broke the seal he put on the gates doesn't mean he's lost all his power. I want everyone to stay together until we're safely out of this valley."

They made their preparations as quickly as possible. But with so many loose horses to round up, children and centaurs to organize, prisoners to free, wounds to bandage, and surrendering Harai to deal with, dusk was falling before they were ready to ride out. Renn rode at the head of the column with the Second Singer, Lord Nahar, Prince Erihan, Shaiala, and Lazim. He clung desperately to the mane of his gelding and tried to look as if he knew what he was doing. In all the excitement, everyone just seemed to assume he could ride, and he'd been too ashamed to admit he'd never sat on a horse in his life. Fortunately, Singer Kherron, still stiff from his ordeal and further bruised by the removal of his chains with a large file, led the way at a slow pace.

Also, Lazim whispered a few tips such as, "Relax, pretend you're a sack of grain, not a crystal statue!" And, "Don't tug on his mouth, just let him follow the others." So Renn managed to stay mounted.

The children they'd rescued from the Tower rode in carts driven by the Kalerei. Most were curled up asleep beneath the saddle blankets Nahar's men had found in the ruins of the stables. Some of the prisoners freed from the dungeons also took advantage of the carts, though a few insisted upon being given weapons and were helping to guard the Harai. If they were rather overzealous in this task, the Second Singer turned a blind eye.

With the shattering of the Khizalace's crystal heart, the storm clouds had cleared. A fresh breeze brought the scent of night from the mountains and a half-moon silvered the surface of the lake. As they drew closer to the water, the horses sniffed the air and snorted. The centaurs muttered excitedly in Half Creature speech. Renn stared at the water with little shivers going down his spine. "What do you suppose Yashra meant by 'if Frazhin reaches the lake, everything's finished'?" he whispered. But Shaiala shushed him and kicked her mount forward to join Erihan's.

"Wait here." Singer Kherron raised a hand to halt the column and rode down the slope to the water's edge. He sat on his horse like a statue, *listening*. The mountains rose on all sides, black and silent. The surface of the lake rippled and shadows moved in its depths. At first Renn couldn't work out why they'd stopped. Then he saw a cart parked on a beach of crystal, hidden from the path by a rocky spur. Yashra stood on the plank seat, her long dark hair blowing around her as she gazed across the water. She did not look around, though she must have heard the Second Singer's horse approaching. Her Harai escort sat on their mounts nearby, watching the lake and the Second Singer with wary expressions. One held Yashra's riderless horse. Two crystal crutches lay abandoned on the shore.

Renn grasped a handful of mane and stood in his stirrups. After a moment, he made out a rowboat far out on the black expanse of water. A lone silhouette crouched over the side and the water around the boat glittered darkly. Renn screwed up his eyes, but the boat was too far away to see what Frazhin was doing. The Second Singer trotted across to the cart and grabbed Yashra's arm.

"What's he up to?" he demanded in his rough voice.

The Harai on the beach dropped their hands to their scimitars, but Yashra shook her head. "He's calling his children," she said with a proud tilt of her chin. "If he succeeds, none of you will make it past the lake."

Kherron frowned at the boat. "His children? But he didn't get any of them out of the Khizalace . . ."

It was Shaiala who provided the answer. Kicking her mount into the shallows, she pointed urgently at the deepest part of the lake. "There a tunnel!" she said in nearly perfect Human. "Under lake! It lead through mountain to place where naga children are born!"

"She means the Fall of Clouds, Father," Erihan said. "We came in that way. We saw their eggs."

Lord Nahar leaned forward with interest, his saddle creaking. "This I have to see! Naga are unpredictable creatures at the best of times. He's crazy if he thinks he can control them."

Even as he spoke, there was a dark glimmer beneath the surface of the lake. Renn's stomach clenched as a long, midnight-scaled tail rose from the depths. More naga glimmered toward the boat, surrounding it with their churning bodies. Frazhin straightened in triumph. His mask glittered in the moonlight as he raised his good arm and pointed toward the path where the centaurs and Kalerei waited. Willing green hands grasped the sides of the boat, and it surged toward the beach, propelled by a wave of wildly lashing naga tails. The amused expressions of the Kalerei turned to alarm as their horses started to panic. Some of the children woke up, saw the naga rushing toward them, and screamed. The centaurs broke into a sweat and a few fillies vanished in glimmers of green, which spooked the horses still more.

The Second Singer shouted for Renn, who was too busy trying to control his terrified gelding to think about much else. He'd been surrounded by centaurs. The path was a confusion of scrambling hooves, warning shouts, and half-glimpsed shadows. His head filled with nightmarish images of Frazhin's mask.

Sparkly! — Sparkly! — Sparkly!

Then there was a shriek and a splintering noise. He wrenched his gelding out of the green light in time to see one of the naga tails smash across the little boat. Yashra let out a cry of dismay as Frazhin, his boat, and the naga disappeared beneath the surface in a stream of moon-silvered bubbles. Nothing came up again.

The centaurs reappeared, looking rather ashamed of themselves. The Kalerei regained control of their horses and stared at the lake, breathing hard. The children stopped screaming and sat quietly. Yashra dropped her face into her hands. She offered no resistance when Lord Nahar's men ran across the beach and dragged her down from the cart. Her escort, hopelessly outnumbered, surrendered their weapons.

As the Harai were led away to join the other prisoners, Renn finally persuaded his gelding to join Shaiala and the Kalerei prince on the beach. The three of them stared at the spot where Frazhin's boat had gone down.

"Do you think he drowned?" Erihan said.

Renn bit his lip. He almost felt sorry for the cripple. "Those monsters probably ate him first."

Shaiala gave him a disgusted look. "Naga not monsters! They help we through tunnel."

"She has a point," Erihan said, frowning.

Renn shook his head. "That's different," he said without thinking. "Shaiala's only half human. They probably thought she was one of them."

The wild girl scowled. Before he realized the danger, her foot shot sideways and jabbed his gelding in the ribs. The stupid horse snorted and leaped a centaur's height into the air. Renn found himself swinging from the mane, staring at cold black water. Only just in time, Erihan grabbed his foot and pulled him back onto the gelding.

"What is it with you two?" he said with an exasperated sigh. "Don't you know when to stop? Look, Yashra's crying."

They all looked at the Harai woman, who was being helped over the crystal shards to where the Second Singer had dismounted. It was true. Yashra's cheeks were streaked with tears, her eyes red and swollen.

"I'm going to listen." Erihan turned his mount and headed back up the beach. With a final glare at Renn, Shaiala followed. Renn would have stayed where he was, except his gelding objected to being left alone in the lake and splashed after them, neighing for his new friends to wait.

The Second Singer frowned at them. "Quiet, you three! I'm trying to decide what to do. Pay attention, Renn. One day you might have to make such decisions yourself."

Renn's stomach fluttered. Part pride at the way the other two looked at him, part uneasiness.

The Second Singer tipped Yashra's chin so he could look into her eyes. She pulled away but he turned her face back again. This time she met his gaze with her proud dark one and endured his scrutiny. Lazim hovered by the Second Singer's shoulder, Anyan and Verris behind him. One dark hand rested on the hilt of his sword. In the other, he held the bluestone pendant that two nights ago he'd given to Renn to try to contact the Echorium.

The lake lapped quietly at the crystal shore. The night breeze lifted Yashra's hair and blew the Second Singer's blood-encrusted curls across his eyes. No one dared speak, though some of the centaurs stamped impatiently. In the carts, the exhausted children whimpered in their dreams.

"What you've done is unforgivable," said the Second Singer.

A sigh rippled along the shore. Yashra bit her lip but did not look away as he listed her crimes.

"You've broken the Half Creature Treaty by making slaves of the centaurs. You've deprived hundreds of children of their free-dom. You've attempted to pervert the Songs of Power. You've conspired to harm an envoy of the Echorium and twist him to your evil purpose. All this you have done freely of your own will, though the fact you were under the influence of another when you wore the mask must be taken into account." He frowned at her. "What I don't understand is why you put the mask on in the first place. Didn't you realize the power it had?"

Yashra had stopped crying. Renn saw one of her hands creep over her distended belly. "He wasn't all evil," she whispered. "You didn't know him. Once he was an innocent, a child him-self. He wanted to be a Singer more than anything else. But your Echorium rejected him, didn't it? They told him he wasn't good enough. It was the Echorium that twisted him back then, and it was the Echorium that injured him in later life. I found him wandering in the foothills and brought him to this place so we could make a fresh start. I nursed him back to health. Piece by piece, we built a new life for ourselves. Since he couldn't travel far with his injuries, he made the masks so we need never be apart even when I had to leave the Valley. Our Khizalace was going to be beautiful, and now it's destroyed forever." Her gaze flicked to Renn and Shaiala, full of something they didn't under-stand. Not hatred exactly, but a massive sadness that swept all before it.

"You cannot be permitted to go free," the Second Singer continued sternly. "However —" He held out a hand and Lazim dropped the bluestone pendant into his palm. "You are carrying a child and that life is, as you say, innocent despite its parentage. Provided you accept the Echorium's Trust-Gift, you will be escorted safely to the Birthing House on the Isle of Echoes, where you will remain long enough to bring your child into this world. Then you will be taken to the Pentangle and given a course of *Yehn*, after which you may reside quietly in one of the Isle villages until your natural death."

Absolute silence had fallen over the lake. The naga had gone now, back into the depths. No sign remained of Frazhin or his boat. Even the centaurs had stopped fidgeting. The Harai prisoners ran their fingers under their sharets. Lord Nahar's men glanced at one another with raised eyebrows. Singer Kherron waited, the bluestone shining in his hand, his bruised face giving nothing away.

"And if I refuse?" Yashra whispered.

"Then my orderlies will execute you here and now and your unborn child will die with you."

"That horrible!" Shaiala breathed.

"Shh!" Renn hissed, still struggling to make his gelding stand still. "I'm trying to *listen*."

Yashra bowed her head. "I accept your Trust-Gift, Singer," she said. "Not for me, but for my child."

A second sigh rippled along the shore. Yashra raised her chin and stood motionless as Kherron fastened the chain around her throat. She stared straight ahead as Lord Nahar's men escorted her back to the cart, which had been brought up from the beach and given a Kalerei driver.

"I don't understand, Singer," Renn admitted as Kherron remounted. "Why did Frazhin think the naga would help him? Did he try to pay them with his mask to take him through the tunnel? Why did they turn on him like that? And how did he know that you're —" He glanced at Shaiala and Erihan to check they weren't listening, then took the deepest breath of his life and added in a pallet-whisper, "— *my father?*"

The Second Singer's green eyes closed briefly. The bruised cheek twitched as he turned his horse's head toward the Pass of Silence. "Not now, Renn," he said softly. "Not now."

17
STONE-DANCER

Seven days later, under the full moon, an unprecedented festival took place on the Purple Plains near the mouth of the Dancing Canyons. A sea of dark tents formed a temporary city where men and women of more than thirty Horselord tribes laid their scimitars aside in favor of a battle of words, fighting to outdo one another with their stories of the Fall of the Khiz-palace. An eerie green light glimmered around the perimeter of the camp as young centaurs practiced with their herdstones, spooking the picketed horses. There were screams and laughter as small children chased the Half Creatures, trying to catch their tails before they disappeared and shrieking in delighted terror whenever they touched an invisible mane or flank. It was a miracle no one was killed — though the story-tellers claimed the presence of the Second Singer in the camp kept such accidents from happening.

"He calls forth Songs from the mouths of children," they said. "He makes Half Creatures visible to the human eye and speaks to them in their own mysterious tongue. He opens a way through the mountains with a single word. Even the rocks listen to his voice!"

Kherron did nothing to discourage such rumors, though Renn grumbled that anyone with half a brain could tell their safe passage through the Pass of Silence had very little to do with the Second Singer's voice, and a lot to do with the simple fact that there were no unstable rocks left after all the recent avalanches. "Who are they calling a child, anyway?" he added, scowling across the camp at where the Second Singer and the orderlies sat with the new Harai leader and Lord Nahar around the treaty fire. "If I hadn't sung the right Songs in that courtyard, we'd all be dead by now."

Erihan touched his throat where Yashra's scimitar had drawn blood. Then he pointed out in his reasonable way that since Singer Kherron was currently overseeing the treaty between the Harai and the Kalerei, it was perhaps just as well his reputation had preceded him because his injured voice wouldn't be enough on its own.

Shaiala didn't care about the treaty or the Second Singer's voice. While the Two Hoofs talked and drank *fohl* and told their stories, those centaur foals still without herdstones had gone into the Canyons to complete the dance interrupted by the Harai three moons ago. Try as she might, she couldn't stop thinking about them.

It had been all right while they'd been traveling. The relief of getting everyone safely through the Pass, the excitement of meeting up with the adult centaurs on the other side, the exchange of stories, the sending of messengers, the gathering of the Two Hoof tribes — all this allowed little time for worrying about the future. At their nightly camps, she'd even taught Erihan and Renn how to do the sideways *Dragonfly* kick, laughing helplessly as the boys attempted to bruise each other. "Centaur foals learn *Dragonflies* before learn to walk," she told them. "You clumsy Two Hoofs will never manage to kick flying target." To which Renn answered, "I don't want to kick a fly. Only Geran and Alaira." Which had Erihan falling over in stitches even without being kicked.

Tonight was different. When Renn suggested another lesson, Shaiala shook her head. The shadowy entrance to the Canyons beckoned. The night held too many memories.

The boys glanced at each other. Erihan touched her elbow. "Come on, Shai," he said gently. "We know you're missing your friends. I'm sure they'll come and say good-bye once they've finished in there."

Shaiala jerked away. "Leave me alone."

"Shaiala —" Renn tried.

"You not understand!" She glared at their hurt, surprised faces, then turned her anger on the whole noisy, *fohl*-drinking, firelit camp. "None of you understand!"

Suddenly, she could bear it no longer. She tugged off the soft boots Lord Nahar's men had found for her and flung them at Erihan. Barefoot, she dodged through the tents toward the canyons, where green glimmers in the sky showed the foals at work.

"Hey!" Erihan shouted. "Where are you going?"

She didn't look back. As the black walls of rock rose around her, time stood still. The wind moaned eerily. Two Hoof ghosts crept through the shadows with drawn scimitars. Shaiala bit her tongue and retraced her steps to the ledge where she'd seen the foals captured by Harai three moons ago. It provided the same view she remembered, though the foals she saw trotting through the canyons tonight were different. She sat on the edge, her legs dangling in space, and watched them through her tears.

By the time Erihan and Renn had scrambled up to the ledge, puffing and grumbling about the climb, she'd stopped crying.

There was an awkward silence. Then Renn cleared his throat. "Er, Shaiala —"

"I know," she said softly, still watching the foals. "It all right. I know I not real centaur. I just want to come here one last time, that all. Before I . . . say good-bye to herd."

"You might not have to say good-bye."

She looked around sharply. "What you mean?"

"Remember the Khiz? Remember how we cracked it? Your feet and my voice working together? And what happened with the gates? It all ties in with what Singer Kherron told me about bluestone and vibrations. Centaur kicks make things vibrate, don't they? So do Songs. They shattered Frazhin's original Khiz-spear twenty years ago, and —"

"I not centaur!" She could have kicked him over the precipice for raising her hopes. "I not manage *Canyon* kick with only two hooves."

But Renn rushed on. "The merlee called you *child of stone-dancers*. I didn't understand what they meant back then, but I think I do now. That's their name for the centaurs, because they can crack stones with their feet. The merlee said I had to help you. They called me *son of stone-singer*."

Erihan's eyes widened. "Oh no. No, Renn, you can't. Look what happened last time!"

"We didn't know what we were doing when we cracked the Khiz. Things got out of hand. This time we'll control it better." He looked meaningfully at Shaiala. "Won't we?"

Shaiala stared at him. For once the Singer boy was speaking sense. It might — just might — work. Her blood ran faster. She scrambled to her feet.

"Quick, then! Before moon sets! Sing!"

"Try here," Erihan said, scraping at the far side of the ledge with his dagger. "The rock's softer. There's already a fissure — look."

Shaiala didn't need to be told twice. She leaped as high as she could, both knees tucked to her chin. With perfect timing, Renn filled his lungs. As Shaiala bore down upon the rock, legs

straight, heels aimed directly at the fissure, a single pure note
rose from the Dancing Canyons to greet the dawn.

There was no aftershock, no pain. As she landed, the fissure
opened softly like a flower beneath her feet. Green light poured
into the sky. A few pebbles rattled into the canyon below. A wind
whirled through the camp, tearing at tent flaps and banners. As
if the mountains had grown tired, the foothills settled into the
plain with a sigh. Then all was quiet and still.

For a long moment, no one spoke. Erihan dusted himself off.
Renn closed his mouth. Hardly daring to believe, Shaiala
opened her hand and stared in wonder at the small green stone
glimmering in her palm.

Then Erihan grinned and slapped them both on the back.
"You did it!" he said. "You really did it!"

*

Their escapade did not go unnoticed.

The entire camp turned out to meet them at the entrance to
the Dancing Canyons. The centaurs took Shaiala on a victory
gallop around the fires. Lord Nahar claimed his son, whispering something in his ear that made Erihan's face light up. People pointed, children raced into the canyons and pushed at the
rock to see if it would move again, mothers called in vain for
them to be careful. Amid all this chaos, Lazim and the other two
orderlies attempted to reassure the crowd that nothing was
wrong. The earth wasn't going to open up and swallow their
tents. It was just a small disturbance, nothing to worry about.
The Horselords squinted into the Canyons, clearly suspicious,
but returned to their tents when they realized that all those who
might once have attacked them were in the camp drinking treaty
flasks of *fohl*.

So it was that Renn finally got his wish to be alone with the
Second Singer, though not quite in the circumstances he'd
imagined.

"What am I going to do with you, Renn?" Kherron sighed. "I bring you on this trip to help me talk to Half Creatures, and find you cracking khiz-crystal and canyons behind my back. Who taught you to do that?"

Renn shook his head. "No one, Singer. It just happened."

"Shaiala Two Hoof didn't ask you to help her find a herd-stone?"

"No."

"Then why did you?"

Renn frowned. It wasn't the question he'd been expecting. "I don't know, Singer. Because she was so unhappy, I suppose. Because she didn't have any friends except the centaurs, and —" He swallowed. Singer Kherron was almost certainly truthlistening. "And I know what that's like."

The green eyes narrowed. "What about Prince Erihan?"

"I —" Renn faltered. Did he mean Erihan was his friend or Shaiala's? His cheeks grew hot. He hung his head, suddenly relieved the Second Singer's voice was not up to singing *Aushan* or *Yehn*. "I know it was a stupid thing to do," he said. "I'm sorry. I promise I won't do it again."

Kherron was silent a moment. When he spoke, his voice betrayed grudging admiration. "What amazes me is that the pair of you haven't brought the entire Midnight Mountains down around our ears. That was a beautifully controlled Song, I must admit."

Renn peered sideways at him. *Praise?* From the Second Singer?

Singer Kherron chuckled. "You most definitely *will* do it again, Renn! I think Graia is going to be fascinated when she hears about this new use of our Songs. But I think it would be best if you and Shaiala Two Hoof didn't crack anything else for the time being, at least not until we get the Lady Yashra back to the Isle." Almost *Kashe*.

Before Renn could take this in, Kherron dropped an arm across his shoulders and steered him into the shadow of the cliff. He pulled out a bluestone and grimaced at it. After a glance around to make sure they weren't being observed, he said quietly, "I need some help with this, Renn. We need to let Singer Graia know what's happened and warn her we're bringing Yashra back with us. Can you sing to open the channel, please? I should be able to take it from there."

Renn eyed the stone uncertainly. "I tried to contact the Isle before," he admitted. "In the Sunless Valley, and —" He swallowed.

Kherron's arm tightened in sympathy. "Don't worry, that won't happen again. It was the Khizalace stopping you. Lazim didn't know any better, or he wouldn't have asked you to try. Now, just think of the Pentangle. . . ."

Renn was surprised at how easy it was. He thought the Second Singer looked a little surprised, too. But Kherron swiftly made his report in his cracked voice while Renn hummed to keep the channel open. Then he smiled and tucked the stone safely back into his robes. "Good! That's done." He sighed, stared along the canyon a moment, then said, "You wanted to ask me something after the battle, didn't you? So now's your chance."

Renn hesitated, thrown off balance by the change of subject. The Second Singer's arm suddenly felt awkward on his shoulders. Yet if what Frazhin had said was true, that would change. Renn would get preferential treatment in class. Geran and Alaira wouldn't dare bully him anymore. No one would laugh at his gift for hearing Half Creatures. He needn't worry about anything, ever again.

In a way, it would be a shame. He'd been looking forward to seeing Geran's and Alaira's faces when he stood up to them and gave them a couple of *Dragonflies* each. The Eighth Years would respect him then just as much as if they knew the Second Singer was his father. Maybe even more.

He hesitated so long that by the time he found his voice, Erihan and Shaiala were coming back to look for him. They were mounted on their silver and gray horses, and Shaiala had hung her herdstone around her neck on a braid of blue centaur hair. She'd even put her boots back on. It seemed she'd made her choice.

Renn drew a deep breath. "Is . . . uh . . . I mean, why did the naga attack Frazhin? I thought they were helping him at first."

The Second Singer gave him a strange look. "I doubt very much they were helping him, Renn. The crystal from the khiz mine polluted their breeding grounds. It got into the lake and killed their babies in their eggs. Didn't Shaiala tell you?"

"Er . . . we haven't really talked about it," Renn admitted. "But Yashra said —"

"Frazhin was crazy. Maybe he really believed the naga were his children, who knows? It's over now, anyway. No one could have survived that."

The horses were nearer now and their riders had spotted them. Shaiala waved. In a moment it would be too late.

"Is it true?" Renn blurted out. "What Frazhin said about you being my father?"

"Ahhh."

Singer Kherron gazed at the horizon, where the night had retreated across the Purple Plains, leaving a pink glow that filled the canyons. "As to that, young Renn, you're a skillful enough novice to hear the truth, so I won't lie to you. I'd be very proud to claim you as my son, but I doubt even your mother can tell you. Rialle did her duty as a Singer, but — Well, let's say she had her own affections." Unexpectedly, he went down on one knee and grasped Renn's shoulders. "You remember Frenn? He and Rialle were very close. She named you after him. The way you teamed up with Shaiala to crack the Khiz, that's not Singer instinct. That's something orderlies and soldiers learn — different skills working together, all equally important. Frenn never made a Singer, but all his life he was brave and resourceful. You're a lot like him."

Renn stared at the Second Singer, his chest tightening. "Frenn?" he whispered. "The same Frenn who was in the pentad?"

Kherron nodded, and all at once Renn was back in the Pass of Silence with the rocks falling and the blue-eyed orderly's arms going around him, protecting him the only way he knew. His eyes filled with tears. "Why didn't you *tell* me?" he whispered.

The Second Singer sighed. "Frenn asked me not to and, anyway, it's not certain —"

"He gave his life to save mine."

Singer Kherron nodded. "Yes."

There was a short silence.

"I'll never be as brave as he was," Renn said, wiping the tears from his cheeks. "I was scared all the time."

The Second Singer smiled. "Those who are never afraid can never be brave," he said gently.

Truth.

Suddenly, the horses were upon them, snorting and stamping. The Second Singer put something into Renn's hand and closed his fingers over it, then straightened and strode off toward the camp with a little smile. Shaiala leaped down and raced up to Renn.

She fingered her herdstone, blushed, then unexpectedly pecked him on the cheek. "Thank you, Two Hoof," she said in Human. "I go to live with Kalerei now. Erihan's mother come back from Southport and promise to teach I how to be real tribeswoman. But I have herdstone, so I still run with centaurs whenever I wish! Good luck with *Dragonflies*. Come back and learn other kicks one day." In a whirl of wild black hair she rushed back to Erihan and vaulted onto the silver mare he was holding for her. The Kalerei prince winked at Renn. Then the two of them wheeled their horses and cantered off across the Plains to rejoin the centaurs.

Renn watched them disappear in a cloud of shining dust, wondering if Erihan's mother realized what a task she had ahead of her. Then he looked at what the Second Singer had put into his hand and smiled, suddenly understanding the gift.

*

As the sun rose over the Purple Plains, Renn settled himself in a quiet crevice, raised the Second Singer's bluestone to his lips, and closed his eyes. He hummed *Challa,* thinking of Singer Rialle back in her sea cave on the Isle threading shells into her hair as she waited for news. He had some apologizing to do and now seemed as good a time as any to start. Also, though he had no idea how he was going to tell her, she deserved to know what had happened to Frenn.

The channel opened in a blur of turquoise and sea songs, flashing tails and excited merlee voices. *Son of stone-singer alive! Son of stone-singer come home!*

Renn took a deep breath. "Mother?" he began. "I —"

It was as if she were in the canyon with him, almost close enough to touch, her wide gray eyes full of love and relief and her silver hair swirling about her. "Renn, I know. Graia told me. Don't cry, son. Shh. It's exactly how Frenn would have wanted to die, giving his life for a young Singer —"

Her voice broke and she began to sing her grief and her joy in equal measure. Hesitantly at first, but with growing confidence, Renn added his voice to hers and their Song spanned half a world, celebrating the Echorium's victory and the dawn of a new day.

GLOSSARY: GUIDE TO THE PURPLE PLAINS

Birthing House   Attached to the Echorium, it is an ordinary slate house in which Singers give birth. Women who don't become Singers attend the singer-mothers during childbirth and care for the next generation of novices until they're old enough to enter the Echorium. All Singers are expected to donate at least one child to the Birthing House. The mothers immediately return to their duties in the Echorium, and the children grow up without family attachments.

bluestone   Stone with magical properties, used by Singers to amplify the Songs and to transmit their voices across great distances.

Crazy   Pallet-slang for a person who is not right in the head and is brought to the Echorium for Song treatment and healing.

Dancing Canyons   Steep-sided canyons in the foothills of the Mountains of Midnight. Site of the annual centaur ritual during which those foals ready to become adults crack the rock to find their herdstones.

Dancing Moon   First full moon of the year.

death-braids   Worn in the hair of a warrior to show how many enemies he has slain, each braid is fastened with one of the foe's finger bones.

Echorium   Home of the Singers. Constructed entirely of blue-stone, this ancient building stands on the highest point of the Isle of Echoes. There is no glass in the windows because it would be shattered by the power of the Songs.

First Singer   In charge of the Echorium, the First Singer always remains on the Isle of Echoes.

Five Thousand Steps   World-famous flight of steps, leading from the Isle harbor up to the main gates of the Echorium.

fohl   A very potent drink brewed from mare's milk by the nomadic tribes of the Purple Plains.

grass serpent   Poisonous snake that lives in the grass of the Purple Plains. They are small and very fast.

Great Sky Plain   Heavenly place where the tribes of the Purple Plains believe humans and horses go when they die.

Half Creatures   Ancient creatures — part human, part animal. Of limited intelligence and shy of adult humans, they sometimes communicate with children. There are many breeds, four of which appear or are mentioned in this book:

— *centaur*   Part human, part pony, they come in shades of blue from palest lilac to almost black. They live in herds, roam the Purple Plains, and use herdstones to conceal themselves from human eyes. They have developed lethal kicks for hunting and defense, including:
Snake: single strike with a foreleg.
Flying Snake: double strike with both forelegs.
Hare: single kick with hind leg.
Double Hare: double kick with both hind legs.
Dragonfly: sly sideways kick with any leg.
Canyon: downward strike with all four legs, used to crack rock to extract herdstones.

— *merlee* Part human, part fish, merlee are found in the Western Sea and in the waters around the Isle of Echoes. Their Songs have power over the wind and the waves. They have short memories.

— *naga* Part human, part water snake, naga are very beautiful creatures that live in rivers. They breed in the flooded caverns under the Mountains of Midnight and have a weakness for sparkling objects, which they hoard.

— *quetzal* Part human, part bird, these Half Creatures are found in the dense Quetzal Forest. They appear in *Song Quest*.

Half Creature Treaty Treaty drawn up between the Echorium and the world's leaders to protect Half Creatures from exploitation.

Harai A renegade tribe of Purple Plains nomads who can be identified by their crimson-and-black-striped sharets.

herdstone Found in the Dancing Canyons, these greenish stones are used by centaurs to "bend the light" and thereby conceal the herd from human eyes. To make themselves fully invisible the centaurs' hooves must be in contact with the earth.

Horselord Leader of one of the nomadic tribes that roam the Purple Plains. The tribes are always fighting one another but will band together if there is an external threat.

Isle of Echoes Island in the Western Sea, about thirty days' sail from Southport. The only place in the world where bluestone is found.

Kalerei One of the most influential tribes of the Purple Plains, they can be identified by their green sharets.

Karchholder A warrior who lives in the Karchhold, an underground system of tunnels and caves high in the mountains of the Karch, north of the Quetzal Forest. For more about karchholders, read *Song Quest,* another title in *The Echorium Sequence.*

Khizalace   Palace constructed of black stone and khiz-crystal. At the top of a tall tower at its heart is a huge, powerful crystal known as the Khiz.

khiz-crystal   Black crystal with similar properties to bluestone, found in the Sunless Valley. If specially prepared, it can be used to control or steal people's memories. Masks made from khiz-crystal can be used to transfer thoughts from one wearer to another.

novice   Child below the age of puberty who is training to become a Singer. Some gifted novices can hear and communicate with Half Creatures, an ability that is usually lost as they reach puberty.

orderlies   Men and (more rarely) women who don't become Singers. Employed in the Echorium as guards, cooks, servants, etc., they may also act as bodyguards to Singers who travel away from the Isle.

pallets   Dormitories where novices sleep.

pallet-whisper   An almost soundless, controled whisper for the ears of one person only. Pallet-whispers are used by novices in the pallets when they don't want their teachers to overhear.

Pass of Silence   A narrow, unstable pass that avalanches at the slightest sound. It is the only overland route into the Sunless Valley.

pentad   Group of five orderlies who are trained to act as a bodyguard to protect the Second Singer while on official business.

Pentangle   The heart of the Echorium where Songs of Power are given for healing, rehabilitation, or punishment. A large bluestone chamber with a five-pointed star (pentangle) engraved into the floor. The recipient sits on a spinning stool in the center. Singers stand on each of the five points. They wear gray silk and dye their hair blue so that bright colors do not interfere with the Songs.

Second Singer The Singer who is in charge of Echorium business abroad and who therefore travels a lot.

sharet Wide scarf worn over the nose and mouth to keep out the dust when riding on the Plains.

Singer One trained in the proper use of the Echorium Songs. A Singer has other, related skills, such as:

— *farlistening* *Listening* for vibrations over a distance greater than the normal range of the human ear. It is greatly enhanced by bluestone or water. Skilled Singers can also project their own voice *(farspeaking)*.

Some young Singers can use this skill to communicate with Half Creatures, but lose this ability as they grow older.

— *truth listening* Sorting truth from lies by *listening* carefully to a person's voice and body language.

Song potion Relaxant given to people before they are given a Song treatment. It ensures the Song will have maximum effect. The recipe is a closely guarded secret.

Songs of Power Five wordless songs that have the power to control emotions and memories:

— *Challa* Dream Song. Most common form of healing. Puts people to sleep and helps them to forget their troubles.

— *Kashe* Laughter Song. Wakes people up, cures depression.

— *Shi*   Pain Song. Forces people to confront their pain and heals through tears.

— *Aushan*   Fear Song. Gives life to inner fears. Makes people scream.

— *Yehn*   Death Song. Closes doors in the head. In extreme cases, leads to a form of *living death*.

Sunless Valley   Legendary valley deep within the Mountains of Midnight, where the sun never shines. It is believed to contain great treasure guarded by demons who swallow souls.

sunstep   An Isle of Echoes measurement, it is the length of time it takes the shadow of the Echorium's flagpole to move between two marks on the outer wall (about half an hour).

Trust-Gift   Bluestone jewelery, traditionally given to those who agree to let a Singer settle their dispute. It is worn as a sign that they are willing to honor the terms of an Echorium Treaty.

Two Hoofs   The centaur name for humans.

Wavesong   Echorium ship, used by Singers when they leave the Isle on official business.